SL∧VE

The Spartacus Rebellion: BOOK II

by Jay Penner

Series

Book I: *Soldier*

Book II: *Slave*

Book III: *Savior* (final)

https://jaypenner.com

Jay Penner https://www.jaypenner.com

Printed in the United States of America

First Printing: June 2022

1.4.1 07-01-2023
Produced using publishquickly
https://publishquickly.com

JAY PENNER

Stay Connected!

Join my popular newsletter

My website: https://jaypenner.com

Follow me on: The Amazon author page

Or my page on: Facebook

ANACHRONISMS

an act of attributing customs, events, or objects to a period to which they do not belong

Writing in the ancient past sometimes makes it difficult to explain everyday terms. Therefore, I have taken certain liberties so that the reader is not burdened by linguistic gymnastics or forced to do mental math (how far is 60 stadia again? What is an Artaba?). My usage is meant to convey the meaning behind the term, rather than striving for historical accuracy. I hope that you will come along for the ride, even as you notice that certain concepts may not have existed during the period of the book. For example:

Directions—North, South, East, West.

Time—Years, Minutes, Hours, Weeks, Months, Years.

Distance—Meters, Miles.

Measures—Gallons, Tons.

DRAMATIS PERSONAE

Spartacus and Antara

Thracian couple from the Maedi tribe.

Gnaeus Cornelius Lentulus Vatia

Gladiatorial school (*Ludus*) owner from Capua.

Crixus, Oenomaus, Canicus, Philotas

Gladiators and slaves in Vatia's *ludus*.

Publius Porcina

Senator of Rome and an estate owner in Lucania.

Cleitus

Scout of the Bessi tribe and now an administrator in Porcina's estate.

Felix, Primigenia, Lucia

Slaves in Publius Porcina's estate.

TERMS

Plebeian (Pleb)

Free Roman citizen not a member of the noble classes.

Gladius/Scutum

A 1.5 to 2 ft. long sword, typically used by Roman legionaries / tall oblong shield.

Sica

A curved sword used by Thracians.

Stola

Garment worn by Roman women.

BEFORE YOU READ

The events in this book take place between 75-73 B.C.

Rome, Capua, Pompeii, Brundisium, and Tarentum are thriving and bustling cities. The great mountain Vesuvius looms over Pompeii and is not too far from Capua. It will be another century before it explosively erupts and destroys Pompeii—but at this time, it is a scarred mountain due to prior eruptions so that the top may have been a fairly barren, flat surface with a caldera, but below the rim, likely lush with forests. In Rome, Sulla, having relinquished his dictatorship and retired, is dead, and new consuls are in charge.

Gladiatorial sports are becoming popular, but it will be a few decades before they take a truly extravagant form, sponsored by the big names of the Republic—men like Julius Caesar. And in about a little more than a century, the games will become the most expansive display of cruelty and depravity that the mob *demands* even if some emperors and senators find them repulsive. Future emperors have little choice but to finance these events if they must secure the loyalty of their subjects.

At this time, *fighting unto death* is less prevalent and certainly far more subdued than the mass executions and butchery in the grand displays of the empire that would come much later. The venues, especially those outside Rome, are not yet the spectacular stone amphitheaters that survive today. One of the earliest structures—the impressive amphitheater of Pompeii (actually called *spectacula*), is constructed a few years after the Spartacus wars and does not exist during his time. The arenas are usually makeshift and include wooden benches. The greatest arena of them all, the Colosseum of Rome, will not be built for another century.

Gladiators live wretched lives. Most are recruited into fighting because they are condemned for their criminality or captured as slaves. Few free men willingly enter the arena–and those who do are trying to escape debt or other vexing matters. Only a fleeting number is likely there for name and fame. Gladiators are lauded in the arena, their names are scribbled on walls, and girls swoon for them, but for the Romans, their worth is only so far as how well they fight, for their life means little beyond the sand of the arena. Keeping gladiators better fed or giving them some latitude in terms of companionship is not done out of compassion or respect for their skills; they fetch good profits and cost much to procure and, therefore, must be preserved in good condition for the show. In some ways, it is like fattening a beast for slaughter.

Even the gladiator types have not evolved as depicted in today's popular media. The principal types are Thraex representing Thracians, Galli representing Gauls, and Samnite representing Samnites. For example, the Murmillo with his heavy tall helmet and spear and the Retiarius with his nets come decades later. Even the armors and adornments were likely basic and simple at this time.

Dear reader, it is essential also to note that this is a *novel* and not an academic paper or a historical journal. I have strived to paint the picture of the time, and any errors, omissions, and dramatic license are entirely mine. At the end of the trilogy, you will find a notes section where I detail my portrayal of the key characters in this book and explain what is known by ancient writers like Sallust, Plutarch, and Appian.

And with that, let me lead you into this ancient world, and I hope you come along as we remember those long forgotten.

ITALY 73 – 71 B.C.

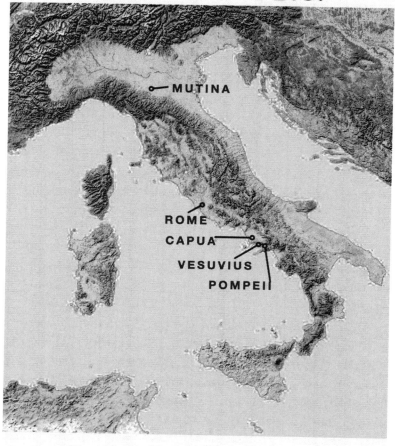

MUTINA

ROME

CAPUA

VESUVIUS

POMPEII

12

RECAP

If you recall book I, *Soldier*, you may skip this.

Spartacus, the son of a Maedi village chief, leads an incursion into their rival tribe's village to steal their god, Sabazios. The raid goes terribly wrong, and Bessi retribution leaves Spartacus' village destroyed, his family killed, and him on the run. Ashamed at what has happened, Spartacus joins a legion belonging to Roman commander Gnaeus Scribonius Curio, and takes part in the Roman attack against the Bessi. On orders of the Roman general Sulla, Spartacus and the auxiliaries he is part of are called to take part in an invasion of Italy. Spartacus learns much about the art of fighting during his march while dealing with a hostile centurion (Florus) and a perennially annoying Cleitus, a henchman of the Bessi man Durnadisso, whom Spartacus kills during the boat ride to Italy.

Falsely accused of deserting after the battle of Colline Gate in Rome, and then escaping a murder attempt by killing Florus, the Roman centurion, Spartacus settles in Capua. But Cleitus is on his trail, and Spartacus is warned by a Roman businessman named Pollio that someone is inquiring after his whereabouts. Spartacus leaves Capua and vanishes into the Lucanian wilderness until he surfaces and finds employment at Senator Porcina's estate. There, he befriends a slave boy named Felix who also happens to be Thracian. When Cleitus finds Spartacus, Spartacus kills the overseer of Porcina's estate but spares Cleitus after severely injuring him. Then Spartacus escapes again and returns to Thrace, where he marries Antara and settles into his new life.

But Cleitus is the hound that Curio uses to find and arrest Spartacus on the charge of killing a Roman officer and causing grievance to a Roman senator. Spartacus and his wife are condemned to slavery and returned to Porcina's estate. But Porcina, in need of money, sells Spartacus and his wife to Vatia, a gladiatorial school owner from Capua.

Now, Spartacus is on the way from Rome to Capua as part of the slave transport.

1

CAPUA

"Keep your mouth shut," the burly, heavily armed guard warned them.

The four in the carriage had no energy to talk, for the shaking carriage, the meager rations, and the raging ocean of emotions in his mind gave no reason to involve each other in happy chatter. The other man, Oenomaus, grumbled time-to-time, inviting the ire of the two miserable guards who rode in the stuffy vehicle. Antara had not spoken for hours. Instead, she preferred to close her eyes and pretend to sleep.

How can she sleep when the shackles chafe?

But the shackles only chafed him, for his wrists were much bigger, and they hung loosely on hers. Outside, the world looked entirely normal. Carts and jostled for space. Men and women, some surely slaves, hurried about holding bags, tools, wood, and whatever else for their day, and the sun shone brightly, with nary a cloud in the sky. They were simply another carriage on its way to something. The familiar smells of cow dung, hay, bad breath, summer leaves, and dry dust all lent the scene the normalcy of everyday life.

It was an odd feeling. A sense of feeling like a prisoner, even if one was not. Why was this different from, for example, being a soldier? After all, he had marched under orders, fought under orders, killed under orders, dug ditches and trenches under orders, built ramparts and heaped corpses under orders. He would do so now—fight under orders and live under orders. So why did this still feel different?

Because he had done all that for the army of his own volition. For whatever misguided sense of purpose. But it was *he* who decided. Not *this*.

What did Zibelthiurdos intend for him? Was Sabazios still angry at his incursions years ago and had not forgiven him? His wife had told him many times that the gods no longer held a grudge, and that they had put him on this path to a great destiny.

He leaned back on the rattling wood posts and closed his eyes. What was it like? Being a gladiator? He had only seen the shows from outside, heard about them, looked down upon them, and now would he be putting on a show in the arena? How would things be different if he did not go to Kintoi's hut but instead ran? His father always said that *when one walks a path, the path is trodden, and no regret removes the imprint of your feet*. There was little to gain from all the *what-ifs*.

They were allowed to relieve themselves once a few hours, still shackled to each other, but with the courtesy of Antara being allowed to disengage. At night, they slept tied to each other. And on the noon of the fourth day, the homes and buildings of Capua finally appeared at a distance. Oenomaus had a habit of speaking to himself whenever he could, would get reprimanded, and then do it again. But no one beat him—an indication that the guards had been warned not to injure them needlessly. But the other man, whose name Spartacus never learned, was quiet as a mute and never uttered a word.

It had not changed much since his stay—just that it had grown larger. He noticed two temples that were not there before. The cart turned into a lonely mud road on a fork from the main highway to Capua. Spartacus recognized Mount Tifata behind him. The ground was flat with grass and shrubbery on either side of the road—and far ahead was the compound and gate of an estate.

A lonely building with tall walls.

Vatia's *ludus*.

2

CAPUA

They were pushed along a narrow passageway. Spartacus did not remember if he was present during the construction of this section, for it all seemed unfamiliar. But then, once completed, structures looked nothing like how they were at the beginning. The passage went through two tall, heavy iron gates, clearly meant to keep one from escaping, and finally opened into a small circular open area that opened up to the sky. There was another door on the opposite side, and here too, the walls were tall, and the surface was smooth, clearly designed to prevent scaling. But at about fifteen feet high, there was a dark window-like opening, possibly for people to look down and address them.

The guards yelled at them to stand in the center and locked the gate behind them.

Just us, but nothing that we can do.

They waited for whoever was to address them. Vatia? One of his men?

Oenomaus was dancing on his feet, and he finally began to curse in his language. It was obvious to all what was happening. Still shackled, they all moved as one toward the wall and allowed him to let loose a long stream of piss on the wall. The guards yelled something but did not come in to administer a beating.

It was not too long before the silence of the space was punctured by noises from the opening on the higher level. A woman's head appeared and vanished.

Eventually, a man's head peeked. *Vatia.* That small head, with a sprinkling of white-speckled hair that looked like someone had dropped salt on it.

Beady-eyed, beak-nosed, bastard slave owner.

"You are now in Gnaeus Lentulus Vatia's *Ludus*," he said in a high-pitched voice with a face devoid of mirth. "You are my property."

What a welcome. Rousing like a general's!

A man beside Vatia translated Latin into the language similar to the twangs he heard in the Gaelic units. Oenomaus was nodding.

"You will make name, fame, and glory. Your wretched life has brought you here, but the gods have given you a chance to redeem yourself."

Spartacus could not control himself. "I am innocent, sir."

Vatia stared at him but did not respond to the assertion. "As I said, you have a chance to cleanse the filth that coats you. And unlike those who toil away on farms or wither away in mines, you will live a glorious life."

Satisfied that no one had an opinion to offer this time, Vatia continued. "You will have a fine roof to sleep under. You will be fed well. You will receive training. And those of you who do well in the arena will have the company of women time-to-time and a feast on the day of victory, all on my patronage. Of course, you can claim innocence," he said pointedly, looking at Spartacus, "and I will gladly sell you to the mines."

He ran a palm over his head and drummed his fingers while the translator completed. Then, he continued, "I am a man of few words. My actions speak for themselves. Conduct yourselves like men and not as beasts, and you will receive just treatment. If you misbehave, you shall experience what it means to be ill-treated."

The ever-present threats.

"You, the Thracian," he said, pointing to Spartacus. "You know the orders for your conduct. Let me make myself clear—if I determine you to be a threat, then I will flog you and your wife, and have you both nailed to a cross for live entertainment in the arena. Or you can bring glory to yourself and this *ludus* and live as a happy man and wife."

This is not the time for dialog. Help me keep my composure, Zibelthiurdos.

He bowed his head and nodded.

Oenomaus had a question. The interpreter hesitated before translating whatever the Gaul said to Vatia.

Vatia's eyebrows knitted, and then he leaned forward on the balcony before addressing Oenomaus sternly. "No, you barbarian. You do not get to fuck every day. Only on days where you demonstrate courage. And if you run your mouth, then not even that."

Oenomaus grumbled beneath his bushy mustache.

"An overseer will see you to your quarters. You, Thracian—your wife will be in the *ludus* kitchen. You will see her whenever I determine and depending on your behavior."

Spartacus kept his voice low, like a supplicant, and asked gently, "Sir,–"

"I am your *dominus*, and you shall address me as such. This is not the army."

Spartacus held his tongue. *Dominus. That ugly word.*

"*Dominus.* I was told that she would live with me."

Vatia shook his head. "She *does* live with you, just not in your quarters—unless you want her to get raped when you are in training. She stays in the kitchen on duty for her safety and your sanity."

Spartacus turned to Antara and translated. She did not look pleased, but he had already warned her to keep her tongue in check. But in some way, Spartacus understood the arrangement even if he was not entirely pleased. She *would* be safe among the women and guards in the kitchen.

"Today, you will be shown your quarters and the training arena. You will meet your trainers. You will learn the rules. Your day in the arena will come—just not yet. I have paid much for you, so make sure I am happy. And if I am happy, you will be happy."

Does he say these words to every hapless man that stands before him?

Oenomaus had something to say, but this time he said it with his head held high, scar-filled chest pushed forward. Spartacus felt a tinge of jealousy for the man's forthrightness and pride in his being. Had he professed his innocence and expressed his displeasure at being brought here?

Vatia smiled at hearing the translation. He addressed Oenomaus. "You look like a skilled man, Gaul. I look forward to your demonstration and seeing you be a champion in the arena. This *Ludus* needs well-behaved fighters who know what is best for them!"

Oenomaus got to his knees and bowed.

What? What did Oenomaus say?

Did the Gaul just supplicate and offer his services? Spartacus had elevated him too high, but Oenomaus seemed only too pleased to get his everyday comforts and do the bidding of the master. *Master.*

Some men were born to be slaves. He looked at Oenomaus with disdain. The Gauls he had seen in battle were heroic to the last man and never so easily bent their knees. And unlike Spartacus, who had a wife and a threat hanging over their heads, it did not seem like Oenomaus had anything to lose.

Was this what Erducos meant when he said Spartacus' mind often thought only of himself?

Vatia's continuation snapped him out of his thoughts.

"There will be more in the days to come. I will be there to watch your progress in training. You will view a few events yourself to see what it is like. You will inhale the headiness of the air and the adoration of the crowds and understand what it means to *please* the crowds. The more they are thrilled by you, the more loved you are, and the better your lives will be."

And the greater your profits will be.

"Wait here. You will have men take you and introduce you to the routine. May the gods be with us," he said and paused. As if he was waiting for them to do something–salute? Bow? Spartacus just looked back defiantly, and Antara's eyes remained fixed on the ground.

Vatia vanished, and it was just them and a burdensome silence.

"Will they take me away now?" Antara asked. Her eyes betrayed fear, which was rare to see.

"You will see me in three days. But be patient. In time, perhaps I can negotiate a better arrangement."

"But what if you die in the fights?" she blurted.

"You said the gods had a destiny for me. Surely dying like a dog in the arena is no great destiny," he said, smiling. Was she questioning her faith?

She looked so frail and afraid. *My fiery wife, brought here because of me.*

"Keep your strength and never show fear," he told her, his voice low. "Because weakness will allow the wolves to devour you. Do not hesitate to bring up the magisterial or Legate's orders to protect yourself."

She nodded.

It was not too long before the other gate opened, and one man strode forward, followed by a few guards. They had thick clubs in their hands, and none looked Roman.

The man in the front had a thick mop of golden hair tied up in a tall bun, lips covered by the yellow mustache, and a generous beard. He had striking blue eyes, the type that Spartacus knew were common in people from the far north. He was only slightly shorter than Spartacus. He was lean and muscular, with long limbs.

"I am Canicus. I am one of the trainers," he said in Latin. His voice had a rough edge, and the words had the familiar accent of Germans in the auxiliary.

Canicus looked at Oenomaus, who stared back blankly. *Surely he understands basic words?*

He pointed toward Spartacus. "Thracian? You?"

Spartacus nodded.

Canicus turned to Oenomaus. "You?"

Oenomaus finally responded, "Aquitani."

"You will take an oath first, and then someone will take you to your quarters," he said. And then he held his fingers to his lips as if to say that they would eat. Spartacus was hungry and tired, and if these fools wanted good gladiators, they would have to feed them first.

A woman came through the gate and yelled at the guards to unshackle Antara. Spartacus held his wife close until she was led away, presumably to the kitchen. She left with dignity, for it would be unbecoming of a priestess of Dionysus to wail and complain.

Will I see her soon?

"Everyone, come with me," Canicus gestured.

They were unshackled and led through the second gate into a dark and damp passage that descended further into a lower level. After about a hundred steps, it opened into a long open corridor with doors on either side.

Barracks.

The cracked stone floor was cool to the feet. But Canicus turned away from the corridor and led the men up a few more stairs into a small chamber with idols of Jupiter and Bellona on a pedestal. Incense filled the chamber with fragrance.

"Wait," Canicus said.

It did not take long before more men were ushered into the chamber. Soon, it was quite crowded with the captives and the guards, including Canicus.

Finally, Vatia stepped into the room from a different door, accompanying his wife. He wore a crisp white toga, and she was in an elegant cream stola and a beautiful pearl necklace. She was much younger than her husband. They stood by the idols.

Canicus stepped forward and bowed to Vatia, who nodded. He turned toward the men.

"You will now perform a *Sacramentum,* a sacred oath to the school and your master. First in Latin, then in Greek, and finally in German."

The oath was simple and clear. They swore absolute loyalty to the master and the school. That they would show no cowardice, involve in no violence amongst each other, and let them be burned if they violated the sacred rules. It felt strange, pledging loyalty to a man who had purchased them to condemn them to a life of servitude and potential death. But there was nowhere to run. The room's smoky aroma combined with the men's solemn tones gave him an odd sense of brotherhood and loyalty–to something greater than one's own.

Once completed, the guards directed them to leave. Vatia called him. "Spartacus," came the voice.

He turned to face his *dominus*.

Canicus waited behind, and two guards stood on each side.

Vatia stepped forward and looked up to Spartacus. He was a slight and short man, and Spartacus looked down. "I have paid good money for you and your wife. Demonstrate your capabilities and bring fame to this *Ludus*. Your wife's companionship, a larger quarter of your own, and perhaps even some coin deposited in your name, will be yours. A few in this *Ludus* have earned these rare privileges."

"Yes, sir."

"Your conduct in this *Ludus*, and in front of cheering crowds in a *spectacula*, will determine your well-being and hers. I expect that they will chant your name and demand your presence. Whatever crimes you have committed, think of this as the chance at redemption. You will bring glory to my house, and through that, glory to yourself."

You expect to make a handsome return on the coin you have paid for me.

"As an incentive rarely shown to a beginner, I have directed that you be given your quarter so you may avoid suffering the company of other men. Eyes will be upon you."

He raised his hand and slapped Spartacus' shoulder. "Now go, join the others and make the *Ludus* of Vatia the most renowned in all of Capua."

Canicus led them down again, back into the dark corridor. He swept his arm. "You will live here. But first–this way."

Spartacus walked with Canicus to a small room where a man waited with a branding iron. *No!*

An angry Spartacus turned to Canicus. "Why?" he said. "We are gladiators!"

Canicus reprimanded him. "You are a *slave*, Spartacus. Like everyone else. Including me," he said as he pointed to the scar on his back just below the neck.

Two guards pushed him forward. "Finish it. We don't have time to wait for you to decide," one of them said.

The process was quick but painful. One of the guards applied a salve on the burn and waved his hand to tell them to leave.

"You may get a fever, but you will be fine in a day or two," Canicus said.

Spartacus tried to ignore the pain radiating from his back. *Just a minor wound.* It was not the pain but the humiliation that burned deeper.

Spartacus noted the characteristics of the barracks. The cells were on both sides of the corridor, facing each other. Some were larger, going by the size of the doors, and others were smaller. There were no windows in the dingy space. The walls were yellowish stone and gray plaster, with much of it peeling away already. *Cheap construction.*

And everything smelled of unwashed humans and damp mold.

They walked past several cells. Each door was made of iron and secured by a heavy bolt. The doors had rectangular windows, making it easy for guards to peep inside.

He heard noises in some. Were there multiple men in a room? Or were they speaking to themselves? Where were those who came with him gone? Oenomaus?

Spartacus felt unusually anxious, like something was growing in his belly and gripping his chest. He had always slept under the open skies, looking at the magnificent stars, or he lived in tents or huts. He was never in a constrained space like this.

He looked up at the ceiling. Small rectangular slots in the roof allowed sunlight into the corridor, decorating the uneven floor with slivers of playful patterns.

Canicus stopped at a slightly open door and pointed to him. "Your cell."

The intensity of *squeezing* in Spartacus' chest increased once the door shut behind him. He *hated* this place. How would it be for Antara? Did they brand her too?

The cell had an army-issue bedframe with a tattered hay mattress on it. An empty earthen water jug lay on its side in the corner. Spartacus lay on the bed, and his feet dangled from the bottom edge. The hay itched his back and irritated the fresh burn—so he had to turn to avoid worsening the pain. There was nothing else in the room—not even a window. The stark walls had lost their plaster long ago and exposed the cracked yellow and orange bricks.

Who was here before me? What happened to him?

His bones weary from the travel and fatigue pulling down his eyelids, and in spite of the branding burn that had now dulled into a throb, Spartacus closed his eyes and sank quickly into the blissful darkness of sleep.

"Get up, get up!" Someone was shaking him. Spartacus had no idea how long he slept—it could not have been long, for the sunlight still dimly lit the corridor, and the man before him, surely a slave, *like him*, had a bowl of porridge.

Spartacus accepted the bowl, a spoon, and a cup of brew made of vinegar and ash. The man had a little bucket of water and filled the jug.

"Will I be allowed to–?"

The man ignored him and brusquely walked out, slamming the iron door behind him and locking it.

Bastard.

But his stomach churned. He greedily gulped the thick concoction of barley and beans and then washed it down with the sour and heady drink. He had sometimes drunk this during the marches–they said it infused a man with vigor, strength, and clarity of mind. The burn no longer hurt as badly and seemed to be healing. He had developed no fever, which he ascribed to the gods' blessings.

And then it was just him and only distant sounds of metal clanging, quiet footsteps, muffled voices. What was it going to be like? A comfortable but cramped living with enough food, controlled visitation, and glory in the arena? What was the nature of the games these days–had they gotten bloodier and more violent? How often did the men here die in the arena? What would happen to Antara if he lost his life? That was one question that had not been resolved with Curio or Vatia. He would bring it up at the next opportunity.

He looked up at the uneven, dark-gray ceiling, and then scanned across the room back to the walls.

A lone scribble was on the wall, far from the stone bed.

VENUS BLESSES SEULLIUS PHYLLIS

Who was Seullius? A gladiator? Was Phyllis his wife? A woman he loved? A mistress?

The cell told a story of those who came before him, and Spartacus thought he would be the story himself someday. He scanned the walls for more graffiti–and there were some, but too hard to decipher, and he was feeling too lazy to get up and inspect.

No hurry.

What was it going to be like–being a gladiator? How fair were the fights? What would one get for a long and worthy performance? How would it be in this *Ludus*? Did men get into fights every day? Did he have to watch his back? He would not hesitate to crush the skull or break the neck of anyone who sought to harm him.

Can I earn my freedom?

The thought jolted him. There were stories of gladiators earning their freedom after several fights–twenty, thirty. But there were no laws he was aware of, and it was entirely up to the owner–in this case, Vatia.

He would bring it up after a few fights. What must he do to earn his freedom? And would that allow him to free his wife as well? Curio had promised nothing of the sort but considering that he was Vatia's property after the sale, surely he was afforded the same terms as any other fighter.

He would leave Italy immediately. Leave this ugly place and its rulers, and find a quiet home–not in Thrace, but some place else. Love for his home had diminished–for was it not them that betrayed him to the Romans? And yet they had lectured him about valor. *Cowards.*

Annoyed by the prickly hay below him, he sat and placed his back to the wall instead. He would probably tear the hay and reshape it.

Baths. Would he get the hot baths he loved so much?

His energy returned. He was becoming restless. But to get up and pace would make him look, and *feel,* like a caged animal, and he would not make himself feel so.

The rage that blazed in his heart for days, seeking revenge on all those who wronged him, had somewhat diminished. Instead, it was replaced by an apprehension, a desire to earn freedom and return to a semblance of structure. The training, which he had heard might take months, would be a welcome departure from the current state.

Who were the other gladiators? From which places? What tribes? How did they come to be here? There were so many questions.

But there was plenty of time. The answers would reveal themselves soon enough.

But no one returned to fetch him. He walked up to the little opening on the door to peek into the empty corridor. Finally, bored, he went back to the stone bed.

The room gradually darkened, and only flickering lamps lit the corridor outside. Someone arrived with supper–no different from the meal before–and Spartacus went back to eating it. The sounds outside picked up–people, talking, noises, but he had no interest anymore in listening.

Tomorrow would be here soon, anyway.

3

LUCANIA

Felix stretched his back and swung the cane around, almost striking the guard who accompanied him.

"Watch it, you bastard," he growled.

You watch it, bastard.

Mellius was long gone, and contrary to waking up in nightmares, Felix had often re-imagined the scene with glee. Of course, one tyrant replaced another, and cruelty was never more than a whip away.

Felix's situation had improved somewhat after the debacle with Cleitus. He had come away as the boy who had saved Cleitus from Spartacus' attack, and with no one to prove otherwise, the master, Porcina, had kept him on. Life had become bearable for a while–with better food, less harsh treatment, and the chance to train a few others to do some of the more physically taxing work during herding.

It had been years since Spartacus had vanished, and then Felix had learned only recently how Spartacus had been returned due to Cleitus. *How I wish I could see him!*

Cleitus! Felix worried every day whether that wretched man would remember what happened. But Cleitus had never come by. All Felix knew was that Cleitus was now employed by Porcina and doing something in the estate– though their worlds never crossed, and he had never seen Cleitus. Felix's world was small–he woke up, spent most of the day in the open fields, went back, had his leg shackled to the wall, and then slept. If he was ever lucky, once a rare while, got a glimpse of Lucia who still lived with her mother.

But like everything else in life, the good days were waning again. The last overseer had taken ill and died suddenly, and was replaced by another one—Isidorus, a Samnite condemned to slavery for his criminality–and he was gearing up to be not very different from Mellius.

Felix had now endured two whippings, threats of having his penis cut off, and constantly pressured to take on larger herds and find new grazing areas. Competition from newer estates was growing, and it was becoming increasingly challenging to find large grass-rich areas all for themselves. More than once, he had been attacked. Of course, the guards saved him not from their love for him but because the master would break their legs if they lost any cattle.

And this guard, one of Isidorus's vicious little dogs, enjoyed berating and beating him and the other boys. It was like entertainment. The slaves merited no consideration at all. Felix knew that once he was no longer one of the prized herdsmen, they would dispose of him. He had survived so far—but how much longer?

"We have to go this way," he said, addressing the guard and pointing toward an uneven section of the area. The mounds descended to a narrow flat path adjoining a crevasse that split the earth in two for nearly a mile. "There is a good grass-bed at the end."

The sweating man cursed loudly. It was rare for guards to accompany herdsmen, but increased banditry and thievery meant the estate had to do something to preserve its valuable commodities.

A few cows. The guard. Him. Surrounded by low-lying hills, streams, and rocks.

When they came parallel to the crevasse, Felix stood on the side to put the beasts in line. *Pofpp, hopp, this way! Hurr!*

"Please walk ahead, sir. I need to bring one more. Keep walking until the path opens up."

The guard nodded, leaving Felix behind.

Felix continued to make his calling sounds, hooting, cupping his palms on his lips.

But there was no other cow.

There was not a living thing anywhere nearby.

He turned and hurried toward the single file above, with the guard in the rear.

The bells on the cows, the hoofs on dusty and rocky ground, and the crowing of a murder of crows all masked the sound of his quiet footsteps as he came up right behind the guard.

And then, with all his strength, Felix gripped the guard's shoulder and pushed him off the edge.

The startled man screamed as he hurtled below and smashed into a sharp outcrop of jagged rocks. His head split like a watermelon, spraying blood on the dark stones.

Some of the cows ran forward, startled by the screams, and Felix, still calming his nerves from the sheer audacity and excitement, had to gather them again.

He waited for the heartbeat to slow down and the ears to stop ringing. He placed his palms on his knees and bent down to retch.

He had waited for this for days.

Felix would wreak his revenge on this estate, one way or another, one little damage at a time.

And he would make love to Lucia before he died.

And nothing on this earth would stop him.

4

LUDUS OF VATIA

Spartacus was woken up before the sun rose and allowed to latrines. A small bathhouse adjoined the quarters, and he was allowed to take a short bath before returning to his cell.

But soon after, the door opened, and another man gestured for him to follow. Oil lamps still burned bright from their wall holders, and it seemed like there were men in their rooms. But he kept his head low and made no conversation as he observed the conditions.

The corridor ended with steps that led up to a quadrangle. The three sides of the quadrangle were the colonnaded estate building, and the fourth was just a bare, fortress-like wall. The soft orange glow of the rising sun suffused the area and made the red tiles on the roof look beautifully grand. The center field was large. Spartacus was surprised by how different this area looked compared to what he remembered from the construction days. A wooden semicircular makeshift arena with three levels of wood-board seating was in one corner of the field. A few men were milling about in the arena and some sat on the benches.

Spartacus observed three distinct groups of men in different corners of the quadrangle. *Divided by age? Skill? Tribe? Something else?*

He was led to the group in the southwest corner, and the man accompanying him grunted as if to say *join them.*

Alone, he walked awkwardly to the group. The seven men standing before another man all looked younger than him. Spartacus was probably the oldest of the lot, except the trainer. And by their features, they were Thracians, Dacians, and a Macedonian or two. About ten more sat on the grass, staring at him. There was no hostility in their eyes, but there was no unspoken *brotherhood* of military inductions.

He stood in the group on the side before the leader—an instructor, perhaps.

The grass was cool to his feet. Were the other men recruits as well? He would learn soon.

"You are Spartacus?" he said in Greek.

"Yes."

"Philotas. I will be your trainer. Come closer and stand behind."

Spartacus shuffled to the back, for he was the tallest man. All of them were in loincloths, and no one held a weapon or a shield.

"You are all here. Hera blesses your families, and Athena seeks to infuse her strength within you."

And Zibelthiurdos watches over me.

"I shall speak, and you will listen. I know not many of you are good at that, but you will soon learn that your ears are as much your weapons as anything else."

The men moved restlessly where they stood. Some scratched their backs. Others rubbed their ears. Some swayed. How many really understood this man? Not all knew Greek or Latin.

Philotas was a lean, muscular man. He was shorter than many others. Golden-brown curls of hair adorned his face like many Greeks. He had a square, clean-shaven face and an erudite manner of speaking that held his audience. Philotas was the oldest of them all, evident by the creases below his eyelids and the silver streaks in his hair.

As odd as it was for the life Spartacus was about to be inducted, about which he knew nothing and had only experienced for a day, the crisp day, the cool morning, and the soft grass made him come alive.

"You are new. This is your first day, and there will be many, many more days. You can make a great name for yourself or live the life of a wretched slave."

One of the men began to say something but Philotas scowled. "Be quiet. There will be time for questions. I said you will listen."

The man grumbled and kicked some grass.

Philotas continued, "I care little for where you came from, what you did, whom you killed, and what you think of this life. Our master, the owner, Gnaeus Cornelius Lentulus Vatia, has paid for you to be gladiators, and gladiators you will be."

How many had a choice?

"Before I speak of the arrangements and training, let me first speak of your basal instincts. We all know that you are not men of rules and discipline."

A few chuckled. Whatever this group was, it appeared most knew Greek.

"Yes, tell them, Philotas. Tell them to be obedient little dogs!" one of the men resting on the grass hollered.

Philotas ignored the man and continued. "The foremost thing is that you shall not fight each other, and you shall not injure each other except inadvertently during practice. You are property, and Vatia has paid well for each of you. When you damage his property, you pay."

Philotas paused and looked every man in the eye. *A trained speaker. What was his life before this?*

"When you finally face your opponent in the arena and win, fine things await you. Excellent meal for the night, with meat. The chance to have a beautiful girl wrap her thighs around you. A hot bath. And maybe even a chance to stroll in the city. But if you fight each other and cause injury, you lose all of that. And you will pay with blood to regain those luxuries. You behave well. You will live better than the miserable millions in Capua or Rome. You misbehave, and you will pray each night for forgiveness. Do you all understand?"

A few half-hearted nods and murmurs were enough for Philotas to continue. "We have fifty-six gladiators in the school now, divided into four groups. You are here: the Thracians, Illyrians, Odryssians, and Dacians. The Gauls, Belgae, Aquitani, and the Celts are the second. They speak their languages. And the third is the German contingent. And the fourth are the Syrians–and by that I mean every barbarian east. Each has its trainer. I am yours. A man called Crixus leads the Gauls—but he is also a fighter, and the master puts him on a show occasionally. Similarly, Canicus leads the Germans and Nisarpal leads the Syrians. We train and eat separately, but there will be many instances where you work together. Your conduct will be closely watched on these occasions."

There was logic in this and some bitter lessons, Spartacus thought. No matter the deterrence and threat of punishment, getting rambunctious, ready-to-fight men of different cultures and languages to cooperate was always a challenge. The units were usually separated even in the army, and this place was no army, and the men were wont to violence and lawlessness.

"You will all receive different roles based on your size, shape, and fighting skills. You will play those roles diligently. You are not just fighters—you are *entertainers*. The audience must *love* you, not just because you sliced a man's thigh or kicked one down, but because you did it with style and great flair! That is what the audience demands," he said, his voice rising, his eyes looking up to the sky. "And nothing is more shameful than a display of cowardice and retreat."

One man in the front scoffed and mumbled. "We never retreat."

Philotas stared at him. "That is what everyone says in the beginning. But I have been here for a long time. You puff your chest and speak bold words. But I have seen men cry, beg not to go into the arena, piss themselves, drop their arms, run, fake illnesses, and try to kill themselves. So, remember that, and never be one of those."

No one uttered a word. Spartacus had seen men freeze in battle, shake in fear before an advance, or go in shock at its end. It was nothing but weakness in their countenance or the curse of the gods. Such men were shamed, beaten, or in the worst case, executed, for they posed a danger to all those around them. Why would going into the arena be much different?

"This training will be long and grueling. Even more so than some of your military service. When in the arena, you are the *lone* warrior. There is no general to guide you. No centurion to lead you. No cohort by your side and no cavalry to your rescue. It is *you* and the one against you. And a few thousand screaming, adoring fans. That is all. You fight to defeat your opponent, save yourself from serious injury or death, and please those who have paid to see you. Get that into your heads and hearts! Nothing else matters."

Philotas loved talking. He allowed no one to ask a question, and he continued extolling the virtues of bravery in the arena and the pleasures that awaited successful gladiators. How much was an exaggeration? Only time would tell. But there was no question that he was well-spoken and knew the sport well.

"When will you finish, Philotas? Will you kill them with your lectures?"

"Go back to napping, Cogitatus. The only language you understand is that of pigs."

The ribbing made Spartacus think that while Philotas was their trainer and sounded strict in his words, perhaps a camaraderie developed over time, giving leeway to some men to engage him in light banter. But what was noticeable was that the rest of the men lying on the grass barely said anything. Or maybe this Cogitatus was a favored one, for some reason.

Philotas turned to them. "That is much of today. We will begin with several rounds of running to get your hearts beating faster, and then settle into training basics."

Spartacus could not help himself anymore. Florus allowed the men to ask a question or two after orders, even in the auxiliary. Men were allowed to ask questions but then obey final orders—but asking was allowed, even in front of senior commanders.

"I have a question."

Philotas narrowed his eyes, opened his mouth to say something, but stopped. He nodded.

"How many times have you fought in the arena?" Spartacus asked.

Philotas smiled. "You are brave to question me on the first day, Thracian. You speak Greek quite well. I have been to Vatia's arena only twice. One was a draw, and in the other, I won narrowly. But I fought before that as an auxiliary in the army, and then as a gladiator who survived nine fights."

That was an impressive performance. Spartacus' respect for Philotas rose. Not only was the man talented, but he also spoke well. Just the kind of man Spartacus could build a relationship with—like the one with Erducos. How he still missed the wise old Odomantean!

It seems Philotas read his mind. He smiled at them and asked. "You wonder if I am a good trainer."

"Yes, tell them!" Cogitatus yelled from the side. Philotas ignored him.

"Not all great fighters make the best trainers. You will find that soon. The fighter knows *himself*. The trainer knows *them all*. The fighter looks inward. The trainer brings the best of all the fighters. He forges them and turns them into the *best*. A man greatly skilled, but not in the arena, will bite the dust if we go up against one who has benefited from a talented trainer. I have shown the *dominus* that I may be a good fighter, but I am a better trainer still. Besides, I am too old to fight in the arena."

Only time would tell if the words had weight. But Spartacus knew the truth in them, even if the others around him did not. He had spent time in Thrace, under the Kintoi, training their men and those in nearby villages. Training required a special skill.

"And why are we good trainers? Because less than one in twenty men dies in this school. Now, you decide whether those odds are wonderful or not."

Philotas put an end to any more questions. "That is enough words for now. Pray to your gods, and prepare to run. Let us see how much you can do!"

It had been so long since he had experienced this burning breath, skin slick with the sweat from exertion, thighs as if on fire, lying flat on the grass trying to gulp air. Philotas was a bastard—unrelenting, haranguing, insulting–as he made them run, run again and again until every man collapsed. Spartacus was the fourth to fall, and the three other recruits lasted for some more time before giving up. His age was catching up.

Philotas went around smacking the fallen men with a flat-based wooden scale. "Get up, lazy sons of whores. Do you think this is as easy as banditry or thievery? We have just started! Assemble!"

One man who raised his voice received a beating–not too brutal, but enough to remind him that there was only one way to respond–and that was with obedience.

After a gulp of water, Philotas had them gather around him. "You will learn to run for long periods without getting tired. You will learn to fight. You will learn to please the audience. And it will be months before you set foot in the arena—so learn as your life depends on it. And everything you do must be to win that first fight—for that is how you will build your legacy."

Spartacus wondered how expensive it must be to run a school like this and pay for the living and training. No wonder the rules were harsh, and there was strict discipline around pointlessly injuring other gladiators. But the games were catching on in popularity and growing in grandeur—and in a not too distant future, he would learn how much.

By the day, he had developed a grudging respect for Philotas. Shorter he may be, his limbs lighter than many he trained, his language too refined for the rowdiness of the men, he was untiring in his efforts to whip them into shape. And in the hands of such energy, there was little doubt that those who persevered would do well.

And when he returned to his room— *cell*, Spartacus was too tired to contemplate anything as he fell into a deep slumber.

5

LUCANIA

Cleitus had a schedule.

He woke up before dawn, offered incense, and prayed to Sabazios. As administrator of accounts for Senator Publius Porcina's estate, his job was to keep the books, record revenue inflows and expenditures, haggle with suppliers and merchants, ensure timely payment for farm workers, and deal with debt collectors. The treasurer of the estate was Porcina's relative named Marcus Vibius, and Cleitus' reports usually went to Marcus who then ordered investigations or approved actions. The two men rarely interacted, for Marcus thought little of Cleitus and was unhappy that Porcina had entrusted estate audits to a lowly slave-like barbarian.

But Cleitus cared little for Marcus.

Anyone had to admit, and as the Senator himself said often, Cleitus' rise was nothing short of *remarkable*. A tattered, damaged barbarian had risen to a sensitive position in the Roman Senator's household—and it had raised many eyebrows. But Cleitus had learned something about himself as he began his life in the estate—that he had an uncanny ability with numbers and could hunt gaps in records even better than how he hunted men. When he applied his mind, he also learned that he was a good learner of languages. And now, more than three years since his encounter with Spartacus, Cleitus had become fluent in Latin and Oscan, and while his broken teeth and severed fingers did not grow, his stature certainly had. The Thracian bastard was gone— sold off as the lowest scum of the Roman society, a gladiator fighting for the entertainment of the crowds, and Cleitus was a rising star in Roman society. The gods had smiled upon him.

What a fitting end.

He absent-mindedly touched his crooked nose, a reminder of the last time Spartacus had broken it in. That was months ago, but the memories still hurt. Some day he would go to a show that featured Spartacus and mock him from the stands—that would be the most joyful moment of his time.

But Cleitus was not wanting for comfort. He had his little quarters in the estate–a room, a kitchen, and even a little portico where he could entertain men that came to see him. He even had two slaves assigned to him–they were hard workers and took most of the manual work away from him. One could easily see the comfort of having slaves around. He had no desire to return to Thrace or back to his people. The more he thought of his wretched childhood and his savage mother, the way Durnadisso treated him in private, the insults and punishments he had endured, the less he cared for his people or their ways of life.

The Romans had treated him far better and fairly than any Thracian ever had. Or at least he had convinced himself of it.

And then there was the question of his desires.

No woman would willingly want Cleitus—not after what war and Spartacus had done to him, but that was little concern. He had paid a part of his salary to procure a pretty Gaelic slave girl called Primigenia who pleased him when he wanted, without much complaint. He had treated her well and had become enamored by her big eyes, beautiful lips, and gentle manner of speaking. She spoke passable Latin, and that was enough—he wanted someone for his bed and companionship, not a tutor.

As he sat in his tall Syrian-wood chair and looked at the bundles of papyrus and parchment records before him, Cleitus' mind returned to the one nagging thought that had bothered him for years.

That fateful evening in the fields.

When their attack on Spartacus had gone wrong.

When the Thracian dog had cut off his fingers like they were beanstalks.

And when he was saved by the boy—Felix, the herdsman—and brought to safety.

Saved?

The day's memories were hazy—most of his recollection was until Spartacus turned on Mellius. It was as if the gods had gripped his throat and froze his mind at that instance—and after that, it was all a messy muddle. All he remembered at the end of it was a haze of pain, stumbling in agony, and the world turning dark.

But the tapestry of violence had some intriguing fragments. A scene of Felix smashing a stone on Mellius' head. A bull charging the overseer.

Had he imagined that?

Did Felix have a hand in it all?

Had that whoremongering herdsmen somehow played a part in Spartacus' attack on Cleitus?

The inquiry into Felix's role in it all had led to nowhere. That the herder boy had sought help which led to Cleitus' rescue was not in dispute, which led to the immediate question—why would the boy have him saved if he were in on it with Spartacus? It made his head hurt.

Cleitus had dropped the matter after he had healed and begun his service in the estate—he had only seen the boy once or twice and let the matter be. What good came of pursuing a slave boy who spent all his day in the field?

But still.

No matter how much he tried to shake it off, the nagging feeling was like a hyena gripping a lion's balls. It would not let him go.

"Primigenia. Primigenia, come here!"

She walked in, so elegant with her auburn hair in a bun. Her eyes sparkled in the morning. The cheeks were red like her lips, and her thin garment barely hid the pink nipples.

She aroused him just by existing. It was embarrassing.

"How much do you know the men in the slave barracks?"

She looked confused. "Know in which way? I am not a whore," she said as a matter of fact.

He shook his hands to say *no, not that.* "No, I mean, do you know them well? Who they are, what they do."

"I know the men in our barracks, but not the ones in the farm and field."

The estate often kept those who worked inside–the cooks, cleaners, tutors, maids, dressers, and so on–separate from the even lower station of slaves that worked the fields and the farms. Primigenia spent some nights with Cleitus, but her "residence" was a slave barrack shared with others of the household. Someday he would just move her here once he was convinced of her loyalty.

"Come here. I have something for you to do."

On the contrary to his worries that she might show no interest in this mission, Primigenia seemed quite excited to unearth some secrets, a welcome respite from the humdrum of her plain existence.

6

LUDUS OF VATIA

The trainers imposed a grueling schedule. The gladiators woke up early and spent hours in the morning and afternoon. Then there was rest and recuperation, a controlled and monitored mingling amongst each other, and finally, before the sunset and darkness began, they were all sent back to the barracks into the cells.

To his surprise, very few were allowed anywhere near a real weapon. All training was conducted under tight supervision, using wicker shields and wooden sticks. The men were also never allowed to assemble in the field simultaneously. Groups of about a third of the full size were let out at a time along with the trainers, and the rest remained confined to their barracks until permitted. This was to ensure that there was never an overwhelming force confronting the guards should there be a riot.

The shields were heavier than real ones, and so were the sticks compared to the swords or spears they would carry. Heavy seven-foot posts dug into the ground acted as practice targets and helped elevate their pulses and fill them with vigor for the mock fights against each other. They spent hours "fighting" the pole. Some of it was reminiscent of his time in the army. But gladiatorial training focused on leg work, movements, "fight-ending thrusts" that did not kill, and theatrics. Only when the trainers were satisfied with the fighters' performance on their posts, would they allow the men to square off against an opponent.

Spartacus found himself at the receiving end of a cane more than once. Distracted fighting, arguing, and missing critical instructions led to being forced to hug the training post and getting caned on the back or buttocks while ignoring the derisive insults from the gladiators who surrounded the victim. The caning was effective—painful, but when administered correctly, it barely broke the skin and did not lead to infections and severe injury, like a good flogging.

Spartacus was also surprised by the lack of chaos and violence on the training grounds. He always imagined the training schools to be dens of filth, lawlessness, and reckless violence where men lived as beasts, forced into their circumstances. But the reality differed significantly. While they all lived like animals–often shackled in their small rooms no better than cages, they rarely fought amongst each other. The few raised voices and occasional blows were quickly settled either by intervention or sharp punishment–flogging, caning, or exercise until collapse. The different cultures clashed sometimes, but the guards and trainers knew how to keep that in check. Rigid discipline and ready access to doctors, regular meals, and a roof to eat under were enough for most men who had arrived here from worse circumstances. Besides, many men came from low stations in their lives and thus saw the arena as an opportunity for glory. They believed that they had a duty to the *Ludus* and thus were amenable to the rigid rules. If there were darker methods to the control, he was as yet unaware of it.

Most men accepted their fate and focused on survival or accruing benefits through their performance. No one raised their hands to the trainers, and all the "students" were generally respectful of others. It became clear why–after all, unlike men condemned to death, these were still given the slightest glimmer of hope.

Of freedom.

Of glory.

Of adulation, fame, and companionship.

Only a few fools would forego the promise and endanger themselves. While living in stifling cells and doing nothing else apart from training to entertain screaming crowds was maddening, it was still better than being hoisted on a cross, drowned, burned, stabbed, or thrown into mines.

But how long could he endure this stifling environment? How could anybody?

"Spartacus and Fortunatus!"

Fortunatus was a good fighter. The Gaul was ten years younger, heavyset, intensely focused, but lacking leg work.

Spartacus walked up to the center of the makeshift arena. A referee stood on the side, a few spectators on the wooden bench, and Philotas was there to harangue and push them. Men trained in pairs in their assigned roles.

Spartacus was assigned the role of a *Thraex*, pointing to his origins as a Thracian. He either trained against another Thraex or a Galli—another heavy gladiator. The men were usually put against those of similar gait and girth, and there were strict rules about what *type* of gladiator went against the other. Philotas had explained how it was in no one's interests—the sponsors, spectators, or the owners—to create lopsided matches that resulted in useless injury or death. One had to protect investment and ensure the best returns.

Since not every ethnic group had all types of fighters available at all times, often, the paired practices cut across them. Language could be a challenge–but so long as the trainers could talk to each other, which they could, the fighters had little to speak, and it mattered little.

He held a heavy wooden fencing stick and a willow shield that weighed more than what a real one would. As the Thraex, he would wield a circular shield and a curved sword—a *sica*—but during training, it was a short, heavy stick. Fortunatus was a Galli with a heavy pointed mask, a tall willow shield covering his chest and torso, and ankle-length guards.

They acknowledged each other and then spent time on their heavy wooden posts dug into the ground.

Spartacus enjoyed these sessions—with one exception.

Crixus.

Crixus' real name was Arvecorix. But the school had a rule—all fighters, slaves, were assigned Latinized names, and they had to adhere to it. This was done on purpose to erode their identity.

The Gaelic trainer and fighter was a loudmouth, vulgar distraction who alternatively infuriated Spartacus or caused him to lose concentration and laugh. His Latin was atrocious, his words often made no sense to anyone, including the gods themselves, and he just would not shut up no matter who admonished him. But he was a talented man, and there was little anyone could do.

Crixus was squat and short, powerfully built, his cascading brown and yellow hair bouncing as he moved about energetically, and his crackling voice alternatively annoying or regaling those around him.

"Beat his bum! Show the strength of your cock, so even pigs pray!" Crixus yelled at Fortunatus, who looked as confused as Spartacus.

What does it even mean?

And then Fortunatus and Spartacus squared again. The younger man was improving–he had learned how to thrust expertly from above the shield, look for exposed body areas, and use the shield like a weapon. But Spartacus, by his experience and height, usually managed to deliver "lethal" blows.

Thud.

Duck and twist.

Stab from above the shield.

Run back, swing and pivot. Punch with the shield.

Thud. Thud. Thud.

Crack!

Thrust from below the shield and strike the ankle.

Crack!

The referee called the match, and Philotas and Crixus came forward to deliver their commentaries. Spartacus noticed that Vatia was sitting on one of the high benches, observing them with his beady eyes.

"You are getting better, Spartacus. Your experience shows that your speed is impressive, despite your age," Philotas said. "In a few months, you will be a truly formidable opponent."

Crixus had something to add. He moved the hair falling on his eyes. "Not much show. Girls not excited. Too boring!" he said, and then he made a few dramatic gestures by swinging his arms and twisting his torso. "Show! This not a battle, but a big show."

Was Crixus doing this as a show to the dominus?

"I understand. I must demonstrate showmanship."

"Yes, yes, showship," he said and turned to Fortunatus. "You did not beat his bum. Leg work too slow, like a donkey on a trip."

Donkey on a trip?

Men often borrowed wisdom from their native tongues and translated them into a new language. Was Crixus, of a tribe of the Gauls, doing the same? Or was this tradecraft—

the crudeness, the loud eccentricity, the terrible accent—all a show?

Fortunatus replied in their tongue, and Crixus shook his head vigorously as he responded with a stream of what sounded like expletives. Then he switched. "Now, speak Latin. Learn!"

"Yes, sir," Fortunatus said. "More nimble movements. More gap and pacing."

Crixus snatched the shield and stick from Fortunatus and faced Spartacus. "You, me. Watch. See fires bloom in women's stolas due to my wind breeze!"

What?

Spartacus had never faced Crixus in training. And he soon learned what facing a showman, and an expert in the art meant. Crixus not only parried Spartacus' attacks brilliantly, but he would run back, put space between them, push out his chest and make dramatic postures before quickly returning to battle. Spartacus failed to inflict a single blow to an exposed body part and had to halt twice to control himself from laughter. There was a wicked cleverness in Crixus' antics—it threw off the opponent and lulled him into complacency. But as time passed and Spartacus grew tired, Crixus found a weakness and thrust the stick straight into Spartacus' ribs. If that were a weapon, Spartacus would be dead.

The referee called the match, and Spartacus acknowledged the defeat by bowing and touching the wicker shield to Crixus'.

"I am funny. You are dead," he said, the slightest grin hiding behind his bushy mustache and his bright, glassy eyes sparkling. Spartacus' impression of the man had already changed with the encounter.

Philotas slapped Crixus' back and turned to Spartacus. "Skill and show. You will learn. And with your impressive physique, you will bring excitement to the masses."

At that point, Vatia rose from his bench and walked out of the arena.

The days passed in rigorous training and each session taught Spartacus the finer aspects of gladiatorial combat. Understanding the opponent and his role. His strengths and weaknesses. The weapons he uses, and the moves he is trained for. Ways to anticipate and parry strikes. How to look for vulnerability. And how to do all this while being *entertaining* and showing a certain spark that the crowd loved. On some days, Vatia watched from the benches. He rarely spoke, and heavily armed guards always surrounded him.

Always afraid. Always suspicious.

When he wanted to send instructions to a fighter or issue a reprimand, he did it through Canicus, Philotas, or Crixus. Spartacus received two commendations from Vatia through Philotas and one reprimand. All of them were related to his presence on the field and his agreeableness to the audience.

"If you are a great fighter but attract no adulation, expect the owner to loan you out to miserable bastards and lousy arenas. They will wear you out until you make money, and then throw you into a ditch if you die," Philotas said after one of the sessions where Spartacus won but failed to impress the trainers. "All eyes will be upon you on your first match. You will hear this until you beg for mercy from the gods—the arena is not just about your skill, but—"

"Your performance. Yes, Philotas, I know!"

Even after weeks of training, the trainers had not allowed him to touch a real weapon. Access to the armory was strictly controlled and guarded by Vatia's men. Only those gladiators who had upcoming matches trained with real iron and bronze, and once the session was over, the weapons were locked away. No one was allowed to the armory or to practice with weapons once the sun neared the horizon–any breaking of the rules meant lashes or worse.

Spartacus also became intimately familiar with the insults and stereotypes of the dominant groups. The Celts were known as the loud rabble-rousers, always ready to fight, quarrelsome, and lacking sufficient intelligence. The Thracians were of a primitive kind with fierce warriors and skilled in swords, but their language was ugly, and they smelled terrible. The Germans? Quarrelsome, arrogant, pompous, and when their women sneered at you, you did not know if they wanted to fuck you or murder you. None of the groups got along particularly well, though some made friendly relations borne of common grievances. But they all had one thing in common—they tried to forget the unfortunate situation of their being and fought hard with hopes of greatness.

In this environment, Spartacus went back to his cell each day, sore from the many strikes on his body, and fell asleep without much thought. His fantasies of thunderous applause and heroic adulation all dissolved into inky darkness within seconds of his head touching the hay mattress. He had so far not seen Antara, and he was not permitted to address Vatia during his rounds. Philotas urged patience.

After one of the sessions, he asked Philotas why he had not been allowed to see his wife.

"He is watching you like he watches every recruit. Your conditions will improve once he is satisfied," Philotas said.

"Have you spoken to him?"

"The trainers have an audience with the *dominus* every few days. He is very invested in our success."

"Is it not part of that investment keeping the men happy and calm?"

Philotas smiled. "Obedience and discipline come first. Pampered men go too soft."

Spartacus controlled his irritation. Philotas had always been by his side. He was a tough but fair trainer, and he knew the ways of the school and the arena well. But he was also a very private man who shared almost nothing about his life beyond the training ground. Philotas, like Canicus, lived in a separate quarter on a higher level, reserved only for the best fighters and the trainers. Crixus had not earned that comfort yet, for whatever reason.

"From tomorrow, your training will pick up a level. In twenty days, Vatia will be present in the makeshift arena, and your job is to show how good you are and what you are capable of. Remember, the happier he is, the better things will be for you."

With Philotas' and Canicus' help, Spartacus had found his authentic manner. After a few failed attempts of flair and dramatics mimicking Crixus and a few others, he realized that their mannerisms did not suit his physical stature or style. Spartacus was a big man. One of the biggest in all the *Ludus* with his commanding height, imposing head full of thick cascading hair and beard, the hairy chest, and trunk-like thighs. His natural brutish demeanor gave him a leader's aura and, combined with his deliberate style, his pedigree having led men in the Roman army, and his Greek training, he was a powerful presence even without having once proved himself in the field.

Finally, it was Vatia who helped Spartacus find his niche. *Affect the manner of a cultured, learned warrior,* Vatia had said after observing one of the sessions. *The people all get brutes, but rarely a philosopher-like warrior.*

So, Spartacus cultivated a new style—the "Thracian thinker," as Philotas called him.

In this style, Spartacus portrayed the manners of a cultured warrior. He developed a distinct gait entering the arena—standing tall, whipping his head side-to-side, exaggerating the polite bow and acknowledgment of the referee and his opponent, and when the men separated to recover, delivering clipped aphorisms in Greek and Latin. He initially found it awkward and silly and then slowly grew into the role. The trainers screamed into his ears again and again—he was as much a dramatist as he was a fighter. Even his limp became an instrument of show—he exaggerated it, thus deliberately drawing attention to physical limitation and thus intending to lull the opponent to carelessness.

Once he settled into the routine and his mind expanded beyond his immediate frustration and focus, Spartacus often fantasized about flowers dropping on him from the stands. Of great adulation and the screaming of his fans. Suddenly his confinement and condemnation did not feel so bad.

But he also began to learn more about the happenings in the school. The first among which was the usage of the small box as punishment.

Men who were deemed disrespectful to Vatia during his visits, or those considered insubordinate to their trainers, were sometimes condemned to the "box." When he heard of it initially, Spartacus ignored it—for he had lived and suffered punishments many times, and such an occurrence was nothing unusual. Such was the order of the world.

But when he saw one of the Germans wail and flail around, begging frantically, his eyes wide open in terror as guards dragged him away, Spartacus inquired a few others discreetly as to what it meant.

The box was a small cement room where a man could not sit without his head hitting the rocky ceiling, could not sleep stretching his legs, and could not turn his full breadth without a struggle. Depending on the climate, it was dreadfully hot or miserably cold, for this room was inconspicuously tucked at the end of the barrack corridor. But Spartacus learned something else—almost everyone knew of it, but no one spoke of it. The experience was like the darkest imagination of Hades—severe cramps, terror in the darkness, thirst, and fear, as a man was left there for two to three days at a time with no food and little water. By the time they were extracted, the victims were delirious and desperate to please. Some shivered at the thought of even returning to their cells at the end of the day. The box broke not the bones or the skin, but a man's spirit.

The men sometimes spoke of a light stutterer named Procamus, who was confined to the box for only a day, and how his stutter had become monstrously worse for weeks after. They all believed that a demon crept into the box along with the condemned men and inflicted torment upon them.

Vatia ran the school with an iron grip. Slowly, Spartacus became aware of the situation of their enslavement—glory was not what men aspired to, as they sought a higher purpose. It was because that was the only way to keep their mind away from their wretched misery. Minor transgressions led to the taking away of basic privileges. Soon, as he would learn, earning the displeasure of the master led to much worse outcomes.

"How are you?" he asked Antara as he held her close. He had been granted the chance to have his wife in his room for a day. Spartacus was ecstatic when she stepped into the cell—looking better than how they had arrived. She wore a Roman tunic, loosely draped around her slim body, and wore her hair in a bun with strands falling like waterfalls on both sides of her ears, a fashion among the local women.

"Dionysus keeps me alive. How are you, husband?" she asked as she felt the many bruises on his body.

"Alive. Training. With a large gap in my chest without you beside me," Spartacus said. The day had been long and brutal, and neither had the energy to make love. *Wish he had been told earlier!* But just the chance to hold her close, smell her, feel her was more than wonderful.

"Do they treat you well? Do they feed you?" she asked.

"They feed me like fattening a pig for pork," he said. She admonished him for the ill-speak. They chatted about mundane things for some more time, remembered their children, and learned more about her life.

Antara was part of the kitchen staff, though he had never seen her during his meals. She said that the women played many roles—as cooks, cleaners, and servers. They worked on rotation in Vatia's villa for household chores. At night, the women were taken to a barrack where they were sometimes shackled before sleep. She showed the mark on her ankle, and he gently traced his finger on it. *What do they think the women will do, foment a rebellion?* They had a male overseer, but he was involved in a relationship with one of the women, and apart from the yelling and occasional beating, he stayed away from them.

Never having lived this way, Antara was still struggling with the life. She cried twice as she spoke of her conditions, expressing the desire that someday they would gain freedom and leave. But even as she said that, Spartacus noticed that Antara's eyes betrayed a different fear, something else beyond the usual concern.

"What is it? Something else ails you," he said gently as he held her chin and lifted her delicate face.

She hesitated at first, and then when he pressed upon her, Antara began to speak. "Rumors. I have heard some rumors—I do not know how true they are or what they mean," she whispered, as if afraid that her words would seep out of the chambers into the ears of malcontent outside.

"Rumors about what?"

Antara snuggled closer so she could speak in a low tone. "The *dominus*, the master, is apparently in deep debt. He is desperate to loan out more fighters, faster, to make some money."

Spartacus was slightly alarmed. Men in debt were nothing surprising in this business—but speeding up fights had other repercussions. "Where did you hear this?"

"No one in particular, but the maids talk. Some work in the mistresses' apartments. They live separately."

He tried to allay her fears. "This is a growing school, and it grows because he can loan more fighters—nothing is surprising."

She looked at him the way she looked when she accused him of something. Spartacus knew the *look*. "Do not think of me as just a maid, husband. I would not have worried if it was nothing to be concerned about."

He grinned. The fire in Antara had not extinguished, and she cared little that he was so much more powerful than her. "I shudder in fear," he chuckled as she punched his chest with her fists.

"This is no matter for casual dismissal," she hissed. "They say Vatia is preparing to send unprepared or less talented men to ugly new events where men fight beasts, sometimes with bare hands!"

Now, Spartacus was worried. He had heard, only in murmurs, that *some* men may be forced to fight animals. And that these were men considered the lowest of the gladiators. But no one knew or was willing to talk about whether the rumors were true. There were limited shows, only inexpensive sponsored events, where animals featured in mock hunting or circuses and acrobatics. Bringing flesh-eating beasts against men was not the norm, for it was far more expensive to manage.

"People like to gossip," he said, but his voice betrayed his uneasiness.

"Not a gossip! Some of the girls have affection for the men training in the arena. And now the master wants to send them to fight others without enough practice, or worse, offer their necks to lions for entertainment!"

How true was this? Canicus or Philotas would know.

He held her close and tried to assure her. "I will speak to trainers. I have built a good relationship with all of them—surely, some will know. Surely many men find it offensive that they are offered up for amusement while being sold stories of glory to make up for their past criminality."

Antara's eyes blazed at his words. "What was our criminality, husband?"

Spartacus had once again stepped into the quicksand of his superiority. He sometimes saw the others as *deserving* of this fate while he was innocent. Even his wife was seeing through it.

"I will inquire about this matter. If something is amiss, surely we have Vatia's ears, for we are an expensive investment. It is in his best interests to keep the fighters focused and motivated. Unnecessary fear will do no good."

It was an interesting situation—how much negotiating power did they have? How far did Vatia see this as a purely business proposition, and at what point would his Roman sensibility kick in?

"Will you have a chance to speak to the master about our freedom?"

It is too early.

"I must first demonstrate my worth in the arena before any discussion."

She nodded. After all, why would Vatia entertain *any* conversation? But how much did Antara know of the conditions for freedom? It was exceedingly rare, for most men died before attaining it. No magisterial contracts resulted in freedom—it was left entirely to the owner. Men usually went to the arena four to five times a year, and the only two examples he had heard from Philotas were of two men, not of Vatia's school, who were freed after twelve fights. *Twelve!*

Men who went past their prime or were no longer fit to fight were often sold off into farm work, mines, or other harsh professions or relegated to back-breaking work in the masters' villas until their end.

"What do you get to eat?" he asked her, steering the conversation away from the depressing topic.

"Sometimes gruel, sometimes bread. Sometimes we steal a little from the main kitchen," she said, grinning mischievously.

"Be careful!" he cautioned her. "You never know the punishments if caught!" Roman law was harsh, and slaves received the worst of it. Surely she knew that!

Antara looked unbothered. "The overseers know. They ignore it, so long as it is controlled."

Playing with fire.

"Vatia is a vicious little bastard, Antara. Exercise caution and do not get ensnared in any stupidity of other women."

It was common knowledge that away from the protection of their men, women did not exercise good judgment and lacked the ability for sensible conduct. The gods had not blessed them with the same ability to think as they did to the men. Surely his wife knew that!

"Of course I am careful," she pouted. "In any case, if I am in trouble, I know that my big husband will ride the horse of Sabazios and rescue me!"

He laughed and tweaked her nose. "Do you quarrel and fight? How are the others?"

"Of course, we quarrel and fight. It seems women from all places—the Gauls, Germans, Spaniards, Romans—are the same," she giggled. "But I have a friend named Methe. She knew a few words of our language, for her lover, now dead, was Thracian. She is teaching me Latin."

"What do you know in Latin?"

"Your penis is small," she said in impeccable Latin and giggled again, very pleased with herself.

He shook his head in mock disgust. "Dionysus weeps for his priestess! Where is this Methe from?"

"She says Hispania. She is a gentle soul."

"Do you know where Hispania is?"

She glared at him and tugged his beard hard enough for him to wince. Their time together would end in a few hours. Spartacus forgot his exhaustion and drew her into a kiss.

Tomorrow, he would need to talk to Philotas or Canicus.

7

LUDUS OF VATIA

"Is it true, Canicus?" Spartacus pressed. "Is Vatia sending men to the arena without adequate training?"

Philotas had stonewalled the discussion, saying he was bound by oath to Vatia not to speak ill of the school or encourage rumors. He had tried to allay Spartacus' fears but had not succeeded. An annoyed Philotas had told Spartacus to speak to Canicus and leave him out of politics.

Now Canicus was tired of Spartacus' insistence. "You have been warned before, Spartacus. Leave the matters of the school to the owner and the conduct of its business to the trainers and sponsors. Where are you hearing these rumors?"

Spartacus did not want to reveal the source—for one never knew whom to trust. "Murmurs in the kitchens and warehouses," he said vaguely. "Is it true? You have not answered my question!"

Canicus, always calm, clenched his jaws. "You take your growing stature for granted, Thracian," he warned. "Do not think that your privileges are assured. Look at the other men. They train, fight, and quarrel sometimes, but they keep their head where it matters. And so should you."

Their reluctance is an indication of the truth of the matter.

But Spartacus returned to Philotas in the evening after a particularly impressive performance where he got the better of two more experienced men, including one who was previously in the arena. Spartacus had heard enough about the experience in Capua's and Pompeii's arenas, and the stories had lost their allure. It was time he *saw* it.

"Are you back bothering me again, Spartacus?" Philotas said. The trainer had expressed his satisfaction with Spartacus' skills more than once, and the two had formed a cautious but respectful bond. Even though Spartacus had never stepped into the arena, whereas Philotas had conquered it, the Macedonian knew of Spartacus' military history and recognized its value.

"Why the secrecy, Philotas? We are surrounded by hard men who fight and belittle each other all day. We have seen death, inflicted it, have been surrounded by it, and yet why the mystery behind how the situation is evolving?"

Philotas retorted. "This is a *Ludus*. This is not a legion. This is not a mountain range with bandits. You are not here of your free will. It is not the same!"

"Let us leave matters of philosophy aside. Is it true? Are men being pressed to the arena without enough training? Are we being sent to the jaws of beasts?"

Philotas sighed. "Come with me. Away from the ears of others, for they do not have your intelligence or inquiring mind."

They walked past Crixus, who howled. "Girls, go walking! Sway bum like horse in the field!"

Philotas pointed his stick at Crixus but said nothing. "He is like a donkey that never stops braying, but he is a sight to behold in the arena."

"He is fixated with bums. How did he come to the arena?"

Philotas shrugged. "He speaks little of his past. I ask little of it. The less you know of your fellow men, the better. I thought you might have realized it by now."

It was true. After all, someday, Spartacus might fight one of his fellow men and might even mortally wound him. But deaths in the arena were rare, though the rumors brought to question whether this was all changing.

They reached the wall at the edge of the training field. "Listen carefully, Thracian. The more you speak your mind, the greater you put yourself at risk. You are older than most, learned, *and cultured*, but you should learn to keep your mouth shut. You are distracted, and I need my best men to focus on the glory ahead of you."

There. They speak of glory.

Spartacus did not respond, letting Philotas continue.

"Vatia wants to grow the *Ludus*, and to grow it, he needs to loan fighters more often and make money."

"And so he loans men before they are ready to be in the arena."

"It is not that simple. The problem with rumors, Spartacus, is that you only hear what you wish to hear. Did it come from the kitchens?"

Spartacus nodded.

"The kitchens are a source for terrible truths, just as awful as the broth and brew," he said, grinning. "Did you know that before you joined, they spread a rumor that Vatia was shipping the strongest to Aethiopean mines and killing off the rest? None of it was true, not even the slightest."

Was Philotas speaking the truth?

"Anyway. The rumor mongers will distort reality and turn a little campfire into a conflagration. Yes, some men will face the arena before adequate practice. But is that in itself a terrible thing?"

"What do you mean? Sending men to slaughter while you speak of glory is a terrible affront to the gods!"

Philotas tugged on his earlobe. "You are a refined man with our mannerisms, yet blind to the truth. What is this slaughter you speak of?"

Spartacus was short for words. *Slaughter* was speculation.

"You have nothing to say, for you have allowed the seed of a rumor to grow into a poisonous weed in mind. How many of Vatia's men have died in the arena in the last three years?"

Spartacus did not answer.

"Four! That is all! Three were from wounds inflicted in the arena. Doctors tried to save them. The other man died in an accident when he backed into a guard's spear. Is that slaughter? I am sure you have killed more men in a day's battle."

"Perhaps that is changing—"

"You think too much, Spartacus. Do you know how this business is conducted?"

Spartacus shook his head. He knew a few details but not everything.

Philotas continued. "A *ludus* loans its gladiators to the organizers. The price a fighter fetches depends on his fame or the quality of the school. The loan becomes a *sale* if a gladiator dies. And the sale is often ten to twenty times the loan price. Do you realize how stupid it would be for an organizer to seek the wanton death of gladiators? It would bleed the sponsors dry, and soon there would be no more games."

Spartacus was learning new aspects of this corrupt business. But he had little to counter Philotas' words.

Now Philotas was in the spirit of the lecture. "Almost every man returns from the arena either as a victor or his ego bruised as the one defeated. What matters is what *valor* they demonstrated on the field. Now, the ones without training? Vatia loans them to poorer locations that pair the men with others from lesser schools. They may not be as trained for Capua or Pompeii, but they are more than adequate for Thurii!"

The explanation was convincing, leaving Spartacus with not much to argue with the man. But Philotas continued. "These men cost money. Sending them against better fighters in larger avenues only puts them at risk. Would you do that, Spartacus? If you were a general, would you send a lightly armored auxiliary against a heavily armored Roman cavalry?"

"My only desire was for my questions to be answered."

"This is not a philosophy school, and you are not a magistrate or tribune," Philotas said caustically. "When you open your mouth and ask questions, men of lesser intellect are swayed and cause trouble. And some ears roam among men and spill poison into Vatia's ears. Do you want that?"

But there was one last question, but he decided not to push his good fortune.

"I thank you and the gods for answering my questions. I am unfamiliar with this world, and yet I have compulsions that I know I must control."

He looked mollified. "Well, that will be it then. I have to address this with the men to contain any damage you may have caused. But see to it that these never reach Vatia's ears."

"Yes, Philotas."

But Philotas was not done. He walked back with Spartacus to the center and assembled all the men—his squad and the Gauls, Germans, and Syrians. To them, he only issued a short instruction.

"Men! You may have heard rumors from the kitchen. Women who should be cooking or fucking can sometimes run their mouths on matters they understand little. No man is being sent unprepared against strong fighters, and no one is going to the beasts for entertainment. Put any questions in your mind aside, and fight for the name that is rightfully yours!"

Some of those who understood him hooted and cheered, and a few others, on translation, did the same. Spartacus caught Crixus muttering beneath his beard, and Canicus had a far stare about him.

"Now get back to your shields and sticks. May the gods look down upon you with pride!"

As the men dispersed, Philotas gestured for him to join. "There is something you should know."

"Yes?"

"The master has ordered that it is time for you to join the fighters in a new event in Pompeii. You will watch and learn. This is the first step in your final preparation to step into the arena!"

8

LUCANIA

Primigenia's smiling eyes betrayed her excitement. Cleitus knew he had to be patient to learn what he wanted, and he knew that she found her "mission" exciting and would do what she could. His day was busy, but it was an interesting one. The investigation into the missing guard had come to an end—scouts had found his remains—just tattered clothes, broken bones, and desiccated skin, in a gorge near the estate. People died all the time. There was nothing unusual about it. But what was interesting in this case was that this man was on guard duty with the boy, Felix, a few days before he went missing.

No, to be accurate, *no one had seen the guard* since his trip with Felix. As was customary in the case of dealing with slaves under questioning, Felix had received a flogging good enough to flay some skin off his back and put him to bed for a week (Porcina did not like that), but he had strenuously declared his innocence and said that men sometimes got lost, were pushed by cows in a stampede, or got drunk and slipped. He had no idea what had happened to the man and that all he did was care for the estate's prized assets as he always did.

And this had only strengthened Cleitus' hunch. The flashes of his memory had returned with a vengeance, now unwilling to rest in the depths of dreams, *howling* that he find out what happened the evening of Spartacus' attack. What had Felix done? What was his role? Sabazios and Apollo, his new god, demanded justice.

Now he looked at Primigenia by his side, naked, her pale skin pink with exertion. He found her beautiful even with one roaming eye and two rotten teeth. Primigenia was always polite and hard-working, and she was enthusiastic in bed. She was one of the many slaves he had seen that had comfortably accepted the life of a slave. She did not lament her condition, made no complaints, and had not even flinched the first time he had ordered her to disrobe. But did she like him? Did she find him repulsive–with his twisted nose, sunken eyes, and a hand with three missing fingers? He was no specimen of the ideal barbarian–like the bastard Spartacus–intimidating in size or with flowing beards and beast-like hair. No one wanted Cleitus. Not his mother. Not his people. And the truth was—not even the others in the estate, for they saw him as an opportunistic foreigner, only a step above a slave. The snide remarks, condescending words, and dismissal of his opinions were daily occurrences. His only protection was the Senator himself, for he saw the value in Cleitus' abilities.

Cleitus brushed away all these thoughts swirling in his head, gently wiped the sweat on her forehead, and pushed the strands of her hair back with the two remaining fingers of his right hand. He had always wanted to, but never dared, ask if she liked… no, loved, him. Perhaps another day.

"Well, you are desperate to say something," he said, smiling. "I am ready to listen!"

She giggled. "Yes, master! It is about what you asked!"

Cleitus' pulse quickened. "Very good. Tell me what you learned."

Primigenia snuggled closer. "Felix is one of the prized herdsmen of the estate. He has been here since his birth."

Cleitus nodded. He had learned only a few scraps of information about the boy–and none of it interesting.

Cleitus did not have a good network within the estate and did not want to go about inquiring about the boy. The books had practically nothing about him except an old entry that recorded his birth. His mother was *Iris*. She had a few other children, none of whom were on the estate anymore, and she had been allowed to go free. But Iris had not stayed in the estate for Felix—she had left for a better life, leaving the toddler to grow as a slave.

His mother was like mine. No love for her child. Just like a piece of wood or rotted meat, only to be thrown away or discarded.

Cleitus had never told Primigenia—or, for that matter, anyone, of his childhood. He had always said he was an orphan—but he was not.

Cleitus' earliest memories were of his mother savagely beating him to within a finger's breadth from death while cursing him for something he could not understand. He was a sickly child, and amongst the Bessi who celebrated strength, any weakness in a boy was looked down upon. It did not matter if the child had greater intelligence than all those around him. She had one day dragged him howling, tied him up, and thrown him off an ass in a neighboring village.

And then she was gone.

A Bessi priestess had taken kindly to him and reared him, protecting him from the baleful eyes of other stronger boys. He had attracted Durnadisso's attention, and the then son of the chief had taken Cleitus under his wing. Cleitus had always feared others, but his scouting skills and relentless pursuit of whatever he put his mind to had helped secure his position by Durnadisso. A few years later, with the mind of an angry fifteen-year-old, he had returned to his village surreptitiously, along with Durnadisso, and bludgeoned his mother to death. He had never forgotten her bloodied, matted hair, shattered skull, and smashed face lying on the village hut. And that rage for unloving mothers had never left Cleitus.

He snapped out of his reverie and returned to the record.

But there was nothing more about Iris or where she came from. There were no entries about Felix except one, in an estate book that recorded misbehavior, something about bringing shame to the estate and conspiring with a slave. But the entry was careless and cryptic—giving no indication of the situation, how long ago, and whom he conspired with.

So, what had Primigenia learned that he did not know?

"They say Felix is very quiet and shy. He does not talk much. He sometimes mumbles to himself and is rarely in the estate grounds from dawn to dusk."

"Well, he is a herdsman."

"But though he is shy, they say he is very stubborn. He has been beaten many times by overseers but does not fear them."

"Nothing surprising. I have only seen him twice under questioning, but he has conviction. Tell me something new, Primigenia!" he scolded her.

She slapped his wrist playfully, surprising him, and drew her hand back sharply, suddenly worried. He found it almost endearing. He returned it with a gentle slap on her plump bottom, and she giggled.

"Be patient, master. Let me tell you all!"

He sighed. Primigenia was polite, but she also liked to talk. If one asked her about the fruits of a tree, she would tell the story of the tree's life, starting with the seed.

"Go on," he said, enjoying her company. He had never once had a woman willingly by his side. Sort of willingly.

After all, she was a slave, but she showed no hatred toward him.

"Remember you said that Felix saved you after that barbarian–Sprotikis–"

"Spartacus."

"Yes, Spartacus. He injured you unjustly," she said, her tone clearly showing her distaste for the bastard Spartacus. How he loved her for that!

"But Felix had a dispute with Mellius, the overseer, during those days."

A dispute with Mellius? Cleitus was now intrigued. He nodded.

"Mellius was a terrible, terrible man. I served under him briefly. He was cruel, and nothing like you, master."

Cleitus smiled.

"But Mellius liked a slave girl in the estate household. She is still there. Lucia. You may have seen her. She works mostly in the *domina's* service."

There were many girls on the estate. He did not know a Lucia, though he may have seen her. But where was this story headed? "What about Lucia?"

"Wait. Let me say," she pouted. The insolent girl! She knew she could be playful toward him with no consequence. But he did not mind at all. Is this how a normal couple would be?

"Fine," he said, though he was immensely pleased that there was more to the story.

"So, Mellius was in love with Lucia, but she cared little for him. They say Mellius was not too far away from being a freedman, but that held little interest for her. He could not force her into a relationship or ravage her," she said as if it was a normal occurrence. "He was frustrated because she was protected by her mother, the *domina's* personal maid."

"And?"

"Felix too had his eyes on Lucia, for she was a pretty girl, and this was before the master had her for himself and made her pregnant."

Cleitus' head was beginning to spin from all the angles of this story.

"But she lost the child, and soon the *dominus* lost interest in her. Some say that Lucia liked Felix. I do not know what she found in him, but they say their eyes met too frequently, and she visited him in his barracks, defying Mellius' orders."

This was becoming more interesting by the minute.

"I do not know the truth, but maybe they even fucked," she said. "So Mellius was outraged and gave Felix a sound thrashing. And Felix, the stubborn fool he was, conspired with the stable keeper to murder Mellius."

There. Conspired. So this was the record in the book.

Primigenia continued. "But it seems Lucia somehow betrayed him, and the master and Mellius found out. They punished the stable keeper severely and put the runaway warning collar around Felix's neck. And there was no question that he hated Mellius with all his being."

But what did any of this have to do with Spartacus? What was he missing? People quarreled about women all the time. Men's cocks caused the greatest dispute, he thought. He leaned forward to inhale her scent–that light aroma of a little rose perfume she had no doubt pilfered from the estate.

"How is this related to Spartacus?"

"Wait, wait," she said, in no hurry. He calmed down when she stroked his stubbled chin. *Did she not find him ugly and undesirable?*

"Now, when Spartacus, the man who did you wrong, arrived, Mellius had the task to' oversee his activities."

Did me wrong? The savage son of a whore sliced away my fingers like they were vegetables and left me to die.

Primigenia continued, now relishing that she had him interested in the story. "But this Mellius complained to others that Spartacus was arrogant and heeded little of his words. Particularly, Spartacus objected to Mellius' treatment of Felix."

"What? I thought Spartacus was assigned as a guard to the different herdsmen and boys in the field."

"He was! But the gossip is that he was somehow taken in by this boy, and instead of beating him to discipline, began taking his side."

The story was getting convoluted and confusing, but very intriguing.

"Now, before you ask, Spartacus was not buggering Felix. At least no one thinks so," she said. "They say it was as if Spartacus thought he was Felix's brother or father."

She had put an end to Cleitus' doubts whether Spartacus was taken into young boys, as some Romans did, but it seems there was no such evidence.

"Was there a relationship between Lucia and Spartacus?"

"If Spartacus wanted to bed Lucia, why would he be favorably disposed toward Felix?"

"Not everything is about someone fucking, Primigenia. Could Spartacus have some kind of history with Lucia or her mother? Where are they from?"

"Oh," Primigenia exclaimed. She grinned. "You are so bright, master. But no, I do not believe they knew each other at all. It seems Spartacus never saw Lucia or ever mentioned her name. They were supposedly Gauls from the far north, and her mother has been here for a long time."

There went that connection.

"You are splendid," he said to her and enjoyed it when she beamed at the compliment. He was no longer that conscious of his "partial palm" when he traced her face–she never resisted or looked bored or disgusted. Cleitus had bitter memories from his past. Of even prostitutes looking down upon him, as if he were a diseased dog.

"How did you learn so much?"

She giggled. "I know many in the barracks. Newcomers and old-timers. They all gossip about everyone. I made it sound like I was just interested. They think I like Felix–I do not care for him at all! He is a low herdsman!"

Low herdsman? The slaves had their hierarchy. The tutors, singers, hairdressers, and overseers were at the top. The herdsmen, ditch-diggers, latrine cleaners, and farmhands were at the bottom, mistreated by those above them.

Cleitus felt a pang of jealousy. Was she sleeping with anyone else? Did she have a lover tucked away–someone with whom she felt real joy, when she merely tolerated him? If there were even so much as a doubt, he would hunt that man down and ensure he was removed from the picture. He had become a gentler master to Primigenia. He no longer slapped or hit her as he did in the initial days when he tried to assert his authority. It was not needed with her, for she complied without question. He was kind to her now, loving even. Where else would she find that? Did she see that?

Primigenia was becoming a distraction! His mind returned to the topic of Spartacus again.

What was he missing?

How were Spartacus and Felix connected?

What did this Lucia have anything to do with it?

Why was Spartacus protective of Felix?

Was Cleitus' fragments of memory–of Felix attacking Mellius–was that real?

He leaned back on his pillow and rubbed her shoulders absent-mindedly.

Primigenia reached between his legs and began to stroke him. This was a ritual–something she thought pleased him greatly.

He pushed her hand away.

Like a special flower that blooms rapidly in the morning sun, a thought began to form in Cleitus' mind.

I know why.

9

POMPEII

Even when shackled and manacled and taken in a wagon like caged animals, Spartacus felt a strange excitement as the carriage swayed and shook all the way from Capua to Pompeii. The journey took a day, going south from Capua, along the side of Mount Vesuvius, and finally to the southwestern corner of the rich town where a large field was reserved for events and gladiatorial shows.

Vatia's school had sent two wagons. One with four fighters participating in the show, and the other with six learners, Spartacus included. Canicus was with the fighters, while a man named Castus, another Gaul of the Aulerci, accompanied the "learners" wagon. Messenius, a bald, stocky Roman, and overseer at the *Ludus*, was in charge. He set the rules, controlled the guards, and was responsible for the security and completion of the trip without incident. He took his job seriously—haranguing them or brandishing a metal-spiked whip, threatening torture for any misbehavior.

How expensive it must be to run these shows!

No wonder gladiators were prized possessions, which was why Spartacus felt a little relieved that the mindless slaughter of men made no sense, and therefore what Philotas said must have been true. Very few died because it was in no one's interests.

Along the way, people gawked at the wagons, disdain evident on their faces. That the gladiators were seen as dangerous animals was obvious from the heavy guard presence and stringent rules during the journey—no talking, loitering, or switching seats. Pompeii was larger than Capua, and they were first brought to the forum. They were led in a line, with guards walking on the side, like a parade, so that the people could get intrigued and excited about the upcoming event. The forum was an impressive place and busy with construction and expansion.

Vesuvius loomed in the background—its top devoured by clouds and center lush with forests.

The men posed by the sanctuary of Apollo and then before the beautiful colonnades of the Porticus of Popidius. Each time, Messenius, the travel supervisor, announced the grand new event loudly and introduced the men as the bloodthirsty warriors of Capua–drawing the required jeers and mocking. The more attention they drew, the better for business.

Near the Porticus was a large Latin poster announcing the event.

ON THE FIFTH DAY BEFORE KALENDS OF MAY FOUR PAIRS OF GLADIATORS SPONSORED BY DECAMANUS GENIALIS FIGHT AT THE SPECTACULA OF POMPEII CIRCUS AND EXCITING SURPRISE AWNINGS PROVIDED SEATING BY CLASS

During his journey with the Sullan army, Spartacus had learned that the general had previously subdued Pompeii, a predominantly Samnite town, and turned it Roman. Sulla brought Roman settlers, the Latin language, administrative rules, coins, and sponsored buildings, turning Pompeii into a thoroughly Roman town in a decade. Like all other towns, dense tenements radiated outward from the central forum and its marketplace–but without question, Pompeii affected greater affluence than other towns.

After supper, they were taken to their quarters beside the *spectacula*. Spartacus could not assess the venue. The fighters went into one room and learners to the other. They were shackled to the wall, given a jug of water, and told to sleep.

The event was two days away. The next day was light with little activity. The fighters practiced in a small open area, and the learners watched. This allowed Spartacus to observe the *spectacula* from outside. It was a makeshift wooden theater, semi-oval and enclosing about two-thirds of the arena. The wooden benches were tiered, similar to but much larger than those in the school. Tall iron posts with thick ropes tied between them acted as the fence separating the arena from the spectators. A stone structure with an iron door abutted a portion of the oval's longer edge, and the wooden benches continued on either side. Workers were setting posts and putting up awnings in the bench-less section of the arena, presumably for standers.

Not too difficult for a good fighter to attack the audience.

He slept well that night, partly relieved that he would not be in the arena and partly excited about what he would witness. He did not know the names of Vatia's men fighting the next day but hoped their gods looked upon them with kindness and imbued them with strength.

They were allowed to clean themselves and pray in the morning. Then each man was tied to the other with a rope around his neck. *You will not go far with this,* Messenius said. The fighters had already been taken away, but the learners were led around the venue to one of the open sections with a tattered awning. They were made to sit on the grass behind the fence–the view of the arena was unobstructed from here. The rope that connected them was tied to a post as if they were cattle held from escaping. Even though he was getting used to the treatment, acts like this brought great humiliation. *Was no one else bothered? Is Canicus not bothered?* Even Castus, who was some kind of trainer or supervisor, was tied with them. He spoke passable Latin and had only talked to them once. *I will make observations. You listen.*

"Sit and do not talk to each other, or you will feel the whip on your backs!" Messenius warned them. A couple of men had received lashes already.

Pompeii was a warm and humid place, and his skin got sticky as the sun rose in the sky. Bugs were plenty—in the grass and the air, irritating. Nothing he had never faced before, but sitting tied in one place while enduring it was certainly a greater annoyance. People gawked at them as they walked toward their benches.

The noise in the air grew steadily, and finally, more people took the benches. *It was time!* The narrow edge of the oval had special, raised benches with a decorated canvas awning—clearly for the high officials. *Where would Vatia be?* The place filled up steadily. He surmised that the benches were for officials and *plebs*, the citizens, and the open spaces were for slaves and foreign workers. Spartacus' section was already barricaded from the rest, and heavily armed guards surrounded them. *Where were the fighters? In the stone structure with the door?*

The entire arena was packed just before noon. Seating sections were dense and filled on all levels, and people jostled for space in the standing areas. Bands played trumpets and harps to silence the crowd and get their attention. Someone made a speech, and he could barely hear what it was—and it all came to an end with cheering and bench-thumping. *Maybe thanking the sponsor.*

The first two acts were to get the crowd warmed up. A drama followed by a comedy mime brought smiles to everyone's faces, including Spartacus'. But the third act, an acrobat on a bull, showed what the crowd was waiting for. The acrobat was talented, running circles around the animal, jumping on it, and riding it with great finesse, but people were getting bored. Some cheered, but many jeered. People threw clumps of clay and a few slippers into the arena, eventually causing the organizers to hastily end the show.

Two announcers entered the arena, and the crowd finally settled into silence. The man closer to Spartacus was easier to hear.

"No more waiting! You will now witness exciting battles like never before by the gracious sponsorship of the honorable Decamanus Genialis and his wife, Servilia! First, a mercenary of Gaul from the *ludus* of Gnaeus Lentulus of Capua against a ferocious Samnite from the *ludus* of Lucius Metellus of Pompeii!"

Two trumpeters entered the arena from the sides, followed by a referee and several armed soldiers who took positions along the perimeter. In loincloths and their bodies glistening with sweat and oil, the men entered next—one a Thraex and the other a Galli. The Thraex held a small wicker shield, and a *sica*, a curved blade, and the Galli had an oblong wooden shield and was armed with a lance. They looked to be of similar height and strength—the Thraex could move faster but had less protection than the Galli, who would be slower but was better equipped. He could not tell if either man was from Vatia's school due to their covered heads.

Great cheers arose from the stands, along with loud baying. There was a certain energy in the air–not the friendly, raucous type he remembered from Capua years ago. This was somehow *different*. He resisted the temptation to ask Castus a question. *Is this fight fair?*

The referee issued his instructions—impossible to hear above the crowd's din, the chatter of sellers, band drums, and trumpets.

A loud whistle began the fight.

What Philotas had said seemed to be true. The two men looked evenly matched as they circled each other and launched sudden thrilling movements. No number of lectures and demonstrations in the school replaced the real event—seeing how the men distanced from each other, faced the viewers to receive accolades, and then turned on each other was as much skill as it was an art. Back home, some tribes held gladiatorial-type games during funerals, but they were nothing compared to what he witnessed here. For a moment, Spartacus imagined himself in the arena, soaking in the crowd's adoration.

Most of the strikes went on the shields or weapon-to-weapon. So it was true as well. Killing the opponent was not the primary purpose. The *craft* of the duel had been preserved. The game ended when the lance struck the Thraex on a thigh, bringing the fighter to his knees. The man laid his shield down and raised a hand, admitting defeat. The referee ended the fight, and two slaves led out the bleeding and injured man as the audience cheered, and a few howled. Doctors waited in attendance, usually paid by the owner of the slaves, and attended to injured men—but only if the man were fit to fight again. Otherwise, they were left to die or given minimal care and put on a different duty until the end of their lives.

It was a satisfying fight and illuminated what a fight in a big venue felt like. *Would the learners stay here until all fights ended?*

Without much ado, the second set came in. Similar in style, but larger men. The game ended when the Samnite inflicted a deep gash on the Thraex's shoulder. Each fighter had their flair in how they moved, how they wielded their weapons and shields, and how they faced the people. The cheers were muted this time.

But by the third fight, the mood of the crowd had changed. The chanting and hoots as the fighting turned dangerous as the men began to tire. Spartacus could hear the screams from the stands: *Stab him!, Bore!, Get his chest!* And the sporadic calls for blood changed to entire sections yelling *blood, blood!*

The men realized what was happening. They tried hard to entertain–running about, with one of the fighters even trying a somersault. The crowd invigorated one of the fighters, who began to try his best to impose fatal blows on the other man, who was now on the defensive. The noise became deafening as suddenly the losing fighter dropped his shield and ran. This was unacceptable by the code of honor.

Fight, you coward! Fight! Spartacus found himself screaming at the man.

The winning man chased the loser, and suddenly a serious fight had turned into a comical travesty–except that there was no humor. Then the runner suddenly stopped, threw his shield, and collapsed to his knees. He raised his hands and sought mercy.

But all Spartacus heard was a full-throated baying for blood, with the entire crowd screaming *death, shame, cut his neck!*

Never had he seen before an audience for entertainment screaming enthusiastically for the execution of a man who had laid down his arms and asked for mercy. The winner stood with his lance raised, unsure what to do as he looked around. The referee was facing the dignitaries, waiting for some indication. Spartacus could not see clearly. In the uproar, he could not hear anything either.

After some back and forth, the referee ran closer to the dignitary section and exchanged some words. By now, the people were back to throwing items onto the field, flinging slippers, fruit, stones, clumps of clay, shards of and drinking pots littering the field. The referee came back to say something to the victor, even as the kneeling man looked around anxiously. He had removed his helmet. His eyes betrayed fear, and with one hand, he clutched his bleeding shoulder as blood seeped through his fingers.

Then the referee stepped back and nodded.

The victor raised his lance. The kneeling man raised his hand in defense, realizing what would happen.

And then the victor swung his lance down with force through the nape of the kneeling man's neck. The sharp tip ripped through the innards and exploded through the chest, causing an eruption of blood that shot through the air.

A great roar and cheer rose from the crowd. The victor pulled out the lance, raised the bloodied weapon, and strutted about. Two slaves ran into the arena, held the legs of the corpse, and dragged it out.

Spartacus found it unsettling—for death came to a soldier against another, death came to a gladiator willingly engaged in a funeral game, death came to a criminal scheduled for execution on account of his misdeeds, but to die for a baying crowd even after seeking mercy, in the event that it was not a dispensation of justice or war? He had been told that the arena was a *show*, and rarely did the men die— certainly not when there was a decisive defeat. Did the man dream of freedom after victories? A meal with meat and salt after a glorious show?

The noise died, and the next event began. Runners with harps played music, and vendors ran through the narrow spaces between benches yelling and selling their wares—snacks, trinkets, little idols, makeup pots–though none came to their section, for it was obvious to all that these men could not purchase.

He wiped a bug off his back and adjusted his position. When was the next fight? Would it be like this again?

The announcers were back. The crowd went silent again.

"Great people of Pompeii! You enjoyed the show and the *end* of a coward, did you not?"

Cheers and appreciation.

"What beautiful music from the talented runners with harps!"

Muted applause. "Next fight!" someone screamed, and many others joined.

The announcer smiled and paused for the noise to die down a little.

"Our gracious sponsor desires even greater thrills and excitement for this wonderful audience!"

The crowd was quiet in anticipation.

"Never before in this *spectacula*, never before in Pompeii, a new surprise for our glorious people!"

10

POMPEII

Vatia had no particular love for these games. Managing a school and dealing with the whims of sponsors gave him no joy, but there was no question that this was a lucrative business.

This humid heat, the baying of the ugly crowd, dealing with slaves and gladiators, he hated it all. But he needed the money, and money gave him respect. And a path to official positions that wielded far more power for far less filth. He had to get there quickly–for his cantankerous wife was threatening divorce, and her powerful father desired to wreck him. She was unhappy that he ran a training school. A *pimp* she often said derisively, peddling in men swinging their swords instead of women spreading their legs. *What prestige is there in calling yourself a gladiator owner? That is like owning a brothel and calling oneself a queen.* While she enjoyed the games, as evident by her excitement watching almost-naked men fight before her, she had no desire to be the wife of the owner of some. But the only way to official power was to first make enough money to stand for elections and sway voters. It all came down to money. And his father-in-law had vowed not to give him one more coin. *I have supported you enough, you worthless idiot! Now it is time for you to do what you must,* he had thundered.

And the way to faster money was to allow his fighters to be fodder for the increasingly violent games–and that meant a greater mix of unworthy criminals fit for beasts' jaws or comic executions and good fighters for prestigious shows. The old days of skill-based fights and dramatic duels were dwindling. Ceremonial games in honor of the dead were becoming rare, and there was no money to be made loaning a man here and there. The people demanded fast, bloody entertainment. And Vatia was going to supply men to the organizers to give it to them.

He watched with some trepidation as the organizers prepared for the next event. The *surprise*. Not something Vatia cared much for, but it had become somewhat of a novelty even in Rome. And now Pompeii would experience it. The problem was, news of these events leaked in the *ludus*, and there was invariably some unrest. Men kept their mouths shut for most parts, but some always had opinions. And those opinions had to be suppressed quickly before any discontent spilled into the barracks. Just seven months ago, a small neighboring *ludus* had a revolt, and soldiers had to be called. All thirteen gladiators had been killed in the fight, and their bodies hung on poles for others to see. While the owner had escaped with his life, he was ruined, crushed under the debt. Vatia had no desire to experience the same fate, which is why he had to have iron control over the men in his school.

Not just that. Only weeks ago, women in the kitchen had spread rumors about sending gladiators to the jaws of death, causing men to ask questions during training. It was unacceptable and dangerous. He had ordered every slave woman stripped and made each one flog the other as a reminder to never comment on the school's affairs. Hopefully, that was the end of them letting their tongues loose.

"If this thrills the audience, Gnaeus, you will make more money than you imagined," said Decumanus, the sponsor, turning behind from his seat. Decumanus was a rising star in local politics and had realized that the games were a good way to curry favor with the people. More games meant more stress but more money for Vatia.

"Let us pray it does not become just a senseless spectacle with poor, wretched men dying for laughing audiences," said Vatia. "There must be some honor in the fights."

"I think it will always be a combination. You know how *these* people are. We keep them happy with exciting fights, fillers, and cheap wine. Look at them. They are bored with the same old acrobatics, dancers, and singers. We need fresh ideas!"

"Indeed. And I have supplied worthy men for your cause, and I hope I have your graces."

The supplication to each of these bastards never ended.

"Bring me the best men and the fodder. Watch your treasury grow," he said and looked at the arena. "Now, let us see how Pompeii responds to this latest thrill!"

11

POMPEII

"Never before in this *spectacula*, never in Pompeii, a new surprise for our glorious people!" the announcer said with gusto.

Now he had the crowd's attention.

"What passions do kings and chiefs of Libya and Egypt, of Gaul and Germania, of Thrace and Syria share? The company of beautiful women? Sailing on the gently flowing rivers? Subduing those that rise against them? Yes. All of it. But something else brings greater joy–the spirit of a hunt!"

Murmurs in the audience.

"Never seen before in this great town, you are about to witness something that will fill you with awe and wonder! And yes, give you some fun and comedy as well. After all, we cannot always be serious!"

What was this about? Hunt? Comedy?

"But first–this needs an arrangement. I shall say no more, for this spectacle is for you to witness!"

Trumpets blared, and the announcers ran away from the field. The audience was utterly silent as they waited for what was next. First, many guards came running in, holding thick ropes and iron stakes and creating a second inner ring, taller than the current protective fence.

Then came workers with a painted canvas that depicted trees, mountains, and deer.

A forest.

They stood up the canvas in three corners of the arena, obstructing the view for some annoyed and frustrated viewers who now moved away and crowded others.

There was silence once again. It was clear that the organizers were drumming up anticipation.

A band showed up near the officials' section and played loudly.

Finally, two men emerged on the field and ran into the center. One was a stocky, well-built gladiator with his hair up in a bun and flowing hair. He wore a loincloth, a small arm guard, and carried a spear. The other was slimmer, clean-shaven, and in his hand was a comically small net.

He had no weapon.

Spartacus was certain that he had seen the unarmed man. They had shaved him—but he was surely from Vatia's school!

The men looked confused, for they were not up against each other. They scanned the crowd that was unsure of what was coming next. The men separated from each other and walked around slowly.

Were they performers? Were they pretending something like a prelude to a comical act?

Spartacus was curious.

"What are they doing?" the man next to him whispered to no one. Castus had no emotion on his face. His eyes were downcast.

That was when they heard it.

The growl.

The distinct, undeniable short *grunt* of a tiger or a lion. Spartacus had seen these magnificent beasts in a display show in Capua.

Now the crowd came alive.

A massive cheer went up, reaching the heavens.

And from the far end, a lion charged through a small narrow gate, followed by men behind tall shields. They brandished what seemed like hot irons and goaded the animal ahead as it tried to swipe them unsuccessfully. The deafening shouts of the audience terrorized the beast, for it stopped in panic and pushed itself against the ropes. It cowered in the corner.

The men poked at the lion with hot irons, and it ran to the field but lay down again, confused and terrified. It took a few more pokes and retreats for the lion to be enraged enough to ignore the pandemonium in the stands.

Spartacus was mesmerized and confounded.

What kind of show was this? This was no ordinary hunt!

The two men, gladiators in name only, realized what was coming.

The unarmed man sprinted to a guard and implored him to hand him a weapon. But the guard pulled back and threatened the man with his gladius.

The crowd was hooting, cheering, *and laughing*.

The armed gladiator hunched and took a tense stand, watching the lion. Had they starved the beast so it would attack the men?

The animal was getting agitated, even as the crowd was whipped to a frenzy. Loud bells, whistles, trumpets, and drums ratcheted their din to push the lion to action, and the iron-brandishers once again ran between the two protective rings to act in case it ran to the ropes again.

The lion began to trot toward the unarmed man, who was frantically running to each guard, shouting, gesturing for someone to give him a weapon.

"Sword! Mercy! Sword!"

What travesty was this? What unfairness! Give him a weapon and let the gods determine a fair battle!

But Spartacus remembered what Philotas had said. The animal fighters were the lowest of the low. He was filled with anger at this gross madness! People were laughing, pointing, and throwing items at the desperate man.

The beast ignored the armed gladiator, who receded, seeing that it was now focused on the man running with its back to the beast. *Never show your back to a wild animal!*

With its mane shaking and the sinews of its muscles tight with tension and pain, the lion finally charged the runner and launched a ferocious attack. It swiped his back, instantly drawing deep gashes and blood, and the man screamed and fell to the ground.

The crowd howled with glee.

A beast cares little for rules. The lion clamped its jaws on his neck and whipped its massive head back and forth, instantly breaking the neck. Blood sprayed all over, and the man went limp.

Does Zibelthiurdos look down upon this with glee? Does Jupiter?

The lion did not feast upon the man. Instead, it lay down again, licking its lips and gently swaying its tail. The armed man was far away from the lion, with his spear ready to launch.

How would they cause the lion to go after him now?

"What kind of fight is this?" Spartacus finally said loudly, causing Messenius to lean forward and warn him.

"Keep your mouth shut and watch, unless you want to join him."

But this time, the hot iron-brandishers did not go to the lion.

Instead, they came behind the gladiator and yelled at him. They argued briefly–Spartacus could not hear. But the crowd's intention was abundantly clear.

Then they poked the man in the back with the iron, burning his skin, causing him to yelp and lunge forward.

May the gods be kind and give him a merciful end. They are forcing him to go to the lion.

Be tortured with brandishing irons, or fight the lion and win. What would one choose?

He chose his path. The gladiator ran toward the beast as the audience encouraged him. He aimed his spear and launched it at the animal with all his strength.

The crowd howled as the weapon flew in a low, tight arc and slammed into the lion's side.

But all it did was to cause the beast to rise in a fury. Now maddened by pain and noise, it attacked the fighter with the spear hanging from its side.

He was no match as it first ripped his thigh and took a large piece of his flesh from the belly. It pushed him to the floor and tore his neck with such power that the head detached from the torso, drenching its mane with blood.

Howls. Cheers. Screams.

Spartacus knew then that the story of glory was just a lie. No one would convince him otherwise.

The rest of the event was a blur.

Heavily armored guards ran into the arena and killed the lion with a volley of spears.

Then the remaining pair of gladiators, fashioned again as a German and a Thracian, fought well until the game ended with a referee call. The audience, who appreciated the skill of the men, shouted for leniency. No one died, and the two fighters raised their hands as they walked away.

But none of that mattered, considering how two events had transpired. One would be blind to not see that this blood lust would grow worse, and people enticed by grotesque displays would demand more.

And when they were all taken back to their cramped quarter and then the wagon back home, Spartacus' mind was a cauldron of thoughts.

Philotas would need to answer his questions.

Or Vatia, even.

12

LUDUS OF VATIA

He walked stoically as they tied his hands behind his back and led him to the "box." Philotas had warned him to be quiet on the return from Pompeii and spare himself from Vatia's ire. But Spartacus would not be silent, for he had expressed his discontent at the performance in Pompeii and how it was an affront to their destiny.

And then *someone* had told Vatia.

He had always seen the box on his way to the kitchen, sometimes wondering what made it so terrible. And now, as they neared it, he felt trepidation, for he never suffered such close confinement by way of punishment. Beatings and floggings were the norm.

They opened the rusted iron gate of the chamber, and a foul odor emanated from it.

"Lie down and get in," a guard barked. "Legs first!"

He felt his breath quicken. *Will I die here? Would they let me die?*

He slid into the stone enclosure, and his feet struck the wall even before his shoulders had entered the space. His skin scraped against the rough stone floor.

"Now flex your knees, get your head in," a guard yelled, pushing his head. Spartacus pulled up his knees, rolled to his side, and then managed to get his head inside. They slammed the gate shut and locked it.

They had not released his hands, still tied behind his back. "Remove my shackles!"

"Enjoy the solitude," someone yelled. "They say it is most joyful! The shackles add to the pleasure."

The laughter receded, and all that was left was silence and the sound of his labored breathing. And the smell–a damp, fetid smell that enveloped him like a dirty blanket.

It did not take long before the spasms in the muscles–the thighs, waist, ankle, and shoulders—changed from discomfort to waves of pain. The suffocating darkness and deafening silence was not the only thing that made the box a terrible place. Not the breathlessness. Demons sprang in his mind, emerging through the mist of panic that began to devour the being.

No amount of shifting or turning relieved the stress and the cramps.

Help me, Zibelthiurdos. For what crimes of mine am I to suffer this way?

But there was something else that cut him deeply, even worse than the shooting agony now radiating from his elbow to the neck.

Antara.

He had not seen his wife since the return. But he had heard something: every woman in the kitchen had received a flogging because they were accused of spreading rumors. And Spartacus did not know if it was because of his words to the other gladiators that made their way back to Vatia. Had he not only condemned his wife to a life of servitude but also heaped more misery upon her because of his inability to quell his displeasure?

Philotas—his trainer and now his friend—had warned him repeatedly not to be vocal, for questioning the norms of the *ludus* or the methods of the master were forbidden. After all, had he not sworn an oath to Vatia to protect the school's reputation? But Spartacus had not listened.

He tried to reason with the reality of his situation. How was this different from the discipline of the army? He swore an oath to the commanders and the generals and was expected to adhere to it. And now, by the angry condemnation of his gods, this was his life–their life.

The previously dull pain in his waist was now beginning to pulsate with a fiery intensity.

He could not straighten himself.

Cannot breathe. Save me, Jupiter! I have long begged for your forgiveness, Sabazios!

Darkness. Unending waves of pain.

He would take being tied and flogged any day over the box.

But his mind fought on. Was this a test from the gods?

Did they see whether he could endure these pains and win?

Cleitus, I spared you, and yet you sought my despair.

Legate Curio, I served you honorably, yet you succumbed to your Roman greed.

Vatia, you dirty scoundrel that lives off the death and misery of men. No gods will forgive you.

He groaned and breathed rapidly, trying to calm himself down. This was a technique the Roman officers had taught the men just before a major battle. He still remembered the shouts of trainers. *Breathe in! Breathe out! Let the air fill your lungs and infuse you with strength! Breathe in! Breathe out! The gods enter your being when you do that!*

His waist was now feeling numb. But a monster had grabbed him by the neck and begun to squeeze the muscle.

He felt sweat running down his face, ears, lips, and neck. He licked his lips and felt the salty drip. He wiped his cheeks on the damp stone floor and tried to stretch his tired arms. *The sons of whores have tied it too tight!*

How long had he been this way?

Had it been hours?

He tried to shift his mind to other matters. He would *not* succumb to this deprivation. The gods had not put him here as punishment but as a test. Had his wife not told him that he was destined for greater things? And great things came to those that deserved it—and gods placed obstacles to see if a man's mettle and strength overcame them.

Yes, that was what it was!

Breathe. Breathe in. Breathe out.

The oppressive heat and dense air were squeezing his neck and choking him.

Wipe the sweat!

Relieve the numbing pain near the knees.

The darkness was like a suffocating hot blanket.

Breathe in. Breathe out.

What right did Curio have to condemn him this way, or for that bastard Porcina to sell him as a gladiator against Curio's wishes? Was freedom even a possibility? He saw no path to walking away—after all, even if he were injured or his bones grew weaker, Vatia would not let him go. He would become a farmhand, or worse, like the demonstration in Pompeii...fed to lions as entertainment to baying mobs.

There was no path to glory and freedom here. There *never* was.

Breathe in. Breathe out.

Or maybe there was, and his pain and misery caused him to fail to see it? Was Philotas correct? Did his anger blind him?

You saw nothing unusual, Philotas said. It was exactly what I told you! Rarely are weak and infirm left to fight the beasts. Did the others not walk away?

Not all of them!

Most of them! And you will be one of those! But keep your mouth shut, Spartacus, spare me the pain of seeing you punished.

But Spartacus had not listened, and here he was.

Breathe in. Breathe. Wipe the sweat to the floor. Twist the waist to relieve the pain. Help me.

Maybe Philotas was right. Spartacus could earn glory in the arena. Bask in the petals thrown from the stands. Make Vatia and the *ludus* proud. And then, one day, hold Antara's hand and walk out to run his own business.

Maybe a farm.

Reunite with his children.

How were they doing? Were they still alive? Had Kintoi's village been kind to them?

Breathe. Breathe. Rotate the shoulder to relieve the pulsing and cramping pain.

That was it. There was no point fighting and coming back to the box, and someday they might tire of him and leave him here to die. What good came of it?

He would seek glory in the arena. Be an obedient but brilliant gladiator.

That was what the gods wanted of him.

Spartacus the Thracian, invincible on the arena, and then a free man.

Eventually, even a king of Thrace.

He pissed on the floor, unable to hold it anymore, and felt the wet urine pool beneath his torso.

And then he was impossibly thirsty. He smacked his lips and tried to swallow. The tongue felt swollen and rough like a buffalo's hide.

The tide of pain was back, engulfing him. Like someone with hot irons pressing on his waist. Like a hook sunk into his shoulder blades and pulled. Like a vice on his neck, twisting.

He knew not how long he stayed that way, but the body had a way of putting men to sleep when their pain overwhelmed them.

He saw himself showered by flowers. A winged golden horse flew in the sky with Sabazios riding on it. His wife floated toward him in cold, deep blue waters.

And Spartacus drifted off to a welcome blackness of the mind.

And then he woke again, drenched in sweat, gasping, moaning, his entire body on fire as contractions gripped him like a powerful vine tightening around a tree branch.

Save me, Zibelthiurdos.

Armies running in the mud.

His head in the jaws of a tiger.

Blackness again.

Where am I? Antara? Where are you? Have you prepared our meals? Where are the children?

I am ready for battle, legate Curio! Give me the orders!

Is the meal ready, Antara? How long should I wait?

And so on it went until he lost all sense of time and place in that fog of terrible pain and misery.

13

LUDUS OF VATIA

"I expect you to hear, listen, and report as soon as possible. And you have been failing!" Vatia admonished the man. "Remember that the comfort of your future is dependent on not just my satisfaction but the safety and growth of this *ludus!*"

"Yes, *dominus*. I apologize deeply for slipping in my duties–"

"First, the rumors and unrest in kitchens. Then that new gladiator, while he is impressive, cannot keep his mouth shut. Why are the trainers not dealing with that more force?"

"He is in the box, *dominus*."

"Good. Keep your ears close to the trainers. To the fighters. Everyone! I must know if someone is angry, sad, frightened, motivated, everything! The games will get harder and bloodier. I have told this to you."

"Yes, *dominus*."

"I have told the others. Ratchet up the training. I already have loan requests from three sponsors with one major game here in Capua. Next time, that shaking man–I forget his name–goes to the beasts. I am not paying for cowards."

"Procamus. Yes, *dominus*."

"I want two of our proven fighters, two fresh and strong—and maybe the shaking Gaul—all of them prepared for the next event. The rates offered are exceptional, and I want no hindrance to the preparation."

"Yes, *dominus*."

"Your service is noticed. Let there be no more mishandling. Your future is bright, and I see many more benefits for you. Better quarters, a chance to keep a woman with you every night, meals from the estate. You want all that, do you not?"

"Yes, and for that, I am grateful, *dominus*."

"Very good. Now go. We shall speak again in a few days. Let no one see that we have conversed in private."

"No one knows, *dominus*."

14

THE SPECTACULA OF CAPUA

Spartacus had not slept well from anxiety and wild imagination in the past two days. But he had finally succumbed to a dreamless, wonderful sleep after drinking a full cup of wine infused with heady herbs.

He would fight in his first game tomorrow, in the *spectacula* of Capua, now set up similarly to that of Pompeii though a little smaller. The sponsor was a Senator of Rome, a name he could not recollect. And unlike the event in Pompeii, a portion of these games was paid for by tickets.

And when people paid for it, they wanted excitement.

Spartacus knew little of the game, for it was customary to keep the fighters in the dark about the event. They had been sequestered days ago and put to rigorous training separate from everyone else. They were taken and held in separate quarters, fed well, and received one visit from their women or prostitutes. Vatia had visited them during training and told them to bring glory to their names and the school.

Philotas would not accompany Spartacus—the trainers were no longer allowed to go with their men. Spartacus could guess why but dared not ask. Not after the box and the reckoning of his circumstance.

They were now all held in a small temporary wooden space beneath the central podiums where dignitaries sat. He saw eight men sitting in close quarters in the dingy chamber, sweating in the hot and humid enclosure, hearing the *thump, thump, thump* of people getting to their benches overhead. All the sounds were muffled, but they were growing loud.

Spartacus had accompanied four others to the game. One he knew—Lanuarius. An experienced fighter who fought as a Samnite. Two others he had seen but did not know their names, for they were in the German sections and rarely mingled with others. The last man was a scared-looking individual that Spartacus thought was carrying water for others but had never seen a fight. Why was he here? Crixus was with them this time, sitting right next to Spartacus. And he was unusually quiet—his exuberance and comical utterances were on pause. He had not said much the previous day, and now, he had only told them to pray and prepare after entering this chamber.

Two heavily armed guards stood hunched in a dark corner near the door, and Messenius, the games supervisor, was talking to them.

"You will get your weapons and shields just before your time. For now, just sit, and no chitter-chatter," Messenius reminded them.

Crixus grumbled something under his breath, but Messenius ignored him and returned to his conversation with the guards. Something about the best bread.

"Are you fighting as well?" Spartacus asked Crixus.

"No. Watching."

"Do you know who we are fighting? Them?" he asked, pointing at the others.

"Maybe. I am not told," Crixus said.

Spartacus felt Crixus had no interest in engaging with him. Perhaps this environment was not conducive to Crixus being—well, Crixus.

Crixus sat with his head low and his elbows on his thighs. The sliver of light from the gap in the door hinge lit his thick hair, making him look like a younger Kintoi.

"Spartacus," he said, his voice low. "Important to do well. Less suffering."

Spartacus was surprised that Crixus addressed him normally, and even his diction was cleaner.

"All eyes on you. Vatia especially. Good gladiators get better quarters and meals. You are talented. He has paid much for you."

Crixus' words were simple. Though nothing he said was new, Spartacus felt a strange kinship with this man. Crixus' words imbued strength in him.

"Real arena is very different from training. Watch the opponent and listen to the crowd. Always listen," he said, tapping his forefinger to his right ear. "Listen. Listen. Listen."

Thump. Thump. Thump.

A small shower of wood dust sprinkled down on them from the ceiling.

Whistles and trumpets.

More muffled sounds, much louder.

More noise near the door.

Two men were swaying back and forth nervously. The others were stoic and calm. The armed guards watched everyone like hawks.

"How do you focus on the fighter and put your ears to the crowd?" he asked, listening to the muffled din.

"Ask gods' blessing. When you fight, watch the opponent. When you break, listen to the crowd. You have trained your character. Play it well. Drama important. Drama spare your life, even if you lose."

Spartacus had never seen Crixus in the arena, and he was not fighting this day. Would he ever get a chance to watch the Gaul?

"Do you know if this is a death match?"

A band playing. Trummbtttttaaaa, Trummmb, Trummmmb, Trummmttaaa.

Sounds of cheers and thumping on benches.

I hope this podium does not collapse.

Crixus turned toward Messenius and, seeing that he was busy, leaned toward Spartacus and spoke in a whisper. "Better to assume. Pray you do not fight our own. But fight for your life and kill if you are told." Spartacus glanced at the other men. What was going on in their heads? Were they full of murderous intent? He did not know them, and they had done no harm to him. But he knew that he must see them as *soldiers*, except in a different setting.

Spartacus prayed to Zibelthiurdos to give him the strength to prevail. His heart thundered in his chest, punching his ribs with fierce determination. It was the same sensation just before the commanders' whistles to launch an attack, except that he was no longer on an open field and could not see his enemy. It was exactly like how he felt in his first real battle. He hoped that his powerful physical stature would give him an advantage over more experienced fighters in the arena.

Keep me alive, Zibelthiurdos. My wife says I am destined for greater things, but I must return with blood still flowing in my veins.

When is my turn?

The noise outside had begun to fill their suffocating space. Had the games begun? But no one from here had been asked to go out–

Another door opened, and three guards walked in. "Quintus of the *ludus* of Avita and Lanuarius of the *ludus* of Vatia!"

Spartacus watched as Lanuarius stood, and then, emerging for the darker far corner, was Quintus. The man from the competing *ludus* was a larger man, both in height and breadth. A chorus rose in the room.

"May the gods give you strength!"

"Beat him down, and fast! Kill him!"

Jeers and cheers.

"Fight well, Quintus! This other man looks like a mouse!"

"Butcher that elephant, Lanuarius!"

As the men took steps to go out, Crixus bellowed. "Eagle of the sky, wolf of the ocean! Swords from your palm like the god's foot! Fight like Zeus!"

Spartacus smiled, and so did Lanuarius.

"May the best man prevail and both return," he said, and Quintus whipped his head in surprise. *Kind words in this hell were rare.*

And then the two men vanished through the door. Spartacus had to wait.

Roar of the Crowd.

Cheers, whistles, shouts.

Silence.

Loud shouting.

Silence.

Trumpets. Whistles.

Someone shouting. Announcer? More noise. Sounds of people moving about on the top. Trumpets.

Silence.

Spartacus' temple throbbed. His back hurt from the tension, and he arched it to relieve the stress. When was his turn? It was better to wield a weapon and face his opponent than sit here and wait. Sweat ran down from his temple to the nape of his neck.

The door opened.

The same three guards entered. The fighters were not with them. What had happened? He would only know later.

Blood rushed to his ears, and his heart beat rapidly again. His turn?

One guard moved forward. "Hercolanius of the *ludus* of Avita and Spartacus of the *ludus* of Vatia!"

A bolt of lightning shot through him.

He could barely hear the encouragement and jeers in the room. Crixus said something and thumped his back. Hercolanius strode ahead of him, his chest forward, cocky. He was a large man, not quite tall, but powerfully built.

"Come on, move!" the guard waved his hand. Spartacus followed them and stepped out of the door into a narrow corridor with tall, rickety wooden walls on either side. The sound was deafening here after all the time spent in silence. He involuntarily closed his eyes briefly in the blinding light of the hot afternoon sun. The path ended in the iron posts and ropes.

Where are the weapons? Was he being fed to the beasts?

Hercolanius seemed to know what he was doing. He waited near the ropes, looked around, and then raised his hands for a round of cheers from the audience. *Did they know him?*

Spartacus realized he was to the side of the dignitary podium. The smell of rich leather and fenugreek wafted down and mixed with the sharp odors of sweat and urine.

A slave walked to Hercolanius, holding a belt, a lance, and a thick leather thigh guard. He tied the leather guard to Hercolanius' right thigh, put the belt to his waist, secured the loincloth, and handed him the lance. And then, his opponent pulled up a rope and stepped into the arena for loud cheers.

Spartacus followed and waited by the rope. He had always trained as a Thraex–would he fight that way?

Waves of doubt washed over him.

What if he was being tricked in some way for the amusement of the wicked audience?

Was Hercolanius so confident because he knew something Spartacus did not?

Keep me calm and bring strength to me, Zibelthiurdos.

Another slave boy ran toward him, holding the implements of the fight. He tied the belt to Spartacus' waist, handed him the *sica* and a thick, circular wooden shield, and secured a thick leather ankle guard to the leg. No protection to the thighs or face.

He tried to calm himself and *listen* to the world around him. The arena was smaller than Pompeii's, and thus the crowd felt closer to him. The dense audience was seated in tight groups of benches placed on four levels. To his left was the taller dignitary section with a red-colored awning. He saw several men and women seated on chairs but could not determine if Vatia was there. *He probably is.*

Unlike Pompeii, the *spectacula* was closed with no open sections anywhere. Were some from his *ludus* sitting somewhere, waiting to see this battle? Were some of the cheers from his men? The din was deafening. He had prepared for this moment, yet when it arrived, his legs felt heavy and his heart pounded like it would box its way out of his chest. He was mesmerized until a guard punched his shoulder with the handle of his gladius. "Move, gladiator! Go inside!"

Spartacus broke from his trance.

He got through the ropes and stepped into the arena.

The people screamed. A referee followed behind him. So far, everything was as he was told during training though it felt entirely different. All his time in the army or training had not prepared him for the sheer madness of this occasion and the assault on his senses.

He walked toward Hercolanius, who stood with casual indifference, leaning on his lance planted on the ground. The referee moved briskly between him and Hercolanius.

"Step back, back. Put some space!"

Spartacus stepped back.

An announcer joined them and waved his hands like a bird, telling the people to quiet down. When the audience shut their mouths and leaned from their benches to listen, the announcer began to read from a wooden tablet.

"Do you want to watch the next magnificent fight between these two hardened warriors from the forests and hills of the world's dark corners?"

"Yes!"

Roars and cheers.

"Witness the Samnite champion Hercolanius fight the brute from the deepest valleys of his barbarian land! Spartacus the Thracian!"

"Fight!"

The crowd was briefly on its feet, cheering. No doubt the betters were busy.

The announcer tried to mention the names of the school and offer his gratitude to the sponsor but was drowned out. Defeated, he yelled some more and then left the arena.

Hercolanius' relaxed demeanor was gone. He stood straight with his chest pushed out and the lance firm in his grip. A stream of cool wind swept into the arena, and suddenly Spartacus felt the finger of a god touch his forehead. A calm descended on him, and the world around was no longer so noisy. Everything Philotas and Crixus told came back to him.

Fight the opponent and listen to the crowd.

He was here for a show, and he would give them one.

In a white tunic embroidered with a black floral pattern, the referee shouted at both. "Engage on my whistle! Fight with great purpose and show your strength. Do not retreat, do not run! And if you can no longer carry on, drop to a knee, raise your hand and open your palm. And when that happens, the victor shall wait for instructions but shall not kill the vanquished. Is that understood?"

They both nodded.

Instructions. Instructions to kill or not.

He took a deep breath, waiting for the referee's whistle. The handle of his *sica* felt wet and slippery, so he rubbed his palm on his loincloth and hunched. He inhaled the warm air and imagined his gods infusing it with their blessing. He imagined his wife smiling at him.

"Move back, back," the referee yelled. "Make distance and then advance upon my whistle."

Spartacus took a few steps back, exaggerating his limp. The audience was quiet, anticipating the *go* and for them to launch at each other.

A few crows made a raucous noise.

Spartacus took a deep breath and gripped his shield.

Phreeeeeeeeeeeeeeeee!

The referee moved away, and Hercolanius did not wait a moment as he strode rapidly toward Spartacus.

How is he that confident?

Hercolanius raised his lance and was within striking distance when Spartacus' training almost involuntarily caused his next move. *The opposition will aim the lance not toward your center but the limbs. Watch for that.*

Spartacus sprinted from his space just in time as Hercolanius jabbed the lance with lightning speed at his thigh.

A cheer rose in the air.

The Samnite's weakness was that it took time for the lance wielder to readjust after a thrust. While a Thraex with a *sica* did not have the reach of a Samnite with a lance, the Thraex could move much faster and swing his sharp and deadly weapon to great effect.

Spartacus strutted to the side, watching Hercolanius, who looked annoyed that he had not subdued this Thraex in the first strike.

Entertain the crowd. I am the philosopher fighter! His role was to make pithy statements and aphorisms when he could.

His throat felt hollow.

Do it!

"A lance into–" he realized that his voice barely came out, and it probably sounded like he was squeaking like a rat. No one, not even those on the stands nearby, had heard him. The slowly pacing Hercolanius only furrowed his eyebrows.

Spartacus' tongue felt like parchment.

He cleared his throat. And then he produced saliva to wet his tongue.

He mustered his voice and willed it to rise. "A lance in the air is like pissing into the wind. Terrible for the owner and pathetic for the viewer!"

That voice in a practiced, clean Latin came out booming. The audience behind him roared its approval. "You speak big, limpy Thraex!" someone shouted from behind. He was pleased, for he had wanted to get their attention to his mouth and limp. *Make them remember.*

Hercolanius was surprised and looked offended. "Bastard," he hissed. And then he ran toward Spartacus again, his lance poised to strike.

All the rigidity and stress had gone from Spartacus' limbs. He knew that Zibelthiurdos watched over him and his wife controlled forces beyond this world. He knew that the years in the military and the months in the *ludus* would not fail him.

Hercolanius' aim was better this time, and the tip nicked the bottom of Spartacus' wicker shield with enough force to jolt him.

"Attack him! Go after him!"

Screams from the audience, who were by now already taking sides.

"Cut his leg, Thraex! Run and cut!"

"Impale the barbarian!"

"Fight, fight!"

Animals in a cage, for the entertainment of their masters.

But there was no other way. He would need to subdue Hercolanius, whose intent was certainly deadly, or he would die based on the whims of those laughing at him.

He parried Hercolanius' attacks twice more, always at the back foot. And then the crowd turned hostile toward him.

"Stop running, Thraex!"

"What kind of barbarian is this?"

"Do not make me lose my bet, sister-fucker!"

Someone threw a rag at him. *Was Vatia watching? Was Crixus out and watching? Were there others from his ludus watching?*

He steeled himself after another backpedaling and hearing the outrage from the stands.

"Hey, big mouth, stop limping and start fighting!" a woman yelled from just behind, startling him.

Enough!

Hercolanius was grinning now. His eyebrows danced as he advanced again. It reminded Spartacus of the real Samnite soldier he had fought years ago, near the Colline gate, but Spartacus had overcome the man.

He hunched, and then he launched at Hercolanius. The speed took the Samnite by surprise, who had no time to readjust the angle of his lance as Spartacus slammed his wicker shield into the larger *scutum*. Hercolanius staggered back, stunned at the attack.

A huge roar went up in the stands.

Yes.

Gone was any shame of being here and gone was the trepidation. If this were his bloody path to glory and freedom, this path he would take.

He sprinted to Hercolanius' side and swung his sica toward his exposed shoulder. But the Samnite was well trained and anticipated the attack—he brought up his scutum, and the impact caused a loud metal-to-wood thud.

"Who wants to bet? Who wants to bet?" somebody was shouting behind him. Even women's shrill voices were as enthusiastic as the men's.

The battle was now no longer on Hercolanius' side. Spartacus struck him repeatedly—escaping the lance and moving with lightning speed to strike his exported parts.

Hercolanius was on the back foot now, desperately trying to maneuver with his weapon and slam Spartacus with his tall wooden scutum. But Spartacus had trained for years and fought legionaries who were adept in the usage of a scutum and a gladius, and Hercolanius' attempts to protect himself and thrust the lance on top of the scutum were hopeless as Spartacus ducked and swung at the man's legs, causing him to dance where he stood.

Spartacus raised his hands when he had a chance, and the crowd went quiet briefly. "A dance is entertaining, Samnite, but one with a *sica* to the leg is even more!"

Howls of laughter erupted from the nearby stands, and those who could not hear joined and laughed, pretending to have. Spartacus felt like his belly was on fire. He was tiring slowly, but was Hercolanius?

How to strike him to defeat?

After a few more futile mutual strikes, he decided it was time.

May your blessing fill me with a lion's strength and a man's cunning, Zibelthiurdos. Give me victory!

Spartacus lunged at Hercolanius. But this time, he did not use his *sica*, but instead, he threw the weapon at a shocked Hercolanius, who brought up his shield even as his exposed lance was angled to the ground but held loosely. Spartacus gripped the lance and pulled it hard, and it was too late for Hercolanius before he realized what was happening.

"Son of a-"

Spartacus dropped, and his bottom impacted the ground. But the lance was still in Spartacus' iron grip, and as Hercolanius lurched forward, losing his balance, Spartacus kicked his exposed belly like a horse kicking its tormentor.

Hercolanius grunted with pain and dropped his scutum, and due to the kick, he pivoted sideways, still holding the handle of the lance, and then fell, losing his balance.

Roars and screams.

Spartacus jumped back to his feet, still holding the bottom of the pointed end of the lance, and before Hercolanius could recover, yanked it with all his strength. The handle had become slippery, and Hercolanius lost possession of the weapon.

What was the rule when the opponent was disarmed?

Hercolanius tried to grapple with him, his face contorted in a snarl and eyes filled with hate. "I will kill you, fucking Thracian barbarian," he hissed.

Pray to your gods, for they have abandoned you.

Spartacus punched Hercolanius' face, broke his nose, and then struck his chest with a forceful thrust of the lance handle. Hercolanius stumbled and fell again.

Just get on your knees and seek mercy!

But Hercolanius would not give up.

So Spartacus swung the lance like a club and pummeled Hercolanius twice more, striking his thighs and torso. Hercolanius was bleeding heavily from his nose and mouth, and his face looked like a beast that had feasted on a fresh kill.

"Give up and signal your surrender," Spartacus growled at him. "Stop!"

When Hercolanius tried to get up again, Spartacus smashed his face. *Let us put this to an end!*

Hercolanius collapsed and lay motionless even as the crowd screamed and cheered and jeered.

"You made me rich, Spartacus the Thraex!"

"Kill him! Kill him!"

Hercolanius stirred again. When Spartacus took a step forward, the opponent slowly got onto his knees. Even as a string of saliva and blood hung from his face, he raised a hand, slowly imploring for mercy.

"Thraex! Thraex! Spartacus!"

"No mercy!"

"Spare him!"

The course of energy had drained off Spartacus, and sudden exhaustion set in. He looked at the kneeling Hercolanius—would his fate be the same someday? How long could he do this? Spartacus was now thirty-eight, among the oldest. He had skill, but the gods slowly drained strength away from men as they aged, and his body could only take that much exertion.

The noise in the arena was deafening, and from the corner of his eye, Spartacus noticed the referee running toward the dignitary stand. People were waving their hands and baying for blood. The calls for *mercy* were smattering few.

They now want every game to end in death.

The referee came running to him.

"Death," was all he said.

Spartacus was frozen. Never had he once killed a surrendered and kneeling man—not even during the worst of his campaigns. He had escaped being part of execution squads that killed captives on a general's or legate's orders. The gods had never compelled him to strike at a defeated opponent. And this Hercolanius—was he not supposed to be a champion? Had he not put his life on the line for the people's entertainment for however many years? And thus was he not afforded the luxury of mercy on failure?

Until now.

"Did you hear me, Thracian? His fight was not valiant. The audience demands a death. Give him a fitting end, or it will be worse for both of you," he warned.

Worse for both?

He did not know what that meant. In what way?

He took a deep breath.

Even as the howling audience watched, Spartacus adjusted the grip on the lance. He kneeled closer to Hercolanius' ears. "Pray. Now."

The Samnite understood. The pride in his heart showed for he begged for no reconsideration, and he streamed no curses. Instead, he hung his head low and muttered something.

The referee nodded.

Spartacus lifted the lance and plunged it through the nape of Hercolanius' neck straight down to the heart, causing instant, merciful death.

Roars.

Hercolanius collapsed, and his blood saturated the sand.

Spartacus turned to the audience that cheered him. And as he walked back to the perimeter, only one thought filled his head. He felt not the taste of victory nor the sweetness of adulation but only the bitter realization that there was no realistic path to freedom from the arena.

This was a well where men were sent to die, not to walk away unfettered.

15

LUDUS OF VATIA

"What do you want?" Vatia asked coldly, eyeing the giant brute who stood before him. The healthy meals were making Spartacus even bigger than before.

The Thracian stood before him with his hands and legs shackled. He had returned victorious from the games. He would fetch good money in the future. Spartacus' first fight had been received very well, and he had put on an exceptional show—learning all the training and even heeding Vatia's words. The *philosopher-warrior* had left an imprint in the minds of the people of Capua.

The problem was Spartacus' perception. A barbarian slave who, just because he spoke some Greek and affected Hellenistic manners, saw himself as greater than his wretched station. And here Spartacus was, after hounding the trainers, seeking his audience.

"A chance to plead my case, sir," he said in that pretentious deliberation. Who did this slave think he was, Pompey?

"And what case is that?" Vatia said. "You fought well and left the arena with honor. You received your reward meal and a night with your woman."

Philotas stood by Spartacus' side. He would get an earful after this discussion.

"My value to you is much higher as a freedman and a trainer than a fighter, sir," he said.

What?

Vatia was confounded that this man even *thought* of such a thing! The sheer delusion! He was at a loss for words and did what he hated about himself–he laughed out of nervousness.

Philotas stood stoically, but Spartacus looked in his eye.

Was he serious?

Vatia composed himself. He had to play this carefully. It was a trivial matter to dispose of vermin like this, but he had paid heavily for the man. There was no point in stroking his own ego and losing money due to unrest. This man was a big mouth, and his complaints would create more trouble. But Vatia wanted to stroke Spartacus' ego and give him some hope, for threats only went so far.

"Explain how," he said finally.

"I am thirty-eight by age, sir. My bones are becoming brittle, and my muscles are getting softer, as it is for men in my situation. But I have many skills and much experience. I can be of service in finding the best men for you, training them, and helping you get the best rates."

"I have many men with skills and experience. This business is not only about how you wield your lance or sword, if you have not noticed."

"But I–"

"I have purchased you with a certain intent, and I do not need a slave lecturing me on how I should run my business. You have shown yourself to be of courage and skill in the arena, and to me, you are an excellent candidate who can earn their way to glory, comfort, and eventually freedom."

Spartacus was quiet. Was he weighing his response? Did he believe these words?

"What good is the promise of freedom if I am dead well before, sir. That is no good for your investment."

"Business is all about risks," Vatia said. "And someone with your experience should not be dying so easily in the arena. You know that, and I know that. You are a condemned man, Spartacus. You should be dead, but I gave you life. You put on a good show and make me money, and I will honor my end of granting you freedom in due time."

Philotas turned to Spartacus. "The *dominus* is generous in rewarding you with this possibility so early."

Vatia continued. "I heard you were in the box. You seem to be a learned man, Spartacus, and punishment only goes so far. If you want to return to a better life with your woman, you must earn it. And do not come in front of me again without a few victories. When sponsors ask for you by name and are willing to pay a premium, that is when you have earned any right to discuss your freedom. Do you understand?"

Spartacus fidgeted. He finally lowered his head and nodded. "I thank you for giving me the audience."

At least he has the manners to show gratitude.

"Fine. Guard, take him away. Philotas, go and bring Canicus and Messenius."

Spartacus shuffled away, the iron manacles making a grating sound as he dragged them on his way out.

Philotas returned with a worried-looking Canicus and Messenius.

Vatia exploded. "Do not bring me these degenerates with demands! Imagine if news got out that the *master* of the *ludus* was entertaining negotiation by his gladiators! Do you know what that can do to business?"

The men hung their heads.

"The next time one of these idiots opens his big mouth, settle the matter there and do not bother me. I have enough to deal with. Is that clear?"

"Yes, *dominus*," Canicus said.

"Messenius, your job is to ensure compliance outside the training ground. Keep an eye on these men, *all of them*. I want to suffer no embarrassment, here or outside."

"Yes, sir."

"And Philotas, keep your man on a leash."

"Yes, *dominus*," Philotas said.

"Now get out. I have to negotiate prices for Apollo's festival. This Spartacus is going to be part of it. Maybe a few fights will calm his passions."

16

LUCANIA

"Let me speak to him, sir," Cleitus asked Porcina. He often met the Senator every six to eight days to go through the books and report suspicious activity or discrepancies. Porcina had his acountants, but Cleitus aided in audits and inspections.

"Why do you need to speak to Felix again?" Porcina asked. "Not that I care, but those affairs are of the distant past. I want no distraction."

"This is not about *this*," Cleitus said, showing his partially-fingered hand. "This is about the guard's disappearance and how he ended up in a gorge."

"Ah, that one. I thought we finished all the investigations."

While Porcina sounded nonchalant, Cleitus knew that it had greatly frustrated the Senator. After much hard work, the estate was recovering, and deaths cost money and made replacements expensive. Labor was harder to procure, and slaves were becoming unaffordable. Every loss was a little cut. Besides, Porcina was *extremely* sensitive to any bad news in the estate—no matter how trivial. That was simply the nature of the man.

"We did, sir. But while you have been gracious in my treatment and seeing my value in the estate, I must remind you that I once lived as a scout and an investigator."

"You can smell bad like a rat. You barbarians seem to be good at that," Porcina said.

Never a sentence away from looking down upon me.

Cleitus only smiled. "You know us. I wished to speak to him only with your permission."

"It is indeed some coincidence that he was present during the attack on you, and the guard went missing while accompanying him. But it has been years, and surely it could be a chance. We have lost many to illness and other matters."

"I worry less for what happens as a matter of course, Senator. It is miscreants hiding within our midst that worries me—and you have entrusted me with the job to find them. Just like this," he said, pointing to an invoice. "Wine sellers are swindling us by mixing promised wine with adulterated garbage."

Porcina sighed. "Fine. If you will torture him again and render him incapacitated, give an early indication to the overseer. It is time we find a replacement for the lead herdsman."

17

POMPEII

Four months after the games at Capua, Spartacus and Crixus were assigned to a new major game in Pompeii once again. Sponsored by some important general from Rome, the festival in honor of Apollo would be a grand spectacle. Dignitaries arrived from Rome, foreign rulers were in attendance, and the venue was grander.

Gone was the wooden-benched semi-open arena. The architects and builders had erected a respectable stone-benched oval arena with four levels in record time. The new *spectacula* had dedicated seating and roof covering for the officials, toilets, multiple entries, and space for men and beasts before entering the arena. Spartacus, Crixus, and other designated fighters had received a tour–a protocol observed only sporadically. There was an increasingly unhealthy obsession with "surprises," which sometimes meant that fighters received absolutely no information on the venue, the setup, or what they were up against.

The men were allowed to stroll in a small field the previous night. The white limestone of the arena shone under the cloudless full moon night. The many lights of the city flickered, and the menacing bulk of Vesuvius rose like a ghostly, shadowy apparition in the background.

Spartacus walked with Crixus. While they had very little opportunity to interact in the *ludus* due to the suffocating and stringent rules, the two had still become a little closer in the months. Spartacus had learned quickly that much of what Crixus did was an act. His terrible Latin and comical manners were deliberately fake. The Gaul was an ill-tempered, impetuous man, but he had a keen mind and was clever in how he interacted with those around him. This night afforded the perfect opportunity for Spartacus to converse with Crixus without the overbearing presence of Messenius or the other trainers.

"Are you prepared for tomorrow?" Spartacus asked casually as they walked away from the others.

"Like a snake that curls around a donkey's bum," he said.

By Zibelthiurdos—Crixus and his passion for donkeys and buttocks.

"Speak plainly, Crixus. We are not in the arena. It must be tiring to keep that act all the time."

Crixus' partially moonlit face hid whatever emotion he felt at that admonition.

"I have–" he paused.

He rubbed his thick beard before turning to Spartacus. "It is exhausting," he said, grinning. His eyes twinkled under the moonlit sky.

"Then let us unburden ourselves. We have trained so long together, yet I know so little about you."

"Why does that matter?"

"Because when men know each other well, they perform better."

Crixus scoffed. "Not perform better when you are dead."

"Maybe it will help us from becoming dead. All we do is fight, sleep, and worry about the next fight."

Crixus rubbed his hair. "What do you want to know?"

"Where you came from. How you ended here."

"Few know of my past. How do I trust you?"

"What difference does it make whether you trust me or not. Can I do anything worse to you with what you say? We are caged like animals and loaned out to fight to the death."

"We have a roof, food—"

"We are animals, and people cheer when our blood springs like a fountain," Spartacus said forcefully.

Crixus was silent for a while as they walked on the graveled path. The wind was getting cooler. Winter would be upon them soon.

Finally, he spoke. "I am a Sequani from lands far north of Italy."

"That is your tribe?"

"Yes. Fierce. We are warriors. Fighters," he said, thumping his chest. "But we are broken with each other."

"Your tribes are numerous, and you fight amongst each other?"

"Yes, yes. That. We saw no danger with Romans. Chiefs go to secure an alliance with Romans while betraying their own."

Not any different from Thracians.

"My village resist. We fight. We kill three centurions. But no help from others, so we lose."

"Did you have a family?"

Crixus nodded. "Wife. Three sons. One daughter."

"Are they with you here?" Spartacus asked, but knowing that answers were rarely good.

"Wife, they rape and hang. Two sons beheaded by cavalry as they ran. Other two missing. Dead? Slaves? Do not know," he said matter-of-factly. "When population fights, revenge is terrible."

"Why did they spare you?"

"See me. Strong. Sold as a slave for a good price. Previous owner tired of me," he said, smiling. *Unsurprising.* "Sold me here."

"How old are you?"

"Thirty-one. Younger than you, old man," Crixus said with his signature accent and slapped Spartacus on his shoulder. "Bones not brittle."

"Not brittle like an old donkey's bum?"

They both laughed.

"Beautiful mountains. Big river. Forests. All gone," Crixus said wistfully.

"So was my home, Crixus."

"Your story?"

Spartacus talked of his past, and Crixus was surprised at the depth of Spartacus' experience and envious that his wife was here with him and that his children may be safe. *While we lament our misfortunes, we often forget the far greater injustices heaped on others right by our side,* Spartacus thought, for Crixus had endured much worse. And if so, why was he willingly accepting his circumstance?

"Why have you not resisted? Have you sought freedom from the *ludus*?"

Crixus slapped his face lightly. It was his gesture to indicate *what you are saying is stupid.*

"No such thing as seeking freedom. Path is narrow and left to Vatia. Please him, and maybe a chance. Or resist and go into box enough times to lose the mind, or get on a cross and die a terrible death."

He has walked my path and decided on the futility of seeking freedom.

"You see no other paths?"

"The gods have given us none. They have abandoned us, Spartacus. We now under mercy of Roman gods, and they no affection for us."

A thousand thoughts swirled in his mind, but Spartacus decided to discuss the fight the next day. Crixus had a few tips, but his voice betrayed his nervousness. The lack of information about who or what they were about to fight was a cause for concern and anxiety.

"Or perhaps the gods have not abandoned us, Crixus. Perhaps they test our mettle and place these odds in our way to see how we conquer them."

"Every gladiator has thought so until their end."

Spartacus was frustrated by Crixus' intransigence and hopelessness. He would bring the man around.

When Messenius finally screamed their names and ordered them back to the stifling little smelly barracks, they wished their gods' blessings for the game. Would they return victorious or lie dead in the arena, only to be dragged by hooks and discarded in a ditch?

Spartacus wondered why he was so consumed by thoughts of freedom. Why not simply accept his fate? Why spend every waking hour thinking of an escape from his circumstance? Perhaps that is how the gods had intended him to be—not to accept his situation.

To obsess about things others would not.

He could be king, yet he was a slave.

18

POMPEII

Cleitus sat on an elevated section right beside the dignitary gallery, a luxury afforded by his position. His skin felt hot even in his cool afternoon. A sensation of dread filled him even in the safety of this arena, surrounded by noisy crowds, guarded by heavily armed soldiers, and invisible in the multitude.

What could *anyone* do to him?

What could Spartacus do to him?

Was he like the winged horse god who could fly and vanquish his enemies?

Was he a demon that could float in the air and descend upon him?

He controlled his breath. Spartacus was just a man—no, even worse, now he was lower than a man in Roman society. A slave. He was a lowly gladiator whose worth was measured by the blood he spilled or how much drained out of him as he lay on the ground.

That was all. He is an animal in a show, and nothing more!

Cleitus often managed invitations to the estate—festivals, games, arbitrations, and more as part of his work.

Just a week ago he had seen the most interesting brochure.

GREATEST GAMES OF THE YEAR FOR THE FESTIVAL OF APOLLO SIX PAIRS OF GLADIATORS COME AND SEE THE TERROR OF GAUL THUMBORIXUS FIERCE BROTHERS OF GERMANIA THRACIAN DEVIL FORMER AUX.

THE BEAST SPARTACUS SYRIAN SWORDSMAN
GOD OF BLADES AMOXUS AND SURPRISES AND
MORE DO NOT MISS SPONSORED BY GAIUS
CLAUDIUS GLABER AWNINGS PROVIDED
REFRESHMENTS PROVIDED SPECTACULA OF
POMPEII

Cleitus' hand had gone cold reading it, but he knew right then that he could not resist coming to watch the man who had tormented and almost killed him.

The bands were still playing, and the crowd was settling in. The dignitary section was filling up and the canvas awnings flapped under the wind. There was much commotion when Marcus Aurelius Cotta, a Consul, arrived to take the most prestigious seat beside the sponsor, Glaber. Porcina would be here soon, not the one to miss the chance to seek favors and mingle with the most influential. The day was cloudless, and he was glad that his sharp eyes would not miss a thing.

Cleitus was dressed like an upper-class Roman, with a crisp white toga with bold maroon borders, golden rings on his fingers, a fine necklace offered as a bribe by an estate supplier, and thick, specially crafted leather sandals that offered comfort to his soles. Could they see it on his face that he was a barbarian?

He had an exceptional view of the arena from here, with little obstruction in front of him except the posts and protective ropes. Since he had arrived at the estate, Cleitus had only been to one gladiatorial game long ago when he was still healing, and while it was interesting, he had left feeling unsatisfied due to the poor form of the fighters and the lack of pomp and splendor.

After the initial comic performances, he sat through two grueling but exciting fights, one ending in death and the other with the vanquished limping away and forgiven by the crowd for his brave fight. It felt prestigious to sit shoulder-to-shoulder with other notable, wealthy Romans and enjoy the match of lowly men who never quite understood how to elevate themselves. Cleitus had taken fate into his own hands and fashioned gold out of it.

Where was Spartacus?

Years ago, he had stared into his tormentor's yellowed rage-filled eyes as he pulled Cleitus' palm forward, placed it on a rock, and sliced off his fingers. He remembered *everything* about it. The terror. The pain. The smell of his urine and the warmth of his blood as it drenched his wrist when he held up his palm. The red-hot agony and the bloodied stumps where his fingers once existed. Spartacus could have just surrendered!

Fucking bastard took my fingers.

And now he would watch this motherfucker fight like an animal for his entertainment. How the gods had turned the tables! He made several short prayers to Sabazios.

Have him gutted, Sabazios! Let his dying eyes meet mine as he lies bleeding. Let death come slowly!

The announcer was back, and the crowd settled down. "Some men may be wretched in their station and worthless for society, but they can still be champions in the arena!"

Cleitus was all ears.

"First time? Exciting, is it not?" the man next to him tugged his toga and interrupted.

I will stab you, monkey!

"Yes," he said and continued to look ahead, hoping that this man shut up.

"I have been to–"

"Not now, sir. Watch," he said gruffly. The man looked miffed but turned away, grumbling something to a woman by his side. Wife, mistress, daughter, who knew?

I should have come here with Primigenia.

The announcer continued. Cleitus knew he would keep it short, for the crowd was impatient and had no love for long speeches.

"Without delay, I invite you to an exciting, never-before-seen performance. The devil from the Thracian hinterlands—"

Cleitus' breath caught in his throat.

"Spartacus! The victorious vanquisher of the famous Hercolanius will show what experience and power are meant to be. Watch this hairy-chested behemoth like never before!"

The crowd cheered and jeered, and all eyes turned toward the opening below the dignitary section. Many stood up, and Cleitus did as well, craning his neck.

Where are you, scum?

And then there he was.

Just like Cleitus remembered, but maybe even larger. He had put on weight, his hair was up in a giant bun, and some of it cascaded down his powerful shoulders. A leather belt held the loincloth that rose high on his trunk-like thighs. Spartacus had shaved off his beard, but the thick mustache had remained. He walked tall into the field, holding a *sica* and a circular shield.

He walked with a limp, just as Cleitus remembered. But he affected a pompous gait, looking around and acknowledging the loud crowd, nodding to the people, raising the *sica* as if he had already won.

Fucking bastard. Die like a dog on the field. I hope the opponent slices off your limbs one by one and wets the arena with your blood.

Cleitus' heartbeat was erratic, and he could not understand why. What could this animal do? He was far away, and hopefully would be butchered like a pig soon.

"I have Thracian slaves," the man beside him piped up again.

Some people simply cannot mind their own business.

He just grunted and hoped the man would shut up.

"Always angry. Good workers, but unless you keep them in control, they are like untrained dogs," the man said, grinning, very pleased with himself. "Of the various stocks, they are the worst. Fitting for one of them to be here. All they do well is fight."

"They are warriors," Cleitus finally said, unable to control himself. *Fucking Roman superiority.*

Enthused by his response, the man had to make his opinion known. "Yes, yes, which is why they belong in the games. From what I heard, all they do is quarrel like rats, and that is how we were able to put our feet on their necks. But great fighters, by Jupiter."

"Those I know are quite agreeable," Cleitus said defensively.

The man scoffed. "Rare. Rare, indeed. They are beastly people fit for slavery and to breed more little strong ones."

If I put out your eyes and cut off your nose, perhaps you will sing a different tune, bastard.

When he received no more responses from Cleitus, he finally turned away.

A conflicted Cleitus adjusted his toga. He so desired to enter into an argument with this whore bastard. Fuck him and his contemptuous nature–did he not see how valiant Thracians were? Cleitus himself had served honorably, fighting every step of the way under Sulla.

But these Romans and how they spoke of others.

Of his kind.

It was the same here with strangers.

It was the same at the estate.

No matter how much he tried, he would never really be Roman.

He wanted to enjoy this event. But as it began, Cleitus felt his gods look down upon him with contempt.

19

POMPEII

Spartacus was introduced to the crowd as the *champion of Capua, the Thracian who vanquished the great Hercolanius with seven fights under his belt.*

The densely packed arena was festive with floral arrangements and banners, loud and energetic music bands, rowdy viewers, and a dignitary podium crowded with important men and women. Red, purple, orange, green, and white dotted the space, and he could see the still fresh and wet splotch of blood nearby. Had the fighter lived or died? The organizers had spread an even layer of husk on the sandy ground.

But there was one difference: he was the only one on the field, and his opponent had not arrived. The familiar worry crept up Spartacus' spine—had Vatia condemned him to a beast-fight? The animal fighters were the lowest of the low—surely Vatia had not already consigned him to the trash heap of the school?

Having introduced Spartacus already, the announcer waited for the crowd to settle. Then he continued. "What man can take on *this* beast? Look at his stature! He was once a famed auxiliary but, like many of his kind, took to a life of crime before falling into the hands of Roman law!"

Cheers and jeers.

"But no, we will not put him to the jaws of a lion, for what entertainment is there in letting a mindless beast tear his throat when he can give us far more thrilling spectacles?"

Far more?

"A worthy fighter must prove himself by taking on uncommon challenges!"

Spartacus had steeled himself to this fight, remembering how he felt the first time and knowing that a projection of confidence was critical in setting up for success. But there was no predictability now–what was the uncommon challenge? Would he be fighting a condemned centurion? Deal with ten snakes in the arena? A lion with its tamer? An archer? Fifty naked women with swords?

He stood straight and turned to examine all the corners. *No one. Nothing. What was the surprise this time?*

The announcer was not done. "Again, for the second time only, witness the power of strength and experience against youth and dancer's limbs!"

Fighting children?

Killing or maiming even thirteen-year-old boys was of no consequence, for they had already developed the hearts of men and learned to kill. He had seen many boys of that age in the tribal armies, and many Roman legions had boys only slightly older, for the minimum age was fourteen.

But what if they were younger?

Were the Romans so depraved that they would put real children out for massacre and enjoyment?

Great applause broke in the stands. Spartacus pivoted on his feet to turn to where the audience was pointing. Emerging from one of the arched entrances were two young men. Their limbs long and lithe, arms and thighs protected by thick leather guards, lustrous golden hair flowing in the wind, and holding narrow wooden, red-painted shields and standard-issue gladii.

Spartacus looked about to see if another gladiator, perhaps someone from his *ludus,* would join him.

But none did.

This was the new spectacle. For him to face two younger men at the same time. Vatia had decided to test or get rid of him. A bitter resentment grew in his belly, and yet the brilliance of the circumstance was that he could give up and die, thus pathetically ending his life, or he could win against this abject unfairness and achieve blazing glory. Either way, Vatia profited.

The gods were sometimes wicked in their ways.

The two boys, perhaps no older than sixteen, their skins still pink from the young blood that still coursed through their veins, but their eyes showing the maturity of those that have been dealt the ugliness of life, bounced on their feet as they came toward the referee and waited deferentially. He could even smell the scented Syrian balsam oil on their bodies this close. Were they brothers? They looked so similar, and sometimes Spartacus could not easily differentiate these men from the cold northern lands. They were Germans who lived beyond the Rhine, of similar stock as Canicus and his people.

The air was charged with excitement—the shouts from the stands already taking sides.

Butcher the old man!

Show the youngsters the errors of their ways!

Cut off their heads, Spartacus!

Chop the Thracian's head and burn his beard!

Who wants to bet a gold coin that experience matters? Come on! Come on!

Some woman was shrieking *Thracian! Thracian!*

Another female voice broke through. *Show your big cock!* Hoots of female laughter followed.

So much for the famed chaste Roman behavior. On the stands, these women were no better than the loud and bawdy Thracian and German women.

Spartacus gripped his *sica* harder and adjusted his stance. The referee was waiting for the announcer to finish.

The announcer raised his hands to silence the crowds and finally concluded the ceremony. "Now we shall witness the battle of duality! May the best win and gain glory forever! The barbarian of Thrace shall fight the German brothers from the depths of Hades!"

When the exuberant roar settled, the announcer left the arena grinning ear-to-ear as the referee gestured them all to come closer. The rules were the same—seek mercy upon injury and leave judgment to the crowds. He hastened toward the edge after asking the fighters to distance themselves before the whistle.

One of the boys shouted something in his language, and the other laughed.

But Spartacus had to hold to his act. He straightened and raised his hands to ask the crowds to be quiet.

"The little puppies snarl at a wolf," he said loudly. He knew some spectators may have seen him before and expected the act. "But the snarl is but a little whimper to its ears!"

Many in the crowd cheered. They loved it when gladiators demonstrated distinct styles.

Spartacus spread his legs and hunched, watching the two like a hawk. They walked slowly, deliberately, confidently, with their shields up to their chin and the gladius' pointed from the top of the shield, just like advancing legionaries.

The two boys moved, separating themselves from each other. The hubris of their age was evident in that cocky display of forward-thrusting chests, the comfortable and loose hold on their gladii, and the way they danced on their feet. *Young fools dying for the greed of older men.*

"Speak Latin? Greek?" he asked, and they only looked at him with disdain and confusion. Neither nodded nor acknowledged his words.

Intentional? Or were they so fresh off the supply lines that they knew no words of these lands?

"Want to live? Fight hard, but do not try to kill. Do you understand? Pretend to kill but not really. And we will all live," he said, his voice low.

One of the boys smiled, and the other had no life in his teal-colored eyes.

"Fight to live. Not to die," he whispered loud enough for them to hear.

The boys looked at each other. And then they both hunched slightly and gripped their weapons hard.

"You die, Grandpa," one of them said in a thick, unmistakably German accent.

Phreeeeeee!

His torso was still slick with the dead boy's blood, and he could taste the iron on his lips. The crowd's deafening roar made it difficult to concentrate, for the boy's companion lay on the ground, with a deep gash on his waist, his hand raised seeking mercy.

Spartacus' heart thudded incessantly, and his body was drenched in sweat even on this cool afternoon. He wiped the blood and saliva off his face and took several deep breaths. His left forearm bled from a cut. A slave boy ran into the arena to tie a thick bandage on it as Spartacus waited for a verdict.

With some difficulty, he raised his hand. "When the wolf walks, the cubs must be quiet," he said, and the crowd roared its approval.

He had no desire to kill the still-alive boy–they had fought hard and admirably, but their inexperience had shown. They were forced into imbalance by Spartacus' deceptive speed despite his height and weight. And they may have also been fooled by the incessant chants of *old man*, perhaps imagining him to be a crumbling gray beard.

One of them had ducked prematurely while parrying Spartacus' *sica* attack and had his neck severed. Now he lay dead, and the other waited.

His thundering heartbeat and the blood rushing to his ears made it difficult to gather what the crowd was baying for. He looked at the sponsor's stand but could not make the gesture with his sweat-blurred vision. Eventually, the referee came running.

Spartacus turned to the man. Another execution?

"Spare!" the referee said. A small course of relief washed over Spartacus. There was no honor or joy in executing a bloodied, kneeling opponent seeking mercy–that was what executioners did, not warriors. That was how the Romans reminded their audience that the gladiators were nothing but low scum.

But not today.

He deliberately walked toward the kneeling boy with a pronounced limp and pulled his head up, exposing the boy's neck. Then Spartacus raised his *sica* high as the crowd screamed and shouted.

Two guards leaned forward menacingly.

He waved his weapon hand to tell the crowd *quiet!*. And they did, for he had already given them a splendid show.

"Experience is the poison in a snake's fang. You may not see it, but by Zeus, you will feel it!"

He aimed the *sica* toward the kneeling boy and launched it, ensuring that it just missed his head and planted itself upright on the sandy ground. The boy flinched, and his shoulders sagged with relief.

The crowd went wild with adulation. The betters had made money, the women screamed his name, and the bands celebrated the win. Two slaves came running to attach a long, twisted hook to the dead boy's feet and drag him, leaving a trail of blood. The neck was attached to the body only by a flimsy ligament and grotesquely bounced on the ground. And then, two others came in with a stretcher to take away the injured partner. What would be his fate? Spartacus could only guess.

As he walked out, Spartacus was filled neither with pride nor relief, for he had come close to death for the profit and greed of his master.

But it was all not over.

He sat quietly in the waiting room, letting his body cool and his heart settle. He drank some water and watched as Crixus prepared himself.

After another round, it was Crixus' turn. He stood and puffed up his chest, and declared loudly in his characteristic swagger, "Every bum shall be beaten to redness!"

Spartacus shook his head but then bowed in acknowledgment of Crixus' success. But what if he could see the man in action? Spartacus always wanted to watch the talented Gaul on the field. It was frustrating that he was here, in this small and smelly room, unable to observe Crixus.

Spartacus could only wonder if Crixus was up against a surprise just as he was. He hoped that the Gaul would prevail.

Finally, he decided to give it a try. He would find a way to watch Crixus.

It took some convincing Messenius to let him join the watchers from the *ludus* so that he could watch Crixus in the arena. *Let me learn from his techniques, Messenius! Surely the dominus would be pleased with my initiative and your willingness!*

By the time Spartacus went with the guards and found a cramped sitting space with others from the *ludus*, Crixus was already taking a stance against another heavyset man who looked Samnite. Unlike Spartacus, Crixus fought with a traditional gladius and an oblong shield. He wore his thick hair in a tall bun and left part of it flying like a horse's tail. One could see that his eyes twinkled even from this distance, and his cheeks showed the creases of a smile.

The opponent had a deathly stare. His dark curly hair had been oiled and shined under the sun. His new blade glinted under the sun.

"Romans fuck you first, and I do second fuck!" Crixus said loudly in his heaviest, more dramatic accent.

That was bold and incredibly foolish, Spartacus thought. Pompeii had many Samnites and no love for Rome!

A chorus of boos rented the air, and people threw items to the field. But Crixus raised his hand—and they went silent.

They knew the drama.

"But Roman's ugly Latin fuck me hardest!" he said and bared all his teeth in a grin beneath his bushy mustache.

Even the Samnite grinned, and the crowd hooted in approval.

Crixus did a little dance, shaking his bottom and thumping the sandy ground. He was pure entertainment, and Spartacus understood what it meant to keep the crowd captivated.

Spurred by Crixus' shenanigans, even the Samnite tried his bit. "The best fuck you will get is with my blade," he said, waving the gladius. "And it will make you forget every fuck!"

The audience roared its approval. Spartacus had to admit that it was not a bad response. But all this ribbing would end bloodily, for they were no brothers behind a shield fighting an enemy.

Then the Samnite charged.

Crixus was a masterful fighter, but so was the Samnite. Unlike Spartacus, an expert in speedy, lightning moves between evasion and circling, Crixus was like an energetic bull. He rarely gave much quarter—instead preferring to rush the opponent repeatedly, hitting him with the shield or striking his weapon and trying to get him off balance. But the Samnite was no slouch, for he had his techniques. When Crixus rushed him, the man deftly often evaded and slammed Crixus' shield so hard that the Gaul had to steady himself.

And when they took a break, Crixus entertained the crowd with his canned, pre-prepared standard repertoire.

"What redder than a monkey's bum and angry donkey's lips? A Roman cheek slapped by Gaelic balls!"

Laughter.

Spartacus wondered what the sponsor—Claudius Glaber—thought of it. Could he hear Crixus? Did he know what the crowd was laughing about? He could barely see Glaber from here, but the sponsor was a lean, pale Roman in a bright white toga, and he sat upright on his seat looking captivated.

Crixus pointed his gladius at the opponent. "Samnite is tired. He practices fighting his grandmother!"

Boos and laughter.

The Samnite became a comedian himself, mimicking Crixus. "What is the difference between Samnite and Gaelic women? Gaelic women think a carrot is a real cock!"

Hollers.

Even Crixus nodded to his opponent, acknowledging the quality of the responses.

But then they were back at it again, trying to beat or be beaten. Kill or be killed.

And then Crixus made a dangerous misstep. When the Samnite lunged, he leaned back, hoping to avoid the rush, but the clever Samnite swung his gladius in a low arc and sliced Crixus' exposed chest.

No!

Crixus, you overconfident fool!

Oohhhhh! went the crowd. Crixus swung his weapon down in that instant arc, hacking the opponent's thigh.

In an instant, the game had changed. Blood poured down from Crixus' chest, and the Samnite fell to the ground, clutching his leg. As Crixus wobbled and the Samnite struggled to get on his feet, the referee paused the game and ran to the fighters.

It became clear quickly that neither could continue the fight. The crowd was in a generous mood due to the entertainment they had received, and the sponsor was disinclined to absorb the costs of death on the ground. Both men were taken away–the Samnite on a stretcher, and

Crixus with the help of two slaves who ran in with a bandage.

It was only by divine blessing that Crixus had not lost his life.

Spartacus waited in the gloomy and dark holding room after the games, anxious to see Crixus.

After what seemed like an eternity, he heard the door opening and feet shuffling.

Crixus!

Crixus was on a stretcher, his chest bandaged yet red with blood. The men lay him down on the floor and left. Messenius ordered someone to come in with more bandages and a salve.

"Why don't these fucking savages die on the field? I have to tend to him now," he grumbled.

Spartacus almost smashed Messenius' head to the wall. *Such an ungrateful mongrel. Wishing death upon the man who had served and fought for Vatia, and made money that fed Messenius and his family.* He controlled himself.

The *ludus* physician removed the crude cloth and washed the wound with hot water. He then tied a tight bandage across Crixus' chest. Crixus winced and groaned but said no words. Why had Vatia sent a trainer into the field?

Messenius addressed Vatia's men in the holding room. "We leave now. Get up, let us go."

As Spartacus, two other gladiators, and a guard carried Crixus' stretcher to the wagon. Two things bothered him greatly. How close he had come to death on this day, well short of whatever number was needed to negotiate freedom, and how easily Vatia was ready to dispose of even his better men–like Crixus. The other thing was that when he returned to the holding chamber after his fight, he had looked up at the dignitary stands and thought he had the most fleeting glimpse of someone he knew.

20

LUCANIA

"You may sit," Cleitus instructed Felix. He had summoned the boy to his residence and office. A guard waited outside just in case, and while Cleitus was no Spartacus, he was still quite effective with the blade hanging from his toga belt.

Felix squatted on the floor even though a cushioned recliner was next. Slaves, especially the lower ones, were accustomed to never using anything considered luxury, for it was drummed into them that they were unworthy of it all.

The herdsman looked tentative, and rightly so. He scratched his back absent-mindedly. He sat and acted almost as if he were on a grassy field watching cows.

"Do you know why you are here?"

"No, sir," Felix said. His eyes showed no fear—there was something in that defiance. Cleitus had seen Felix's back—it was a tapestry of violence, worse than most slaves, for scars lined every inch of his bony back. Years of lashing, flogging, beating, all telling their story in the ruptured, burned, torn, flayed, and healed skin. Did he fear pain? What was his threshold?

"Fear not, Felix. I have no plans to torture you for new information."

Felix tried but failed to conceal his relief. While torture was the accepted and normal way to pry information from slaves, Cleitus knew from his past that it did not always work. Men admitted to all manner of things, even fantastical ones, under pain. He had seen it too many times to trust the method of gouging eyes or breaking knees to extract truthful confessions. In the end, the victim gave up nothing of value but instead was rendered incapacitated and valueless.

"The *dominus* has allowed me to ask you some questions. But it may please you to know that I will not have you lashed only to get an answer."

Felix looked confused but nodded.

"Tell me again about the missing guard. You said he was nowhere to be found, and yet he accompanied you for many days, on the same routes, in the same manner, did he not?"

"Yes, master. But sometimes, he wandered away."

Cleitus nodded. He knew that Primigenia was listening from behind the curtains—she wanted to know what was about to happen and had begged him. It excited Cleitus that someone was interested in what he did.

"Tell me again, in as much detail as you can remember, the last day he came with you," Cleitus said, pointing his intact forefinger. He knew that Felix remembered the story behind the remaining missing digits.

Felix seemed almost relieved to be asked to repeat without blows accompanying them. He described the responses to Cleitus' questions on how many cows and which one was in the front, and where they were at different points of the day.

"You know the land exceptionally well, do you not? No wonder the master values your service despite your questionable behavior."

A little smile curled up Felix's lips and vanished.

But Cleitus *knew* Felix was lying. No one remembered such details from quite some time ago when nothing was unusual about the day. After all, if Felix was truthful, the guard had simply not shown up at some point. Felix had constructed an elaborate story for the day, and many liars never understood that truth was rarely so complete and precise.

When he was a scout and did all manner of cunning things for Durnadisso, Cleitus had become an expert at remembering places, routes, sequences, times, and everything needed to find and investigate runaways and derelicts, traitors, and other mischief-makers. He learned that it required immense practice and skill to remember *ordinary* days. And what separated the honest and the liar was the extent of *certainty*. An innocent man was often certain of his guiltless position but struggled with details, but a man most certainly guilty proclaimed his innocence loudly and was *also* very certain of every detail that proved his innocence.

The dead guard was not why Cleitus was here; he was a pretext to get to Felix. What role did Felix have in Spartacus' attack? That flame burned in Cleitus, and he could not let it go. If Felix was up to no good, this was a great way to curry favor with Porcina.

"Let us leave the subject of the guard behind. It seems you are innocent of any charge."

Though I am now certain you had a hand in his death, but have no way to prove it.

"I know we spoke of this before, long ago, but I must return to the subject of Spartacus to clarify a few details. Things I never asked."

Felix's eyes fluttered, but he said nothing.

"You remember him, do you? The story is that he was quite protective of you."

"He was just another guard, master. Some are kinder. Some are not."

Liar. A confident, cocky liar. All that leather on your back has taught you nothing.

"There is a difference between kind and protective."

"He was kind, master."

Stubborn liar who thinks he is clever.

"Do not lie, Felix," Cleitus said in a kind voice. "We know when a man argues with an overseer to be lenient to a low slave, it is not an act of kindness alone."

Felix's eyes turned toward the floor.

"The question is, why? Was he buggering you? Does Spartacus have deviant desires?"

Felix looked offended. He shook his head. "No. No, sir. He said he had a wife."

Liar. Spartacus had no wife then.

"If he had no affection for you, why be so kind, even to a herdsman?"

Felix flipped his palms as if to say, *I do not know.*

"Was he trying to become one of you?" *Unlikely, but let us see what he says.*

Felix rarely smiled. But this time, he did as he rocked back and forth, gripping his bony knees with his hands.

"He was a powerful man and not a slave. Why would he want my life?"

"Maybe he tired of his guard duties."

Felix shook his head and said nothing more.

Insolent bastard.

"Come closer, Felix. Come here, sit before me."

He looked unsure but meekly came near Cleitus' seating and sat before him.

"You have no idea why he sought to keep you safe from Mellius."

"No."

"And you just stood and watched when he killed Mellius?"

"Yes."

Cleitus swung his arm and slapped Felix so hard that the boy lost his balance and sprawled on the floor.

"Get up. Come here, sit by me. Come."

Felix had his palm on his cheek, and he struggled back to his feet and sat before Cleitus.

"So, no reason for him to protect you."

Felix looked fearful but made no admission.

Cleitus slapped him again. Felix fell but uttered no word. He did not confess and said nothing.

"Back. Come and sit beside me now. Come."

Felix was back again.

"Did you know I watched your beastly *father* in a gladiatorial game two days ago? He was running around like an animal."

Felix's eyes flickered this time, even if only for the briefest moment.

"Yes, he is alive. So far. But who knows for how much longer?"

Spartacus had fought brilliantly, and Cleitus had to admit that he was a sight to behold. He had been unfairly put up against two younger Germans, yet how he overcame them! He ducked, ran, swung, parried, stabbed, knelt, defended, and in the end, killed one of them and subdued the other. The speed of his movements despite his size, the bobbing hair that flew in the wind like the gods guided it, the power in his attack, it was all spectacular. For all his intense hatred for the man, Cleitus had conflicting emotions watching the exemplary gladiator. And when the crowd screamed

Thracian, Thracian! Cleitus had beamed until he realized that he had been trying to pass off like a Roman.

The son of a whore had not died. Instead, he had somehow kindled pride in Cleitus' heart.

Do not be fooled by that. Remember what Spartacus did to you!

Yes, but was he not magnificent, bringing such power to our name?

Quiet! Quiet!

These *feelings* Felix did not have to know. The boy's face showed a mixture of hope and concern.

"You still say there was no compelling reason why Spartacus went against Mellius on your behalf."

This time Felix only looked at him defiantly.

Cleitus flicked his wrist, and the boy flinched, and then Cleitus hit him again.

"Get up. Up. Come here. Sit next to me."

Somehow Cleitus was no longer enjoying this, for something was becoming more and more certain.

Felix, disoriented from the strikes and possibly half-deaf by now, slowly staggered closer to Cleitus and sat again. His face sagged, now deep red, and with a welt on his cheeks. A line of blood appeared where Cleitus' ring had scratched the skin.

But this time, Cleitus did not hit him. "There is so much I can do to hurt you, boy. But it seems you have such a loyalty to a man so long gone that you will accept jeopardy but refuse to divulge the reality."

It was unclear if Felix could even hear him. He kept rubbing his right cheek and ear, smearing the blood.

"I know a lot about you. More than you think you know."

The boy said nothing as he swayed where he sat.

Cleitus reconsidered his approach. It was normal for the Romans and even him to resort to violence when dealing with slaves. It was the most natural thing–to beat them, flog them, rape them, whatever it took to get truth or compliance. He had intended to have a calm conversation with Felix but had quickly descended into hitting this arrogant, stubborn boy and had gotten nowhere. And it was too early to kill him, for his replacements were not all yet ready.

He watched Felix as the boy steadied himself and squatted again, looking defeated.

"Can you hear me?"

Felix nodded.

"I sat there for hours, watching the fight. I watched him fight until the end."

Silence.

"You have never seen gladiatorial combat, I know. Warriors fight each other as thousands watch and cheer them. It is thrilling. Something like a drama or play," he said, but seeing Felix's blank stare, he realized that the herder had never experienced anything. Not a drama, not a play, not a comedy, not a fight, absolutely nothing that was entertainment.

Felix woke up, worked, and went to bed shackled.

Cleitus wondered how it might be for Spartacus. Hopefully, something similar or worse.

"Anyway, you do not know what it is. But just imagine two men putting up a show for an audience."

Felix nodded, unsure but now wanting to please Cleitus and avoid another strike.

"I will admit, he was magnificent."

The boy continued to stare.

"They put him against two German boys. Two! And yet they could not touch him."

Just like how all of us went against him and lost. Like how he led the auxiliaries against the best legionaries and still prevailed.

But he cut off your fingers and left you for dead.

But he let you live, unlike how he slaughtered the others. He gave you a chance. And that too after you went with the centurion to have him killed. He had done nothing to you then.

He insulted you before.

But that was because you followed Durnadisso, who had a personal vendetta. Spartacus spared you twice, and his leadership kept you alive during the marches.

Quiet! Stop it!

Cleitus pressed a palm on his skull to calm himself down. The back-and-forth of his emotions was like a foaming ocean.

Felix was watching with rapt attention.

"They tried to stab him, went at him from both sides, and still it was impossible. The gods have blessed the man for his speed despite his age."

The boy's lips curled up in the slightest smile.

"And then, against all odds, he won. Again. Apollo rode to his rescue. And the whole crowd kept screaming *Thracian!*"

He watched the boy carefully.

"*Thracian! Thracian! Thracian!,* they kept shouting! It was a roar that reached the heavens."

Felix's eyes opened ever so slightly, and his chest rose and fell.

Cleitus was sure.

He leaned forward and asked quietly. "Now, tell me, Felix. Are you a Thracian of the Maedi?"

21

LUDUS OF VATIA

Spartacus huddled with Crixus, Canicus, Philotas, and an excitable Celt called Procamus. He was one of Crixus' men and would not leave his side, and while Spartacus did not know this man, he could not have excluded him, for Crixus demanded that he be present.

Crixus had recovered in the last month, still not ready to enter the arena but good enough to yell at the fighters. The *ludus* physician had done a commendable job, though Spartacus was surprised that Vatia had not discarded the Gaul like a rag. There was rarely hope if the wound was a deep puncture. In the army, men suffering from such injuries were given a merciful death, and their earnings were sent to their families. It was a different matter in the gladiatorial schools. There were terrible stories of how such men were sometimes simply thrown off the wagon on the side of the road and left to die. They had no protection.

"Is Messenius anywhere here?" Spartacus asked. The supervisor had become a thorn by their side. It was getting darker, and the leaders had sent the rest to their barracks.

"He is away today. Canicus is the overseer," Crixus said, and Canicus nodded.

Excellent.

"Who here believes we have a path to freedom?" Spartacus asked the men. It was time to confront the harsh truths of their enslavement. He had gathered them all after broaching this subject before, and now they were willing to listen.

No one spoke a word until Procamus opened his mouth. "Vatia will k-k-kill us all. W-w-w-w-We will all have our li-li-limbs eat-eaten b-b-by hungry tigers!"

Procamus had a stutter which became pronounced when he was agitated. He was subjected to mockery, for the gods did not inflict stuttering upon men of intelligence. Such was the way of life. But all that had not stopped Procamus from holding a sword and fighting the Romans and ending up in this *ludus*. What was surprising was his friendship with Crixus. How did he tolerate this tactless dullard? Procamus was a good fighter, but he had no talent when he opened his cursed mouth. Besides, his stutter had gotten worse recently, making it hard to understand him.

But then Procamus was right.

Canicus, the thoughtful and quiet German of the Sugambri tribe, scratched his chin. "There is no question Vatia is putting us at greater risk than he ever did before."

But there was something more he wanted to say.

"What is it, Canicus? Do not hesitate," Spartacus pressed.

"Vatia sent three of my men and a Gaul to beast fights two days ago. No one returns from those."

Spartacus turned to Philotas. "You said–"

"I am not told of everything," Philotas cut him short. "I am not Vatia's confidante!"

"I am n-no-no–"

"Procamus–"

"Q-q-quiet! Not d-dying ripp-ripp–"

"Ripped apart. No one wants to," Crixus said kindly as he clasped Procamus' shoulder.

"This is what I believe," Spartacus said, keeping his voice low. "Vatia seeks to increase the number of low, weak men inducted to the *ludus* to sell them off to these execution matches fetching more money. And when we weaken, there will be no retirement, no glory, no freedom—just the mockery of running in the arena as a lion chases us, or as we are butchered by a gang of lunatics for the audience's merriment. His strategy is clear. He will extract the most value from his best fighters, and when they are reduced to a shell, send them away for a cheap fight and convert the sale upon their death."

Philotas nodded. "To think he put you against two boys and Crixus against an armored man. It broke all rules of fair battles."

"There is nothing fair in these games," Spartacus said. "It has always been an illusion. Which one of you has a contract with Vatia guaranteeing your freedom?"

No one acknowledged having that.

"And yet here we are, training, fighting, knowing more by the day that this will be an inglorious end. Why have you not resisted Philotas? Canicus? You have been here the longest!"

Canicus looked offended. His jaw clenched tight, and his golden hair shined under the fading orange sun.

"Do not think you are the first to ask these questions, Spartacus!"

Clearly, none of you have done anything beyond asking questions!

"Should we not go beyond *asking questions?*"

There was silence. Spartacus knew he had to tread carefully now.

But Canicus was not done. "Whether we are gladiators or not is immaterial. We are *slaves* and this is our destiny, having escaped execution!"

"That does not mean we are treated like animals for entertainment and given false promises. Why not execute us, then? Surely you had notions of justice in your tribes! We kept our word, and while our punishments were harsh, they were just!"

Canicus turned away, not responding.

Procamus slapped his chest. "B-b-burn the f-f-f-fucking school, is what I-I-I s-s-say!"

"Procamus!" Crixus admonished his man sharply. "Do you want to get us all killed?"

"You stuttering idiot! Be quiet," Spartacus admonished him. This was always the challenge when sensitive subjects were discussed among larger groups when there was no deep connection amongst the men. There was always one fool who failed to understand the methodical nature of planning.

"N-N-No you be q-quiet," Procamus responded. "Every-every-everyone is alwa-always qu-quiet un-until they die screa-screaming. Wa-warriors, you say, but all f-f-fuc-fucking co-cowards."

Procamus was right again. The silence was what would kill them eventually.

"You speak what is in our minds, Procamus," Spartacus said gently. "But if there is no tact, we will die well before we do anything. Besides, many of us, including you, have our women in service of the estate. Some even have children. What use is getting all of us condemned to death or a worse fate?"

Procamus grunted, mollified.

"What are you suggesting," Philotas finally asked to break the uncomfortable silence.

"Is there a chance for us to have a united front and refuse to fight until we are heard?" Spartacus asked.

"He will put us to death," Crixus said. Canicus nodded.

"But this is not an army," Spartacus countered. "Mutinous behavior would result in certain death. But *this* is business, and Vatia does not have legions to put us all down without resistance."

"He does not need legions to kill unarmed men," Philotas said. "All he needs is a gang of thugs with weapons. What are we going to fight them with, sticks?"

"We can grab their weapons."

"Who is willing to walk forward and die in sacrifice for others?" Canicus said, and no one had an answer.

"Do we not have a way to access the armory?" Spartacus asked.

Philotas and Canicus scoffed at the same time. *What a stupid question,* they seemed to indicate.

Procamus was hugging himself and muttering something. Spartacus saw this as a warning sign that the man did not have enough control. He had seen men in the army conduct themselves most unexpectedly, and often the precursor to such behavior was increased agitation and anger. Was he losing his mind?

Crixus said they had made many prayers for the man and that his wife spent time before the gods every week, seeking a cure for his impediment. *One day, the gods will fix his tongue,* Crixus had assured him.

"The armory is impenetrable. Ten-foot thick stone wall with two locked heavy iron gates. None of us have keys," Canicus said.

"Ju-just bu-burn his es-es-estate down. Get fire, w-w-wood, and s-some kniv-ves from the kitch-kitchen!"

Spartacus looked at Procamus. His disdain for the man had turned to respect. While Procamus was clearly becoming unhinged, behind that stutter was cunning and gumption.

Everyone ignored the Celt and turned to Spartacus. *They looked to him for direction.*

"Setting fire to the estate or attacking guards using kitchen knives may feel good for an hour but is futile," he said. "What happens then? Will the Romans just let us take a happy stroll down Capua's streets? We have to be careful and wait."

Canicus remarked, "You are contradicting yourself. The more we wait, the less chance we have."

Spartacus' cheeks burned at the slight. Canicus was right.

"When I say wait, I mean until we know *exactly* what we can do. We can burn everything down, or we can break out and run, or we can refuse to fight and seek an audience for our grievances. Or, we can see if there is a way we can get sold to another *ludus*."

Suddenly their interest was piqued.

"What do you mean get sold to another *ludus*?" Crixus asked. This was the most enticing option that had no violence in it. Vatia was a harsh bastard, but Spartacus had heard of other, smaller schools that still relied on skilled games.

"If there is some way for another school to buy us and make a profit for Vatia."

But reality set in soon. How would one even go about it? How did you find such schools? And then convince them to visit Vatia. And then for Vatia to accept offers. And then that school to be more considerate. What sounded like a clever idea was only an ephemeral hope.

Dispirited, they returned to other possibilities, and none seemed practical.

Meanwhile, Procamus was becoming increasingly loud and angry, repeatedly pushing them to *do something* and it always ended up with the demand to burn the estate. Eventually, Crixus screamed at him in his language and sent the subdued Procamus away. While he had nuggets of clever ideas, the man lacked the stability for the brewing conspiracy.

"Keep an eye on your man," Spartacus said sternly, turning to the Gaul.

"It is my business," Crixus countered. "Stutterer maybe, but he clever."

"Clever he may be, but he poses a risk," Spartacus said. "I have seen men of such affliction and behavior. He will die or get us killed."

"He is right, Crixus," Canicus said.

"I take no orders from Germans," Crixus said testily. It was known that much bad blood flowed between the Gauls and the Germans, and now, even so far away from home, they could not settle their differences easily.

Canicus was a poised man and not given to bursts of emotion, so he said nothing, the point already made.

"Crixus, can you not find a way to remove Procamus from the roster and let him be a trainer?"

"Vatia will not accept. He has already said that Procamus must fight."

Must die.

"Was he always this restless? His stutter is worse."

"His affliction is worsening. He is volatile. Why did you bring him here, Crixus?" Philotas asked.

Crixus lost his temper. "Maybe he is worse now, but he always has my back! I protect him! He was once a great fighter!"

"Keep your voice down," Spartacus cautioned. "And your temper in check. We cannot have anyone betray us through impatience."

"Procamus listens to *me*," Crixus insisted, and Spartacus decided to drop the matter. He knew that it would always be a challenge managing the many tribes and their loyalties.

"If we do anything, do you think your men will follow?" Spartacus asked them.

"Mine will," Canicus said. Crixus affirmed. Philotas was unsure but relied upon Spartacus to lead the Thracians.

Spartacus did not want to argue that any action would not work with three or four leaders; it would need one. It was too early and led to conflict.

Philotas changed the conversation. "What next?"

Something else was brewing in Spartacus' mind. If the solution was violence, in which they had much experience and expertise, then the key to success was *weapons*. The armory was inaccessible, the kitchen was useless for a violent breakout, and no matter how skilled, they would not last long against wooden shields, spears, and real gladii. The guards were almost all men with military experience and would butcher them like fowl. Even the strongest hand was useless against steel.

But how to get weapons?

"What is outside the wall?" he asked the men. The *ludus* were buildings on three sides of the training field, but a tall wall on the fourth. "Does anyone know?"

After some hesitation, Philotas spoke. "A gravel path, and a swamp beyond that. Do you think we can scale the wall?"

They all knew that scaling the wall was impossible. It was too tall and smooth, and the men had no access to ropes, grappling hooks, or ladders. The top of the wall had sharp spikes and embedded nails to prevent anyone from trying a foolish escape.

"No. Just because men cannot climb it does not mean something cannot be thrown over."

22

LUCANIA

"Now, tell me, Felix. Are you a Thracian of the Maedi?"

This time Felix's eyes opened wide. Cleitus knew without a doubt then that the connection between the boy and Spartacus was that they were born of the same tribe. It had to be.

Felix struggled with his words. The boy was incapable of deception as much as he tried.

"You are, are you not. Your mother was a Maedi."

Felix was still quiet.

Cleitus switched to his language. *"The question is, how did Spartacus find out? Do you speak their language?"*

Maedi was slightly different from the Cleitus' Bessi dialect, but both could easily understand each other.

But Felix stared blankly. *He does not understand.*

"How did Spartacus find out you are of his tribe?" Cleitus asked again, but with a softer tone. "I am a Thracian too. Surely you know that."

The boy struggled with admitting the truth. He pulled his knees up to his chest and gently began to tap his forehead on his knees.

"I hold nothing against you, for Spartacus is a forceful man. I do not know how he found out you are of his kind. Tell me, Felix, and I seek to do you no harm. See, I am your kind too!"

Would Felix trust him? The herdsman did not answer. But that was acceptable, for Cleitus now had the upper hand.

He continued. "I never thought you would be one of *us*, and I would be kind to you if I knew. You no longer look like us, do not speak our language, and know nothing about our ways. And these books," he said, vaguely pointing to the tomes behind him, "say nothing of your provenance, or your mother's."

Felix's eyes lit up.

"She left me," he said. "I was nothing to her."

And I was nothing to my mother, either.

"I killed mine," Cleitus said suddenly and was surprised by his revelation.

Why am I sharing this with this low slave? He is no Thracian. He never was, except by his mother.

But our blood flows in him. Our gods still see him as their child. And surely everyone borne of our lands is imbued with that boldness, and it shows in this boy.

Stop it! You are now beginning to think favorably of both Spartacus and Felix. What evil air emanates from them?

There is no evil. They are your people, unlike the Romans here.

Cleitus shook his head in irritation. The noises in his head would not stop!

Felix was taken aback by this utterance. "Why, master?" he asked, as his finger traced the drying maroon smears on his face.

"She left me. But before that, she tried to beat me to death."

Felix was still.

He seemed to want to say something.

"Go on. I will not hit you," Cleitus said.

Felix had only the slightest smile on his beaten and blood-smeared face. His cheek was beginning to swell. "But she left you free, master. Mine left me in a cage to die slowly."

That is what the gods ordained.

How could a god ordain a child to such a life?

Quiet. Be quiet! Remember what you are trying to do!

What are you trying to do?

Justice. Justice for yourself. To find the truth of that day. To find the truth behind Felix's involvement in Spartacus' attack. In Mellius' murder.

But Felix brought you to the estate to live. Spartacus spared you. And Mellius, in his supreme foolishness, got himself killed. Why did he matter to you?

He does not. He—

Cleitus shook his head again and caught Felix watching him curiously.

"Some of us are unlucky," Cleitus said drily. "And the gods have given you this life and this," he said, lifting his finger-less hand, "for me."

Cleitus was suddenly at a block on what to do next. What *was* the point anymore?

And then he regained all his faculties.

The point was to find everything about Felix, implicate him in the conspiracy of siding with Spartacus, and then in the guard's death, of which he was certain the boy had a hand. And use all that to further himself with Porcina. The Senator would be ecstatic at Cleitus' cunning.

"Well, Felix. Tell me about Lucia," he said.

23

LUDUS OF VATIA

"Are the gods keeping you well, my friend?" Pollio asked. The Roman contractor and businessman were now healthier than ever, having put on considerable weight that his jowls sagged and his belly stuck out prominently beneath his toga. Spartacus had worked for Cleitus when in Capua before Cleitus pursued him. They had become close, and while Pollio had no qualms in scamming others, he had developed a connection with Spartacus. And finally, when Cleitus the hound smelled him in Capua, it was Pollio who had warned him and helped him escape.

Spartacus stood before Pollio; his hands held wide to allow the Roman to inspect him.

But it was all a pretense. And both knew it.

The little conspiratorial discussion weeks ago had yielded one action. Canicus had a connection in the kitchen, a rather pretty local pleb who was taken in by his looks. They had arranged for Pollio to pay a visit under the guise of a legitimate event sponsorship through her. Pollio was shocked to learn of Spartacus' fate and hastened for a visit.

"As well as they can," Spartacus said. "Now go and look at a few others, Pollio. Make some remarks and talk to Vatia before you return to me."

Pollio loved the charade. He went about the arena, berating or praising the trainees. He sat on the benches and shouted encouragement. He got into a pointless argument with Vatia, who was present as the host, about why Romans should "rotate" the fighters after only two games.

Eventually, Vatia left, leaving Pollio to spend the next few hours assessing the *ludus*. This was not uncommon—sponsors often visited a *ludus* before deciding to loan or buy fighters. They watched the training, interviewed the trainers, and inspected the men. Sometimes they brought their wives, mistresses, or daughters for a show. Pollio had arrived alone.

And finally, with Messenius away on an errand and Vatia no longer around, Spartacus gestured at Canicus to send Pollio his way.

The roly-poly Roman ambled across the field and came toward Spartacus, grinning ear to ear. "I have never been to a training school before. Not what I imagined."

"What did you imagine?" Spartacus asked. No doubt the man thought the schools were some kind of filthy madness where men ran around fighting and murdering each other.

"Well, something different. Certainly not a place you would bring your woman. You look better than when I saw you at Capua so many years ago."

"Better is an illusion, Pollio. You certainly look much healthier."

Pollio laughed. "My profits are fat. I am fatter," he said and held up his fingers to show his rings. "But my life is now decadent boredom. I will admit that."

Such a luxury to have!

"And when I received this hush-hush invitation and that too with your name attached to it, I could not resist rushing over. I was angry at the gods for putting you here!"

"Do I have your confidence?"

Pollio looked offended. "We spent much time in the trenches, Spartacus, do not forget that."

Pollio's trenches were construction ditches, but Spartacus would not contest the man. He continued. "But first, tell me what got you here? How did you end up in this mess?"

Spartacus sighed. "It is a twisted story."

"I am all ears for twisted stories, not your grandmother's tales."

Spartacus laughed. And then, he recounted his journey culminating in Vatia's *ludus*, and Pollio protested the unfairness at appropriate times. And when Spartacus finished, Pollio's exuberance had somewhat dampened. He looked around, and the *ludus* no longer looked like an exciting place with happy trainees and fighters.

"I never knew Vatia was such a vicious bastard. The man's whining hides his vices. I tried to get into this business, but he and Asina have a stranglehold in Capua."

Spartacus nodded. "He is worse than most other *ludus* owners. Of that, we are certain."

"And your wife toils in the kitchens?"

"Yes."

"Is she beautiful? She must be!"

Spartacus laughed again. There were certain things about Pollio that would never change. "Yes, she is. But shall we talk about why you are here before you are escorted out?"

"Ah, yes. Tell me. It better be something exciting. I think I can imagine but let me allow you to speak."

Spartacus hesitated. Suddenly all this seemed like a poorly imagined idea from a desperate mind. Pollio was Roman through and through. His view of slaves and gladiators was no different from anyone else's—and he could very well be one of the screaming hoards in the *spectacula* thirsting for a fighter's blood.

Pollio was also an astute man. He stepped closer to Spartacus. "I see your hesitation. I saw you as a capable nobleman, and I still see you like that. I place you in high regard for whatever misgivings you may have for me as Roman. Even if our laws have unfairly condemned you to slavery, I do not see you as a slave. Do you think I am so foolish that I believe you asked me to see you here for a casual chat?"

"It has been years, Pollio. Surely you see that people change, and it is the truth that I worried much about seeking you."

"You have nothing to fear from me. What is the worst that could happen? I listen to your hare-brained scheme, laugh at your face, sleep with your wife, and go home to my pretty slaves."

"Leave my wife alone and do the rest of it," Spartacus said, though he was feeling better. There was not much to lose. More from the *ludus* had not returned from recent games, and the influx of weaker, less talented men was increasing. It was the only time. "Pollio, what will you get out of aiding me?"

Pollio shrugged. "I have some ideas," he smiled mysteriously. Sure he had some nefarious schemes of his own. And in time, Pollio would extract his worth.

"Now, tell me, Spartacus. We both know we have limited time."

This was it. He took the plunge.

"Can you help us break out of the *ludus*?"

Pollio did not look surprised. All he did was knot his eyebrows and rub his chin. "What do you have in mind?"

Spartacus was surprised by the lack of reaction. Did he not realize how *serious* this was?

"Do you understand the gravity of my ask? This is not about just helping me escape."

Pollio scoffed. "I asked you before. Do you think I am a fool? I always guessed that, knowing you, an audacious request was most likely. I have thought about it all, Spartacus. I need excitement in my life, and Vatia has fucked me in business more than once. This is my time, and I now have enough influence and money to keep official busybodies at a distance. And like I said, I have some wonderful ideas, but do not ask me yet."

Spartacus was now filled with hope. "What do you think?"

"Well. I am sure you have given it considerable thought, given your military background. But I can tell you what is possible and what is not."

Spartacus pretended to show Pollio a few gladiatorial moves to avoid suspicion, and then they sat together on a bench, away from others. Canicus and Philotas watched from afar, and Crixus was nowhere to be seen.

"Tell me now."

Pollio seemed pleased to have his opinion heard. "The good news is there is no Roman legion nearby. Not in Capua anymore. With peace in Rome and its surroundings, they have moved military garrisons further east and south. Only a small detachment on the edge of the town. So, if you manage to break out, you can disperse before there is action."

That was good news. But it was never only favorable tidings, for the gods always had something wicked in waiting.

"But that means little. Businessmen and owners of schools, like Vatia, usually have a large private guard. They are usually former soldiers, the leaders are often centurions, and they are heavily armed. And a collective security arrangement means that when one is in trouble, the others respond to it. It keeps everyone safe."

You lift me and bring me down, Zibelthiurdos!

"Now, do not despair. Listen to me. Usually, if a fight breaks out in a school or rioting threatens an influential businessman's property, messengers rush to the collective members who dispatch support. It can take hours before all order is restored–but be aware that reprisal is vicious, and those captured and implicated face the harshest punishments. And you know *what it means* to slaves," he said, throwing his hands out.

"How large are these guard contingents?"

"Oh. You can never say. I am part of the collective, and responses can range from ten men to a hundred. A hundred, armed, trained men."

"Have there been other attempts before?"

"From a *ludus*?"

"Yes."

"There have been. I checked before coming here. But in one case, six men escaped, and I do not know if they were ever apprehended. In another case, thirty tried escaping but were caught."

"What happened to them?"

"Do you want to know?"

"I must know what fate awaits us if we fail."

"Very well, then. Twenty were sent to beast fights and died. Four ring leaders were hoisted up on crosses. The rest died during apprehension."

How different would their fate be the longer they stayed, anyway?

Spartacus saw that Messenius had returned to the field and was talking to Canicus. It would not be too long before his attention turned to Spartacus and Pollio.

"What do you know about the layout," Pollio said, sweeping his palms around him.

"This complex has barracks on two sides of the quadrangle, the wall on the third, and Vatia's quarters, kitchen, and other facilities in the main building, making the fourth part of the perimeter."

"Where is the armory?"

"Secure corners separate from the barracks, under heavy lock-and-key, and behind thick stone walls."

Pollio looked at the wall and said to himself. "Pretty tall. Is there a way out of the building from the barracks?"

"Only through the kitchen. The barracks lead up to the eating space, from where one corridor goes into the rest of the building. Surely there is a way out from there. The rest are heavily secured."

"We may have to stop soon," Pollio said. "It seems you have sixty to seventy here, and you seem to be fit men. But without weapons, you have no chance."

"I recognize that. Is there a way you can get us weapons and haul them over the wall?" Spartacus asked urgently.

Pollio looked at the wall and shook his head. "You cannot just haul heavy weapons over the wall. Do you think I have access to siege equipment? They have guards watching the outside of the wall. They will sound alarms well before anyone even starts an attempt. Even if we kill a few, it will be too late."

All hope was draining. "Can you not bribe some of them?"

"And expect them all to keep their mouths shut? Or risk being executed? I wish to help you, Spartacus, and get some thrill. But I have no interest in dying like a dog or losing everything I have. We need to be clever and tactful."

What paths were left? It seems like nothing is possible!

"Perhaps this is all entirely futile. The gods have put me here, and I shall go to my end after I slay men who have done me no wrong."

Pollio's eyes narrowed. "You speak like a coward. What happened to your grand ambitions of becoming the king of Thrace or even Rome? And yet you give up because you cannot rally men to get out of a fucking *training school!* Was that how Sulla fought, tucking his cock between his fat thighs and crying mummy?"

Spartacus felt ashamed. Had this place crushed his spirit? "Is there a way?"

"Yes, there is, you idiot! But it requires much planning. I have a brilliant—"

Suddenly there was much commotion. Whistles! More than twenty armed guards rushed into the field. A red-faced Messenius was screaming.

Had they been caught? Did someone leak the news? Spartacus panicked. Was this it?

Messenius sprinted toward a frightened Pollio.

The supervisor's face was scrunched in fury. "Pollio, sir. You must leave! Now!"

"What—"

"We have an incident. You cannot be here, for your safety. Your man is here to escort you!"

A man appeared from the entrance, and Pollio looked relieved. He turned to Spartacus, who was now on his knees. "You are a good fighter. I will see you in the arena," he said and blinked twice. A signal that he would find ways to be in touch.

And then Pollio was gone.

"What happened—"

A guard struck him viciously on the back, causing Spartacus to stumble and fall on his face. He lay there, unsure what had transpired.

Then he heard Messenius speak to Canicus. "You sons of whores will pay."

24

LUDUS OF VATIA

A few minutes ago...

Antara scooped a ladle of the barley porridge and filled the large wooden bowl. The first group of fighters was seated for lunch on the long wooden benches. Guards stood watch on either side, knowing that the men often made lewd attempts at the women who served. So long as none tried to rape one of them, minor indiscretions were laughed away. She had lost count of how many times someone had grabbed her breasts and buttocks or tried to kiss her. Every woman, even the older ones, suffered this unending harassment, but it was accepted. Some of the younger ones even enjoyed the attention. Antara never brought it up with her husband–surely he knew, for he watched others. Only when he was seated for lunch did the rest behave and leave her alone, and she had never seen him indulge in vulgarities. Even Crixus, a man her husband spoke highly about, was wont to grab when he could, though he avoided her.

Her day began before the sun rose, cleaning the utensils, scrubbing floors and benches, and preparing the basic breakfast of bread chunks or barley porridge. Then it was time to serve them into the cups that other slaves took to the barracks. Then it was back to cleaning, scrubbing, and preparing for the afternoon meals. The cycle repeated with little respite until dinner was usually served before sunset. After that, there were usually sundry tasks within the house, whether in the estate kitchen, rooms, bathhouse, or elsewhere as ordered by the supervisors on duty. She and Methe did most of these activities together, often chatting away or making snide remarks. The days were exhausting, but abuse beyond the usual verbal tirades or occasional slaps from the female overseers was rare. Some women willingly engaged in sex with the guards in return for leniency and minor conveniences, while others were coerced with little protection. Antara had managed to escape from both because she was a good woman and the wife of a prized gladiator.

"Is your man here?" Methe, her friend asked.

"No. Later," she said. Her Latin had improved, and she could now converse in simple sentences and understand what was being said.

She went about serving the porridge to the men who chatted amongst themselves. But when she arrived at the stutterer's seat, she noticed that he was agitated.

Procamus was muttering something to himself and tapping the table with his knuckles. He did not lift his bowl. He often came with Crixus, who was seated two benches away. Antara knew Procamus well. The man used to be cheerful and took all the mockery without a complaint. The girls mimicked his speech. The men ribbed him endlessly. Some heaped scorn. Yet nothing bothered him.

But all that had gradually changed in the last few months.

Procamus had become sullen and ornery. He no longer took the teasing in good spirit, and Crixus had to often quell fights that broke out because Procamus took offense. She was sure no good would come of it. She knew that Procamus' wife made many prayers to cure his affliction, and Antara had joined too sometimes, but none of that had borne fruit.

His stuttering had gotten progressively worse, and it was becoming impossible to understand him anymore.

She filled his bowl and hurried away, avoiding a hand shooting out beneath a bench. *Leeches.*

When she was safe behind a small barricade that separated the seating area from the kitchen, she heard one of the guards loudly admonish Procamus. "Shut up and stop murmuring, you retard."

She turned toward Procamus, who was gripping the bench's edge and now muttering something even louder.

Crixus stood, looking concerned. It was rare for fights to break out in the kitchen, for they all knew the consequences. Antara had heard her husband speak of the beatings and the terrifying punishment known as the box. And not to speak of starvation and losing even minor privileges. Even these hardened men, many of them criminals, understood that.

"Hey, you. I said shut up," the guard said and swatted Procamus' head.

"S-s-s-stop it," Procamus said sharply, drawing gasps from the kitchen staff. No one raised their voices at the guards—it never ended well.

"S-s-stop it, s-s-s-s," mocked the guard, whose nickname was Buffalo. "Fucking retard, s-s-stop what?"

He hit the poor man's head again.

Procamus kept his head low and began to sway, gripping the edge of the bench.

But the guard bared his yellow teeth and would not stop. "F-f-f-fuck m-my moth-ther, she is-is-is an id-idiot like me, but s-she i-is tight!" he said and swatted Procamus' head again.

Procamus snapped.

He shot up from his bench, pivoting on his feet, and pulled Buffalo's gladius out of its sheath with stunning speed. And before the shocked onlookers could react, he grabbed the guard by his upper garment and sliced his neck like a melon.

Blood sprang like a fountain from Buffalo's neck and drenched the nearby table, some of it staining the barley porridge and turning it red. Procamus left Buffalo, who collapsed to his knees, his eyes wide open with disbelief and his hands grabbing his neck, trying to stem the copious bleeding.

Antara's heart thudded with terror. *No! You fool!*

Procamus had his back to a wall and waved the gladius even as two other guards rushed toward him. They did not attack—instead, they held their weapons out. "Put it down, you filthy rat! Put it down!" one of them shouted. Perhaps they knew the danger of attacking a trained gladiator who may be an idiot in his mind but was lethal with a weapon.

"One more step, and I will dr-drop you," Procamus warned. "Not one step. I told him to stop."

It was as if peace had descended upon him in this moment of violence. His stutter had almost vanished.

"Put your gladius down," the guard snarled. "Or we will cut you down like a fucking dog."

Buffalo kicked where he fell. His face turned white, and his blood left patterns as his feet wiped the floor. A low hiss of air escaped from the deep gash on his neck, and frothy bubbles formed in the blood. No one paid heed to him.

Antara was frozen where she was. More guards entered. Messenius came running and warned everyone to stay where they were.

"Do not kill the bastard," Messenius shouted. "We are not allowed to gut them. We need to wait for the *dominus*."

"Wa-wait all you want. You will all die soon," Procamus said cryptically. "Your cruel-cruelty is no longer sanctioned b-by the gods. No more!"

Messenius tried to mock Procamus but failed. The gladiator kept shaking his head as he kept the gladius firmly pointed outward. He had also grabbed an iron lid cover with a small bell on top and held it like a shield.

"Put your weapon down, Procamus. The master might still forgive you for this transgression," Messenius said.

"Forgive? No, he will not. I was always d-dead."

Crixus bellowed at him rapidly in his language, which Antara did not understand. The two exchanged sharp words, but Procamus would not drop the weapon.

Messenius turned to someone and barked an order.

Meanwhile, Procamus continued again. "Matter of time. Just see."

And soon, as everyone watched, a guard came dragging a woman by her hair.

Procamus' face dropped. "Leave l-leave her al-alone! Sh-she has nothing t-to-to d-d-d-"

The terrible stutter was back.

Messenius' eyes were cold and hard. He grabbed the crying woman and pulled hard on her stola in one swoop, stripping her nude. Holding her tight, he moved the tip of his gladius down, grazing her navel and then resting the tip on her inner thigh. The woman began to tremble with fear.

"Drop your weapon, or I will fuck her with my gladius," he said, unsmiling, even as other guards made lewd gestures. He pressed the blade and drew a thin bloody line on her thigh. Anticipating outrage from the gladiators in the seating area, the other guards began clearing them, sending them away. Crixus continued to shout at Procamus in his language.

"Tell your man I have little patience," Messenius told Crixus. "They both die, or he surrenders, and she may yet live. His fate is in the master's hands. Tell your pig fucking idiot to stop stuttering and give up. Now!"

Crixus addressed Procamus gently this time and began to advance on the man. Procamus' lips quivered, and whatever he wished to say died in his throat.

Suddenly his shoulder sagged, and all the fighting left him.

Procamus dropped the gladius and collapsed to his knees. The guards landed blows on him until he lost consciousness, at which point they tied his hands and legs and took him away.

Antara barely breathed during this period.

Then Messenius shouted. "Come with me to the field! Make sure nothing mischievous is afoot!"

And they all ran out.

Dread washed over Antara. How would all this unfold?

25

LUDUS OF VATIA

There was not a sound except the distant chirps of birds and the incessant hum of jitterbugs in the afternoon. Fifty armored guards surrounded the gladiators, none of whom carried a weapon or any kind of implement that they may use to cause harm.

Messenius walked to the front. "You, you, you," he kept on, pointing to the leaders and the senior gladiators and ordering them to come to the front. Philotas, Canicus, Crixus, Spartacus, Oenomaus, Castus, Nisarpal, and Urbanus all made the first line of the arc of men forced into close quarters. They faced another set of guards with their gladius' pointing out from the top of their shields. Messenius vanished back into the building.

What was going on?

"Everyone stay still and wait. The *dominus* will be here soon."

Vatia emerged from one of the entrances to the field, followed by more guards. He looked harried and angry, barking something to Messenius, who was now shaking his head vigorously.

And then, behind him, his arms tied and dragged by a rope to his neck was Procamus. They had not killed him yet. Behind him was his wife, crying, her hair disheveled and her hands bound. Spartacus had since learned what had happened in the kitchen—what a fool. What an abject idiot who could not control his mouth and temper. And now he would die, and Vatia would make it a spectacle. Would he make Procamus fight here in some ugly way and get himself killed?

Procamus kept his head low and looked at no one. He was naked, and his body bore the marks of a good beating. Once they were all assembled, Vatia got on a stool to address the assembly. The thrifty bastard seemed to think he was on a podium for his voting masses.

"You know why you are here," he said in his high-pitched whiny voice. It grated Spartacus, for he had developed a severe distaste for the man.

Vatia scanned his beady eyes on them. "We have rules in this *ludus*. Rules to ensure everyone's safety from those here for their many wrongdoings, who have been given more than most citizens can aspire for—food, shelter, and a path to glory."

Path to death.

"I have been a benevolent man. Merciful. I have paid money to take you from death's jaws and give you life. Your gods abandoned you, and ours have given you kindness, yet all I see around me is hubris, arrogance, and now the utter gumption of a man to raise his hand to one of my guards— not just to inflict wounds but to take his life. Yes! Take the life of a man protecting those whose lives must have been taken long ago!"

Vatia had lost further weight in the last several months. His eyes were sunken, looking like hollow dark pits in his sickly, wrinkled face. Most of his hair had fallen away, leaving a prominent bald pate and strands of willowy silver hair. Spartacus had heard rumors about Vatia's influential father-in-law threatening to have his daughter leave him and financially ruin him. Was all that getting to Vatia?

"The softness in my treatment of men little more than animals has turned them into snakes that bite a master's hand. And I speak not just of this stuttering vermin's murder of one of my men, but of the hubris and arrogance of those who see themselves as leaders among gladiators," Vatia said. This time, his eyes settled on Spartacus before moving on. "Many here seek freedom and glory without the sweat and blood required to earn it. They wish to lay with their women and strut about in the cities without *earning* their redemption. They think of themselves as masters in this business and spread rumors. They think that I will become bankrupt if they refuse to fight or cause their deaths—and I can assure them that no such thing will happen. Those are just minor inconveniences. Like a benevolent master with his errant slaves, I have been patient, but no more. Today, every man and woman will witness what happens when you lay hands with impunity on one of my men. And you will stand and watch."

Benevolent and merciful? A death profiteer with no sense of justice.

Vatia nodded, and soon four men emerged from the barracks entrance holding a tall wooden beam. Spartacus knew instantly what it was. *Sabazios be merciful and end Procamus' life soon, and take him with you!*

Procamus' wife began to wail loudly and collapsed to the ground.

"No, master, please, no, master! Forgive us!" She tried crawling toward Vatia, but a guard lashed her several times until she lay motionlessly in a heap, sobbing. Several other women in the back began to cry, and Vatia looked around with smug satisfaction.

A large loin-clothed man wearing a black mask and carrying a flogging whip made his way and summoned several gladiators to dig a deep rectangular hole in the ground to hold the beam. All through this, Procamus made no protest, instead choosing to stare at the sky and speak to himself. They stamped the earth around the fixed post to ensure it held firm.

Spartacus had watched floggings, including severe ones where the men died soon after, and knew it to be a terrible ordeal but deserved by those who abandoned their men or put others at risk. He hoped this time that Procamus would die quickly during the administration. The gladiator was a skilled fighter and had lived a hard life, and thus his body had the strength to withstand violence longer than most men. Sometimes, that was a curse.

The guards dragged Procamus to the post and had him wrap his hands around it. They tied his hands and legs. Procamus' back already showed the damage inflicted upon him since his surrender.

The masked man swung his whip to test the leather strips. The small metal pieces attached to the strips clashed and made an ominous *tinkle*.

"Begging your gods is worthless, for they have condemned a treacherous bastard like you," the masked man said through the fabric. *Why the mask?*

Absolute silence reigned in the quadrangle as the gladiators and the tense guards eyed each other and waited for the events to unfold.

And then, as they watched, the man lifted the whip and brought it down sharply on Procamus' back, and even Spartacus winced. A guttural howl escaped from the condemned gladiator as an angry, bloody red gash opened instantly. The tips of the leather strips were already decorated by pieces of flesh and skin ripped from Procamus' back.

Thwack!

Thwack!

Thwack!

Thwack!

Procamus pushed back and screamed. His legs almost gave up as his back became a bloody mess with deep cuts and large sections of muscle exposed and ripped. His bowels loosened. The stench mixed with the acrid smell of urine and the distinct sharpness of fresh blood. Deep anger rose in Spartacus, and the inner ring of guards fidgeted nervously as they continued to point the gladius' over the shields.

Thwack!

Thwack!

Thwack!

Procamus' wife, who was wailing, lost consciousness. Vatia stood resolutely, scanning everyone around him as if to say, *dare try a thing.*

The vicious flogging now ripped off a piece of muscle near Procamus' center, exposing his spine. The leather strips were bloody red, and his entire back was nothing but a mess of velvet. Procamus lost consciousness as well, and his legs collapsed.

Die, brother, die. A day will come when we shall inflict this on these godless people.

Crixus stood nearby, and while his jaws were tight and his face without emotion, Spartacus caught the moistness in the Gaul's eyes. He sensed the restless energy amongst those around him—Vatia had miscalculated. The field was *sacred* ground, where men, even in their abject misery, forgot about their situation and station and trained to pursue redemption and freedom. And now, all they would remember was the fickleness of their fate and the monstrosity committed for one among them.

Procamus had fought for Vatia and made him money. And this was now his reward.

Violence was no stranger to any of them, for they had all killed and maimed—but who among them had inflicted this injustice on another?

Guards untied Procamus and left him on the ground. Then they went inside and brought a wooden crossbar with a notch in the center. They used a short ladder to affix the crossbar to the top of the beam, forming a T.

The masked man ordered stools to be placed around the beam.

The chosen gladiators were forced into the terrible job of turning Procamus so that he could be lifted. With men on either side and one behind, holding a moaning Procamus' bloody body, they had him standing on the stool. The man behind lifted Procamus' right hand and held it against the crossbar, and the masked man stood before Procamus. He placed a long, rusted nail on the wrist and pressed it, positioning to hammer it in.

All the wailing around had subsided into silence.

Procamus' bloodshot eyes were open now, but he barely registered the violence inflicted upon him.

The masked man slammed the nail with the hammer, driving it through the wrist into the bar. Procamus let out a low moan. Then the executioner repeated it on the left wrist, ensuring that the nails were deep enough. He then ordered the men to tie Procamus' extended arms to the bar, at the elbows.

He stepped down from the broad stool and removed the other on which Procamus stood. And before Procamus sagged from his weight and broke his shoulders, the executioner ordered the men to hold his legs to support the weight.

He pulled out another long, rusted nail and placed it just above the ankle bone. He then slammed the heavy hammer on it, nailing Procamus' right foot to one side of the beam.

Spartacus could hear the nail's *rrrrskkk*, the sound of the metal grating the bones and cracking them as it was rammed through until it penetrated the wood.

He then did it on the other. Procamus let out loud animal screams throughout it all, yet death was no closer to him than it was at the beginning of the crucifixion. They tied his legs to prevent the weight from dislodging the nails.

Why do you punish him so, Zibelthiurdos? Let his spirit leave his body!

Satisfied with his vicious work, the masked man barked at the other fighters to return to the group, and then looked at Vatia for approval. The Roman nodded.

Procamus was whimpering now, his shoulders straining from the downward pressure causing difficulty breathing, even as his legs shook uncontrollably.

"Let this be an example to all the slaves who decide that they are greater than what they are and lay their hands on one of *us*. I have said that my mercy is greater than most, thus sparing his wife from this wretched end. But she will remain in the estate and continue in the kitchen, and let her be a reminder to all the men and women of what happens if one of you decides to let your urges get the better of you."

Spartacus could barely breathe in anger. If Antara and other members of this *ludus* were not in service of Vatia, he was certain he would inflict harm on this man at the first available opportunity.

"And the next time," he said, the threat hanging like a noisome toxin in the air, "it will not be just the perpetrator. And now you shall all return to what you must do. Train, bring glory to yourself and the school, and ensure that you do not end up like him. Remember that the choice is yours—adoring crowds, better quarters, perhaps even freedom, or something else you wish not on yourself or anyone else."

Satisfied at his screeching speech, Vatia turned to the masked man. "Leave him there, and keep two guards next to him. May no one come to his aid or hasten his death."

Procamus' body was shivering. His eyes were partially rolled up in the sockets.

The unending cruelty of Roman bastards.

With that, Vatia and his entourage left the field, and slave women lifted Procamus' still incoherent wife and took her with them. The masked man turned to them. "If anyone raises a hand as we leave this field, they will find themselves next to him."

They all stood still as the inner ring of guards walked back cautiously, still holding their shields and gladii. And once they receded, those behind left in an orderly fashion. The two beside Procamus sat on the stools and stretched their legs. One of them grumbled. "Now I have to sit here until this pig fucker dies."

Spartacus looked at Procamus, who was repeatedly trying to hoist himself up. His arms and shoulder joints were already painfully extended. His breathing was labored, but much fight was left in him.

Spartacus thought death would not come early to the poor man.

But when he looked around to see the men, he saw little anger in the eyes and faces. Instead, their heads hung low, their shoulders sagged as they walked away, and some were already chatting with others as if nothing had happened. *They are defeated. And they are numb to the cruelty and accept it as their fate.* This was no surprise—those who toiled for years in slavery simply accepted their station.

But the gods had given Spartacus a different mind. Not one that would accept this easily.

All this reminded him of that boy in Lucania–Felix. Was he still alive?

Spartacus looked around to see if Messenius was around, and the man was nowhere to be seen. There were more than the usual guards on the perimeter, but except for the grotesque display of a crucified man in one corner, the situation was quickly coming to normalcy. He walked briskly to a slowly trudging Canicus and came beside him. Canicus said nothing and pretended not to notice.

"Are you not outraged?" Spartacus asked in a low voice. "What message is this?"

"Be quiet!" he hissed. "There is a time and place, not now."

But Spartacus would not listen. "The least we owe our *brother* is a merciful death. Do not tell me that you can claim to be a leader of men and allow him to die a slow and torturous death as we pretend otherwise."

Canicus turned to him. His eyes blazed. "And what would you have me do, Spartacus? Hang beside him? That *idiot* killed a citizen guard, and are you surprised by his fate? Be glad no one else joined him."

Spartacus was surprised by the utter indifference. He grabbed the younger man's shoulder. "And thus we give reasons to the Romans why they think we are barbarians, devoid of any human nature. It is because we simply allow ourselves to be treated this way!"

Canicus turned to Spartacus. His face was red with indignation. "You have been here less than a year, so do not lecture me, you old bastard. If it were not for my discipline and calm mind, half of the men here would have died!"

"Well, soon we will all be dead, while you keep telling me why we are better off this way! How blind are you to what you see around you? Why do you think Vatia is now so bold as to *crucify* one of our men in front of us and expect us to continue as if nothing happened? Why?"

Two of Canicus' men had now converged near him. And Crixus was now watching from a distance.

Canicus calmed himself by taking a deep breath. "We had this conversation just a few days ago, Spartacus. I have not forgotten it. We have to wait. What about your friend Pollio?"

Spartacus searched Canicus' eyes to see if he was serious. It was a heartening sign that the German had not escalated the argument but instead seen the wisdom in his exhortations.

"Pollio said he had an idea, but we were interrupted. He said he would find a way to be in touch–through your contact. Will she continue to do your bidding?"

Canicus smiled. "She will do anything for me. But I will not put her at extreme risk."

"There is nothing risky. She is a citizen and has every right to meet Pollio. You make sure that your interactions with her raise no suspicion."

Canicus nodded.

By then, Crixus had joined. "If we stand here and argue, we will cause concern."

"He is right," Spartacus said. "But we shall talk every day, even if only briefly."

They nodded.

"What can we do to end Procamus' life?" he asked, and everyone turned to see the hanging man. The two guards were sitting near the stool, with one dozing off.

"I have an idea," Crixus said.

Most guards switched an hour before the sunset, sometimes leaving only one or two in the field. That was when few fighters were training, and the weapons were all back in the armory. While Philotas and Castus had returned to the barracks, Spartacus and Canicus remained on the field. Crixus, who had hatched the idea, had left as well by orders of Messenius, who was now anxious to have as few senior men on the field as possible. One of the guards with Procamus had left, and the other one leaned on the wall nearby and picked on his teeth.

"It is time!" Spartacus said. With only twenty men in the field, it was now or never. It was risky, but he was no longer willing to play Vatia's game. And he had learned during his time in the army and even during his days in the *ludus* that a leader is not born of easy decisions.

Sometimes, showing men that he cared for them came from putting himself at the front. After all, even in the terrible battle of the Colline Gate, well after many thought the battle was lost, General Sulla had ridden up and down the lines, exhorting men and encouraging them to fight. Every commander who led from the front risked dying–leaving their families and anyone else at risk, yet they did it. How could he hope to fulfill the destiny his wife said the gods had planned for him if he simply *accepted* everything as is?

On cue, a group of Canicus' men began to brawl, and two men accompanied Spartacus as they ran toward the lone guard on the field.

"Sir, stop the fight! Stop it!" one of the gladiators yelled at the guard. Surprised, the man scrambled to his feet, for rarely did a group of strong men come to *him* for help.

"Fucking savages," he muttered as he adjusted his helmet and ran without glancing at Procamus.

The dying man was still letting out torturous breaths, gasping and moaning as he kept trying to relieve the immense pain and stress on his joints as he hung and tried to support himself on his nailed and buckling legs. Spartacus had learned that when crucified men began to sag, the body continued to fight to breathe, causing the men to try to stand up to relieve the pressure on their lungs. Often, the soldiers broke a condemned man's legs, forcing him to collapse and die quickly from asphyxiation. As terrible as it was, it caused a quick death to what might otherwise be a much longer ordeal.

Procamus' shoulders had swollen purple, and his tongue protruded from the cracked lips. The areas around the wrists were turning black.

"May Zibelthiurdos and your gods take you to their arms," Spartacus said. He swung his heavy wooden stick hard and struck Procamus' temple with such force that his head smacked and bounced off the crossbar. He did it again to ensure Procamus lost his consciousness.

Procamus' legs gave up entirely, and his body sagged, almost breaking him at the tied elbows. But with no faculty to be conscious, it would not be too long before his life left his body. Spartacus had done this so quickly that the guard had still barely reached the brawling Germans. Spartacus gestured at his men, and they left in a hurry.

They joined the guard in dragging the men away from each other. Some were terrible actors, howling senseless obscenities and even suppressing grins, but the lone guard was too harried to notice. Once Spartacus joined, and Canicus kept yelling at them to stop, it ended quickly. "Always something about insulting another man's tribe," Canicus said with as much bitterness in his voice as he could muster. The guard cursed them all roundly, but he was no longer interested in litigating this matter since his day was ending. More guards had arrived on the field but went to their posts after noticing that things had calmed quickly.

With light fading, Spartacus knew that the new guards near Procamus would never realize what had happened.

The lead guard for the night blew the whistle. "Time to go inside. All of you!"

As they began to walk inside, Spartacus turned to Canicus. "I am not dying here. And none of us should," he finally said resolutely. "Zibelthiurdos demands that."

"Old bastard you may be," Canicus said. "But a convincing one."

26

LUCANIA

"Well, Felix. Tell me about Lucia," he said.

Now Felix's face came alive. He almost stumbled back from his squat. The boy's lips sputtered, and Cleitus had a special satisfaction that *something* evoked a strong response from this stubborn mule.

"I - I know she is a slave girl in the estate."

Cleitus laughed. This boy was so comically inept at hiding certain things while he may be a master at others. That was the power of women.

"Only a fool would be bought by your answer," he said, grinning ear to ear. "Now, she makes your heart soft and your cock hard. Do not lie!"

Felix, unaccustomed to friendly banter, was unsure how to respond. He suppressed a little smile, but his lip's tiniest little upturn gave him away.

"Do not be shy. There is nothing to be ashamed of what a beautiful woman could do to one. Primigenia, come here!"

Cleitus knew she hovered nearby. She was a busybody and extraordinarily curious about Cleitus' story–after all, she had given him the lead on Felix.

Primigenia walked through the door and stood beside Cleitus. Felix stared at her, but they did not acknowledge each other. After all, Primigenia was of much higher status amongst slaves, having found employment within the house than toil in the fields and manage herd animals.

Cleitus held her by the waist and pulled her toward him. He gently separated her stola, exposed a breast, and ran his hand over it. "Look at that. How beautiful. I bet this is what you fantasize about every day. But with Lucia, of course."

Primigenia giggled. He covered her again but placed a hand on her crotch. "I know you want to be there with Lucia, Felix. I know it very well."

Felix, stupefied by this but unquestionably strangely excited, tried to hide the erection beneath his loincloth. He hung his head low and began to draw imaginary lines on the floor.

"How do I know? Well, everyone knows. These things are hard to hide. But have you considered your station, Felix? You are a low herder's boy, you still have that ugly collar around your neck like a dog, you spend all your time with buffalos and sheep, and who knows - maybe you fuck them too."

Primigenia giggled again. He enjoyed making her laugh.

"So, how can a boy like you aspire to be with her? Maybe you get to see her sometimes, from a distance, so near and yet so far. Maybe you rub yourself in the fields fantasizing about her, but that is all you will get. Until you die, or she gets sold elsewhere as someone else's whore."

Felix's chest rose and fell. Cleitus knew he was inflicting conflicting and yet powerful emotions on him. The promise of what *could be* and yet what *it was*.

"I *know* that the estate is growing, and we no longer have to rely so much on a few people—especially herdsmen like you. And that is bad news. No one will tolerate your strangeness anymore."

No response.

"We both—we are the same people. I can help you."

Felix looked up, his eyes quizzical.

"But there is a problem, boy. Many distrust you, even if some events are years old. You are like those bad slaves—always getting themselves into trouble. But you, especially, have been up to no good or found yourself in questionable circumstances more than once. Very few slaves are that way—they mind their own business and do their work."

Felix finally uttered a few words. "I did not cause any trouble."

"That is what they all say. *I did nothing.* We both know that to be a lie. You did conspire to run away with Lucia—I now know that. You made a bond with Spartacus and were there when Mellius got murdered, and I was attacked. And now a guard disappears while watching you," he said, still smiling.

Cleitus turned to Primigenia. "Leave. I have more to discuss."

She was disappointed. He pinched her bottom as she turned to leave and then turned to Felix, grinning.

"Now, having someone of my blood working for me, away from all the terrible fieldwork, would benefit you and me. Does that not sound like the gods have finally favored you?"

Felix nodded slowly. He was hopeful. Cleitus was sure no one had ever offered to help this boy. Except perhaps Spartacus.

"I can have you run errands. Maintain the ditches and garden. Even milk cows and help in the kitchen. Imagine how wonderful your life will be. And maybe if not Lucia, there will be other slave girls you might even get to..." he said, making a lewd gesture by putting a finger through the gap made of his thumb and forefinger.

The boy sat cross-legged on the floor, his hands on his thigh and leaning forward with curiosity. It was so easy to entice these wretched things.

"But if it is Lucia you desire, I know she still works in the estate. I might even request to have her transferred to me for some time. Does it not sound like music from the heavens?"

Now that he had Felix's rapt attention, Cleitus made his next move.

"Do you want all that, boy?" he said and intentionally switched to his dialect, even though he knew Felix could not understand it. "*Imagine how your life will change.*"

Felix looked uncomprehending.

"What I said was, imagine how your life will change. I said it in your language, but obviously, you do not understand. I–"

Felix spoke. "My mother sang to me in that language. I knew one song though I never learned what it meant. It sounded like your words."

Cleitus realized how Spartacus might have recognized that Felix was a Maedi in that instant. That was how! Felix must have sung the song in the field, not knowing what it meant, only to have Spartacus realize it.

"And that is how Spartacus recognized you, did he not?"

Felix knew he had given away that little secret too. He nodded reluctantly to a proud Cleitus.

"So, do you want to work for me, Felix? I have the influence to talk to the master or the overseer."

The boy nodded. The blood on his cheek had crusted, and he peeled off the flakes.

"But there is one thing. I cannot seek favors on a sullied name like yours until I have all the truth and clear your slate through forgiveness."

He glanced slightly at the guard who stood a distance away, and the man stirred, preparing to come forward.

"Do not lie to me again, Felix, for that will end any hope for you. I have bared much to you, seen you as of my kind, but I will not stand for deception played on me," he said sternly.

Felix nodded. The boy spoke so little.

"Will you tell me the truth when I ask you the next question?"

"Yes, sir."

Cleitus leaned forward and smiled reassuringly. "Did you kill that guard? You pushed him over the edge, did you not?"

27

LUDUS OF VATIA

"Come in. Sit down," Vatia said to the man. Some days felt like an elephant was tugging on one arm while a lion was gnawing on the other. His bitch of a wife and her father were making his life miserable. Her nagging that he run for the office of a Tribune, an expensive, miserable affair, was wearing on him. Her father, an influential Senator of Rome, had somehow decided that Lentulus's growing business was smelly and unworthy of his stature. All these pretentious bastards wanted to sit on a high chair and watch the marvelous games, but may the gods forbid someone *actually* makes it happen!

He was losing his little remaining hair and sanity, but his treasury was growing, and so was his influence with the powerful men of Rome. Curio and even the ridiculously rich but exceedingly unpleasant Marcus Crassus had heard of him. They were not his allies or friends yet, but he would change all that. And when he was beginning to gain a foothold against Lucius Asina's larger school, trouble was beginning to brew in his. *Fucking animals.*

The crucifixion had gone off quite well, and things were quiet since then. The only unfortunate thing was that the stutterer had died the same night—which was surprising. He hoped Procamus would live two days in full view, reminding them of the fate they would endure if they crossed him. He had left the man's corpse to rot for another two days, until the stink of his dead flesh became a distraction.

The gladiator sat before him, always polite, always well-spoken, but not terribly effective these days. He leaned forward and took a date from the plate, and even that annoyed Vatia.

"What is going on? Your effectiveness is in question now," he said, with a tinge of irritation in his voice.

"Only a minor hiccup, sir," the man said. "To be expected when many hotheads and experienced men get together."

"We have not had these issues before."

"But the *dominus* has never procured expensive, talented, and experienced men as he has done recently. And with that comes the usual annoyances of those thinking they are greater than their circumstance."

Vatia nodded. It was true. In the first few years of his *ludus* he had brought men cheaply—mostly errant brigands, thieves, deserters, low-life thugs, and criminals who were stupider than monkeys but knew how to brawl and fight. Having lived years in hardship, many often saw the *ludus* as a luxury with its comforts of a roof and meals. But as his business grew, Vatia had purchased better-qualified men— with Spartacus and Castus being among the most expensive. But these men were no common thieves and came with the risk of running their mouths and letting their minds wander where they should not. Lucius Asina, his competitor, had confessed to the same in a rare moment of candid conversation. *The more talented they are, the more the headache, but it is usually worth it. Always find ways to keep them in line. The best way is to give them women and wine and keep their families hostage.*

"Now, tell me about this recent affair you wanted to talk to me about."

The man adjusted his loincloth and picked another date while simultaneously reaching out to a jug of wine.

"You can drink all the wine you want when you are done, Philotas. Now talk," Vatia said testily.

Chastised, Philotas hurriedly chewed the date and spat the seed into the bowl on the side. "Yes, sir. This may be something worth paying attention to."

"Go on."

"You admitted a man named Pollio to come and inspect the *ludus*."

"Yes. Pollio is a businessman, and it is customary to allow them to inspect if they wish to loan fighters from the school. What about him?"

Philotas smiled. His eyes twinkled with the mirth of someone who knows something of great value to the other. "It seems there is a history between Pollio and Spartacus."

Vatia was taken aback. "Pollio and Spartacus? Are you out of your mind?"

Philotas leaned back. "No, *dominus*. While I do not know all the details, for he is a cagey man not wont to share everything about his past, it seems Spartacus worked for Pollio when he lived in Capua."

"Spartacus lived in Capua? When?"

"Years ago. It seems he arrived there after the battles in Rome."

Maybe they had mentioned this during the auction, but Vatia could not remember.

"And how did he become acquainted with Pollio?"

"I only have the very slightest of details. He may have acted as a supervisor for some of Pollio's construction projects."

Vatia took a swig of the fine wine. Locally made, truly the best. "And how does all this matter? Many of these louts worked for someone or the other before they got themselves in trouble."

Philotas nodded. "True, sir. But it seems this Pollio has greater affection for Spartacus than usual."

"Affection? In what way?" he narrowed his eyes. Were they lovers?

"No, no, sir. No indication they were involved in a vulgar way, but perhaps there are unspoken debts to be paid between them. I do not know what."

"Go on. I still do not know if this has to do with this school or me. Is Pollio looking to purchase Spartacus? Let him go ahead. I will sell for a hefty multiple."

Philotas rubbed his curly hair. The Macedonian had made good of his value to Vatia. The men trusted him with his deceptively gentle demeanor, good-natured behavior, and a past in the arenas. And then Philotas made sure to keep Vatia informed of it all in exchange for a good living and a real potential for freedom. They might even make a good team. Most recently, he had learned of the rumors from the kitchen through Philotas' warning. And it was Philotas who kept the restless men in check with all the lofty promises. Managing a *ludus* with gangs of mischief-seeking, always angry and miserable men was a combination of lies, hope, punishment, and threat. It was not as simple as simply dragging men out and cutting off their heads or nailing them to crosses.

"No. I have heard no such thing. But what is curious is Spartacus has been speaking about breaking out of the estate."

Vatia raised his eyebrows. "Really? But is that unusual? Men fantasize and speak of it all the time. They have done it every week here, and nothing ever comes of it. And knowing a fake noble like Spartacus, I would be surprised if he were not."

"What I meant is Spartacus has been speaking to Pollio about potential plans."

Vatia put his cup down. *What?* "Did you say Pollio is conspiring with Spartacus?"

"Yes, master. It seems the businessman is not visiting the *ludus* with any intention to sponsor the games," Philotas said, grinning ear-to-ear at revealing this delicious information. *What an idiot.*

Vatia laughed.

Philotas' smile disappeared. "I am being truthful, sir. I say this to serve your interests!"

Vatia nodded and took another sip. "I laugh not at your sincere attempt, Philotas, but at your naiveté. You believe Pollio is trying to *help* Spartacus?"

The trainer looked confused now. His ballooning chest deflated somewhat, and rightfully so. How stupid were these men?

"Do you know who Pollio is? Do you know the man?"

Vatia stood and began to pace. He loved telling stories, and he would tell Philotas one, just to put some sense to his backward mind. "Pollio is a true Roman son-of-a-whore. And I meant that really–no one knows who his father is. Many years ago, he came to Capua seeking fortune and made his money thieving like there was no sunrise. This town is littered with men and women he has not paid, failed to honor contracts, broken his promises, and taken advantage of. His wife divorced him, for she could not bear to see him putting every whore against a wall with no shame. He even tried starting a little gladiatorial school, lost control of the men, and sold them to their deaths. Have you heard of the canal bridge he built? The bridge is *in* the canal now, and the man who financed it to make money from tolls is now on the street begging for money. He is always looking to leverage one man's weakness against another, but I can assure you it is not me whom he wishes to cheat. He has too much to lose now."

Philotas' face looked blank. Did he not register it?

Vatia continued. "It is possible he came here knowing Spartacus is in the school. And whatever the history may be, imagine how valuable it is for him to take this knowledge that a group of men is trying to foment trouble and bring it to me? Pollio will rile up the men, fill their heads with all the juicy information, and then come to me with a proposition."

He enjoyed his theatrics and display of his acumen on the businessmen—after all, was that not the life he lived?

"He will come to me one day, saying, '*Gnaeus Lentulus Vatia, your men are up to no good and will only make it harder for you. Let me buy the school at a big discount!*' and he will switch his tone when I laugh at him. He will then seek a fat fee for revealing all that he knows. The money to stab Spartacus and every other big-headed scum in the back. The Thracian idiot does not know it yet, but Pollio is no one's friend."

It slowly dawned on Philotas. He nodded. These slaves lived their lives in their little worlds and knew little about the world outside.

"Let me tell you another story," Vatia said, now glad that someone was listening to him with attention, unlike his bitch wife. "Have you heard of Marcus Crassus?"

"No, sir."

Of course not. "Well, Crassus is a very famous and very rich man and general. Probably the richest man in all of Rome, but an unpleasant man nevertheless. Do you know how he made a lot of his money?"

"No, sir."

"When homes caught fire in Rome, he would send in his fire brigade—men with pails of water—and then haggle with the homeowners to buy their property at knock-down prices if they wanted it saved. The owner had one of two choices—watch his home burn and lose everything as this fire brigade stood nearby scratching their balls, or get *something*. And then Crassus would fix and re-sell the property for a hefty profit. Do you think Crassus was the homeowner's friend?"

Philotas nodded more vigorously now. He was finally seeing it.

"Whatever he is up to, he will appear before me sooner or later, and I will have a good laugh. You make sure that the men are only talking and not trying anything else. And report to me anything new. If Pollio comes again, I will humor him. You make sure to be by Spartacus' side to know what they are talking about. The more they get into their fantasy world, the better leverage for us. I can use this in the Capua councils to turn everyone against Pollio."

Vatia was beside himself with glee. This was such an unexpected gift, and he would now not only watch as the slave leaders made utter fools of themselves but also take a powerful shot at Pollio. One less competitor in the city was good for the rest. Cunning scammers like this taking aim at someone else's enterprise had to be put to the ground.

"You did well, Philotas," Vatia said, finally. "Reward yourself with an outing. Spend a day in the town, but do not even think of anything else."

Philotas laughed. "Not at all, thank you, *dominus*! May our gods shower their blessings on you. You have given me a life I never imagined I would have, and I shall jeopardize it for nothing!"

"Very well. So, what do you propose about this undercurrent of unrest? Is it worse than usual?"

Philotas looked thoughtful. The man was a learned Macedonian—and there was some merit in listening to his thoughts. While he may be naïve about the complex affairs of businesses, he understood the mind of the criminal and the slave.

The gladiator scratched his thigh. "A little worse, *dominus*. Like I said before, they are now under the influence of multiple men, led by Spartacus who, if I may say boldly, thinks I am his friend."

"How much sway does he have?"

"The Thracians listen to him, and in that, there is no surprise. He makes a big show of having functioned as a centurion and his learned Greek. He is a good fighter and stands tall, and that is always an advantage."

"What about the others?"

"The Gauls listen to Crixus, not so much to Spartacus. Most do not even understand what he says, and there is always a competition on who is braver and who fights better. The Germans listen to Canicus."

"But?" Vatia knew that it was never that simple.

"Both Crixus and Canicus listen to Spartacus. At least they pretend to. And they participate in his treasonous conversations. If they get bolder and come under his witchcraft, it could worsen."

"Is the Thracian going to be a real problem?"

"No worse than others, but he is more influential than most. They are brought in by his stature and words. Can you get rid of him *dominus*? Maybe just sell him and be rid of his influence?"

"He is one of our stars now. The sponsors ask for him. He inspires the others, so why let him go when you can keep an eye on him and peal the others away from his grand ambitions. Why do they listen to him? Because he tells them that their lives are worthless and there is no prospect of freedom or greatness, does he not?"

Philotas nodded.

Vatia continued. "Douse those flames. Take away his incentive to inflame others. Assure them that their grievances have been heard—no more beast fights. Wine with meals. Maybe even meat once every few weeks. And then we shall loan Spartacus, Crixus, and every other troublemaker out. Again and again. Until they make all my money and their blood seeps into the sand."

Philotas grinned. "You know the ways of the world, *dominus.*"

"Nevertheless, I shall have a word with Spartacus and peer into his thoughts. But he should not see you with me."

"I agree, *dominus.* And once you speak to him, I shall report to you his reactions once he is back on the field."

What a snake.

"For now, you have earned your pleasures and vices," Vatia said, satisfied, and nodded at someone.

A slave girl brought out the freshly washed and attired widow of Procamus. Her hair was braided like Roman girls, her cheeks made pink by cosmetics, and her mirthless eyes adorned by kohl.

"Take her, enjoy yourself," Vatia said.

Philotas bowed to him and gestured for her to follow. She went with him meekly, for what else could she possibly do? Her husband had been crucified, yet she had to put those memories aside to continue living.

What a twisted man. Still a base animal behind that affectation, Vatia thought of Philotas, and hoped that this banal talk of uprising and rebellion would die quickly.

"You have summoned me, *dominus.*"

Vatia turned from the window and faced the Thracian. Whatever his misgivings toward this troublesome character, he never ceased to marvel at Spartacus' presence. His thick hair, a strangely attractive yet large and ugly face, and the hairy and muscular torso combined with limbs like trunks inspired awe, and it was no wonder most men listened to him. And to add to it was his skill of language and a colorful story–he might almost fashion himself as a king.

"Your name spreads far and wide. I have organizers asking for you specifically. Your drama, the limp, and stature are good for my business and you."

"Yes, *dominus.*"

"And yet I hear from observers that you have a troubled mind. And that you voice your dissatisfaction without caution, thus poisoning the thoughts of others around you."

Spartacus' eyes narrowed only momentarily. He gave a curt nod. "Recent events give pause, *dominus.* The crucifixion–"

"Was deserved. What would you do if you were in charge of the school? Do the Thracians let miscreants away with flowers?"

"A swift execution, *dominus,* away from the eyes of men who train to fight for you," Spartacus countered in his annoyingly deliberate, thoughtful fashion, drawing out his words. *Who did this slave think he was?*

Vatia raised his voice and pointed at Spartacus. "You are no one to tell me how to conduct *my* business. Your job is to bring glory to the school and yourself so that you and your wife may earn what most other slaves are never allowed to. Do not forget that you live *because* you are here!"

Spartacus nodded curtly, but he had more to say, and he said so coldly. "Procamus was a disturbed man, and his actions came of an unsound mind. The men believe that you are sending them to undeserved deaths."

The nerve of this man!

"Undeserved? You say *undeserved?* Most of the degenerates who fight about you are criminals deserving nothing else, and yet they have a chance to redeem themselves beneath *my* roof. Did you know that Canicus was once a bandit who murdered innocent travelers on highways? Or that some of these men raped young girls to death and threw their babies into fires? Do not speak to me about who deserves what!"

This conversation was not going the way he hoped. Spartacus still had fight to spare and had not yet earned all the profit.

The Thracian bowed again, but this time, said nothing in response. His thick face and chest glistened with sweat. *A beast.*

Vatia calmed himself. "I called you here so that I may calm your mind. You should speak to others and tell them to remain focused on their purpose. Your feats will give you a path to a good life, perhaps freedom one day as you yearn for it. But do not think that my patience is infinite if you continue to foment disturbance."

Spartacus looked surprised. "I am fomenting nothing, *dominus.* I speak what any slave dreams of. Surely there is no surprise in that."

"It is not that you dream, but you raise your voice to act on it. Remember the clause of the contract."

The threat required no mentioning. Spartacus knew entirely well.

"Yes, *dominus.*"

"A sponsor from Rome wishes to return. Pollio. You may have met him last time."

Spartacus' eyes flickered only for the smallest fraction. *The bastard knows him well.*

"He was impressed by you and may seek to have you in one of the upcoming games."

"Yes, *dominus*."

"Pollio is a crook and a cheat, so no one knows whether he is serious. But that sponsors are asking for you is an excellent sign. You keep me happy, and I shall make your life comfortable."

"Yes, *dominus*."

"Were you not in Capua at one point?"

Spartacus shifted on his feet. "Yes, I was."

"Did you know Pollio? He was active in construction."

Spartacus shuffled again. *Would he lie?*

"I was a lowly worker, *dominus*. I knew no one of station."

Conniving bastard. Philotas will keep an eye on you.

"Ah. I thought perhaps Pollio knew you, given your physical presence. Now return to the barracks, Spartacus, and keep your tongue in control. Do not heed rumors and spread unfounded fears, for your good and the others'. You seek glory and a comfortable life, do you not?"

"Yes, *dominus*."

"You may leave."

As he shuffled away with three guards trailing him, Vatia wondered how long he would suffer this man.

28

LUDUS OF VATIA

Pollio was back. He had refused to send any messages through Canicus' girl, stating that he had to deliver them himself. And here he was, pretending once again to make a great show. Vatia was with him, so was Philotas, and Spartacus accompanied Canicus, Oenomaus, and Crixus to meet the businessman. While Spartacus had not been designated trainer, he and Oenomaus had proved themselves on the field and in their ability to inspire the men and thus often joined discussions.

"Well, you ran me out last time, Vatia," Pollio said. "I barely had the time to watch the savages go at each other!"

Vatia seemed to be in good cheer. "Well, what they do is train. This is not where they fight, and there is no savagery except the occasional brawl."

Pollio laughed. "Ah, yes. Brawls. It is just as common as cheap Sicilian wine with these barbarians. So, what happened last time? Do you have control over your men?"

Vatia turned to him. "These men are content to be here, and an infrequent occurrence of violence is nothing surprising. Surely you know that from your construction enterprise and news in other schools."

"Of course. I was only humoring you. Well, my visit was cut short. When I visit these ludi, I really like to observe the quality of the men, how well they train, how well behaved they are, and so on. I want to sponsor a good show and cannot afford to borrow from schools that say much but deliver little."

"Indeed. And you will find that my men are as good as, if not better than, Asina's. We are the best two in Capua."

"Asina's is twice as large. How many do you have now, Vatia?"

"Eighty-six. We are growing rapidly. I had a new batch come in just two days ago. Not all are exceptional fighters–many go out to smaller events. We will be as good as Asina's soon."

"Of that, I have no doubt, no doubt at all," Pollio said, nodding vigorously. His eyes briefly connected with Spartacus and returned to Vatia.

Spartacus was tiring of this entirely fake, collegial banter. He could see that the men hated each other with a passion. If Pollio were not an influential man himself, Vatia would have him stabbed in a back alley or buried in the *ludus*. But all this pretense was necessary for Pollio to have permission to stay on the field, unsupervised, so that he could speak to Spartacus.

Vatia's question about whether he knew Pollio had thrown him off in surprise.

What had made him ask that? Capua was a big town.

Did Vatia know something about their past?

How?

Spartacus was troubled by these questions but decided to leave it to chance.

Vatia and Pollio exchanged more strained pleasantries until the *dominus* was finally tired. "Well, Pollio, I will leave you to it. Leave before sunset for your safety."

"I will, Vatia. You have been a gracious host," he said, bowing.

"I hope you will loan many of my men for your esteemed sponsorship," Vatia said with an exaggerated smile and a bow.

They watched as Vatia left.

Philotas exhaled loudly and exclaimed. "Anyone else tired of it all?"

Spartacus laughed, and Pollio joined. Messenius was nowhere to be found. They were free to speak.

"Let me watch the men for some time," Pollio said. "Do not get the guards too suspicious."

The charade continued. Groups of men fought vigorously as Pollio exhorted them and offered his expert opinions on how they should conduct themselves. This time, for his safety, he had brought two heavily armed men of his own, and they hovered nearby without speaking a word.

When it was all over, Pollio gestured to Spartacus. Crixus and Philotas stood to join them, for Castus and Canicus and Oenomaus had to return to barracks.

"May we speak privately," Pollio said, eyeing the others. "Do they need to walk with us?"

Philotas looked offended. "There are no sacred conversations here. We are brothers, and we bleed together."

Pollio was not convinced. He looked at Spartacus for affirmation.

"All our plans are together, Pollio. They can be trusted."

The Roman reluctantly agreed. Crixus and Philotas tagged along as Spartacus walked beside Pollio.

"When you were here last time, you said you had an idea," Spartacus asked Pollio.

"I did. Or I thought I had an idea, but it is no longer viable. What is the mood here?"

"The energy has reduced," Spartacus said, somewhat deflated. "It seems Vatia has heard of the simmering discontent. The loans to beast games have reduced, the meals are a little better, and most men get to stay outside the barracks and rest a little longer. The physician seems more caring about wounds received during training. There is some overcrowding, but it is limited to newcomers' barracks. So most no longer care that much to rise against the benevolent master."

Pollio looked surprised. "You do realize these are temporary measures."

"The men are simple, sir," Philotas opined. "They react to what they see. Most do not think beyond today's meal and a night's sleep."

"And that is how they all die," Pollio said wryly. "And here I was, looking for some enthusiastic reception, but it seems that gladiators are all ready to blaze their paths to glory and afterlife."

Spartacus did not know how to react. They were at an impasse.

But Pollio continued. "Maybe not all of them want to leave. How about some of you?"

And before Spartacus replied, Crixus asked what was burning in Spartacus' mind, and certainly in Philotas' too. "Why helping us? What you get?"

Pollio turned to Crixus and stopped. "Why does it matter if I help you leave? I have my reasons."

"What if benefit you is terrible for us?"

Pollio ignored Crixus and looked at Spartacus. "Is he an idiot? He asks if it will be terrible for him? Is he living in Apollo's gardens now?"

"It is not a surprising question, Pollio."

"Stupid, nonetheless. Vatia is a bastard, and I have unfinished business with him. His ruin is good for me. You do not need to know more than that."

Crixus grumbled. Spartacus placed a hand on Crixus' shoulder to assuage him.

Pollio seemed a little disappointed. "Well, I am not sure why I came here. If the appetite for freedom has dulled, then there is not much I can do. What about the leaders—all of you—do you want to stay here?"

"I wish to leave. I have no desire for this place," Philotas said with force. "Tell us if you have any ideas!"

Pollio raised an eyebrow and looked at Spartacus.

"If I run, it is with my men and wife," Spartacus said. "I will not condemn them, her, here."

Crixus nodded. "We must act as one. Not running alone."

Philotas cracked his knuckles. "How long will we endure this? Perhaps we can get help once we get out."

"You live better than us all, Philotas," said Spartacus. "And how would we get help if only four or five of us? And if we run, leaving others behind, no one will ever trust us again, regardless of what we try later."

"At least let us find out his plans if we choose to!" Philotas said.

They stopped walking and stood in a tight cluster. It looked like the Roman was delivering a lecture to them as they stood with their arms crossed and heads bowed around him.

"Well, men, we are stuck in the swamps of uncertainty. It seems we must be wary yet wait for favorable times. If we do something stupid, then all of us will suffer terribly. I am a businessman, and I will not accept monumentally risky propositions without a proportional reward. If you must know, influential men are investing in Vatia's venture, so things are no longer that simple. Anyway, may I speak to Spartacus alone? Let me reminisce about simpler times and talk to this man as if we were together in the trenches."

"It would be entertaining for us to listen in," Philotas said.

"Leave them," Crixus said gruffly. He offered a curt bow to Pollio and turned to leave. "Return in a few months, sir. Perhaps here changed."

Pollio nodded in acknowledgment. Philotas looked unhappy that Spartacus had not asked to stay, so he turned and began to walk away, trailing Crixus.

"So, Pollio—"

"Be quiet. Wait until they are out of earshot."

What is in his mind?

Finally, it was just them.

"Forget about our time in Capua," Pollio said. "Do you know Gaius Claudius Glaber?"

"He was a sponsor for one of my games in Pompeii. Was he in the army?"

"Apparently. Well, he is an influential man. He rose through military ranks and became a legate under Sulla. He sponsors some minor games. He is likely to be elected praetor in the next election."

"And?"

"Praetors are powerful men, Spartacus. Second only to consuls. They receive military commands."

"What are you implying, Pollio?"

"Well. It seems that Glaber is now an investor in Vatia's ventures. As you have noticed, the games are becoming more and more popular, and there is money to be made. These men are beginning to spread their wings—from slave sales and running *Latifundium*, large estates—they are now putting money into gladiatorial schools. I would not be surprised if these so-called reputed men began to sponsor the schools themselves even though they thumb their nose at it now as it is nothing but pimping fighters."

Spartacus considered this worrying information. The situation was more complicated if men with legions behind them backed Vatia.

"You are a smart man. You should know that this means I cannot overtly support you. I cannot send thugs to beat your guards and help you break out. And not when it seems your support is shaky."

"What about your roster of influential men?"

Pollio laughed. "Jupiter knows I am trying. But these money-grubbing sons of whores are becoming too greedy. Real estate is not that attractive anymore, and the big men are not putting out contracts for large buildings, so my wallet is not expanding that quickly. They simply hire the necessary men and use slave labor to get the work done. We need slaves to do our work cheaply, but we are fucking ourselves out of living wages."

Spartacus smiled. That was a strange twist of Roman economics. He knew that the large slave labor benefited the wealthy but made things much harder for the *plebs*. Now Pollio, who certainly made good money from this travesty, felt the heat. But Pollio was also the only key to any plan of escape.

"Do you want to escape, Spartacus? Does that fire burn within you? Why not find a way to get away with just your wife? Maybe I can arrange something, even if risky."

Spartacus shook his head. "Honor is a slippery concept for you," he said, and Pollio laughed. "I cannot leave my men. If I go, they will crucify my Thracian group as an example. I will not let that happen."

Pollio nodded. "Spending time in the auxiliaries as a supervisor has ruined you with these fancy ideals."

"What then?" Spartacus said, laughing. "It seems we must wait."

"Yes. But you keep yourself alive, Spartacus. Shall I come to your next game to cheer you on?"

Spartacus shook his head vigorously. "No. I do not want the man who once saved my life to come and watch a spectacle. There is no honor in it, Pollio, and I will not be the animal you pity."

Pollio struggled to respond but then accepted. "I struggle to reconcile the station of gladiators with that you are one."

"You must leave now. But can I trust that I have your ear and can send you missives?"

"Of course. And I will find more people who can communicate with you."

"There is something in particular that you may assist me with without endangering yourself."

"What is it?"

"When you hear of the games nearby, big or small, and if you learn of anything unusual that may involve this *ludus* or us in particular, will you be able to send word?"

Pollio's eyes narrowed. "You clever bastard. Yes, that is a good way to know if you are being put at risk. But remember, I may not always know the details—and if I do not believe it to be of much value, I will do nothing."

"That is understandable."

"You must act in haste, Spartacus. Rally your men. If Glaber wins, then your chances diminish significantly."

"I will do what I can. May Zibelthiurdos bless you, Pollio."

"Let him keep his blessings until you are free. But there is something else."

"Yes?"

"Vatia was too friendly and too eager to allow me in. I am suspicious by nature. I do not like his behavior."

"What do you think?"

"You have a snake in your midst, Spartacus. You should run before it strikes."

29

LUDUS OF VATIA

The days following Pollio's departure revealed the nature of men averse to risk. Few were interested in engaging Spartacus on any rebellious ideas. Only Oenomaus, who had grown in stature by his recent game victories, and Crixus, who was perennially angry, were still of the mind to escape. Philotas had somehow changed his mind and was now adamant that they wait because conditions were improving. But the most powerful reason for the men's ardor to cool off was Philotas' speech after Oenomaus' splendid victory at the games in Thurii.

With men gathered about him as he recounted the Gaul's valor, Philotas surprised everyone with a shocking revelation.

"Listen, men. No free man wishes to be placed in confinement and sent to the games for the entertainment of others. I did not enjoy it during my time, and I know most of you do not. You may even overlook that your lives are better today than months ago. Or even the adulation Oenomaus has received, like many others, and their rich meal on return. But today, I bring you another very interesting rumor–the *dominus* does not confirm it, but he reluctantly allowed me to share it."

Spartacus stood nearby, curious like everyone else. He admired Philotas' relentless energy in trying to bring peace and calm to the crowd. As more fighters were inducted into the school, the crowd grew. More and more men shared their tiny quarters, for Vatia had not added living space.

This brought unrest, but nothing alarming so far. And it was Philotas who was usually called in to settle disputes.

Philotas continued. "The rules that govern our lives are made in the Roman Senate. And I have been hearing that with the increased popularity of the games and the adulation showered on the valiant fighters, there will be a special status for the most accomplished gladiators and their trainers!"

There were many murmurs amongst the men. Spartacus was surprised but held his skepticism as he did not yet know the details of this status.

Now that he had everyone's interest, Philotas urged them to listen carefully. "What does this special status mean, you wonder? Why would any of us, men who were once free and roamed like proud beasts amongst weak men, care about *any* status except freedom?"

Many loudly applauded the sentence. Spartacus found himself nodding at Philotas' firm and expert delivery.

"Which is why this news was bewildering. Now, if any of us must inhale the sweet air of earth as a free man, we are at the master's mercy. He, and he alone, has the power to grant the copper plate that declares our freedom. And while he has been better to us than most school owners are, we are not freed at the rate we want!"

He has been better to us? Spartacus wanted to intrude but knew better that this was the time to listen. If there was indeed positive news, it might afford a bloodless path for everyone.

"The Senate is preparing a decree that grants automatic freedom to a fighter on the culmination of a certain number of combats or years in service of a school as a trainer. It means that the discretion to grant your freedom is no longer in the hands of the *dominus*, for he is compelled to let you go!"

Spartacus felt his spirit rise and saw the hope in the faces and eyes of the men who stood in rapt attention. *Could this be true? What were the terms?*

He exchanged glances with a stupefied Crixus.

"What are terms?" Crixus asked what was probably in everyone's mind.

Philotas smiled. "Be patient, Crixus," he said condescendingly. "I have more to share."

"We do not yet know all the rules. But what I have heard is that a man should have endured the *spectacula* for at least five years and won eight fights at least. Alternatively, if he is injured and out of commission but talented to be a trainer in any capacity, then the length of service is ten years. Surely, those who have toiled in the army know that this is a very generous set of terms," he said, grinning broadly.

It was a generous term. After all, auxiliaries had to walk with the army for more than twenty years if they were to receive citizenship. While this did not confer statehood, it would matter little for each man who left this cursed land and returned to their homes far away.

The excited conversations amongst men got louder. Philotas yelled at everyone to be quiet. The next question came from a German who stood nearby.

"Do we get credit for our time here?"

Philotas made a sad face. He rubbed his curled hair and clucked. "The gods are not always so just and fair, and surely you do not think the Romans would suddenly become kind. We do not get all the credit for our tenure, only for two years. So those who have been here longer, you have three more years. I must wait. You must. Such are the rules."

It was not a terrible rule, for letting men leave would ruin the schools, and surely the men who ran them had enough influence not to allow such a thing to happen. Three years or five, it was still a clear path to life outside, assuming one lived.

"What happens to someone injured and unfit to be a trainer?"

Philotas' face hardened. "What do you think should happen? They have earned no fame and have no skill, and their life is no different from any other slave. What happens to them is what has always happened."

Life in servitude or discarded in a ditch somewhere.

Philotas' speech had changed the mood of the entire school. Most men came from the lowest classes of their societies and lacked the faculty to critically examine Philotas' assurances, Spartacus thought. For them, throwing themselves into the vigor of training and staying out of violence was the way, and there was little patience to lend an ear to anyone who questioned the validity of these fantastic stories from the Senate.

"Do you believe this?" he asked Crixus. The Gaul was unsure, but he was willing to wait and see. *If it is just two to three years, why do something risky? Let us get our glory and our freedom!*

Spartacus gave up trying to debate after a few attempts. Philotas would not entertain any conversation, stating that Spartacus was risking himself and everyone around him. Only a few other men—Oenomaus and Castus—were still suspicious of the news. Even Canicus had become subdued.

Vatia had achieved compliance and peace without a single skin-tearing flogging.

The fever wracked his body.

The physician barely did his job, leaving Spartacus groaning and sweating in his hot and humid cell. There was little care—only disdain that he had lost the previous game in Herculaneum and lived only through the merciful gesture of the crowd and the sponsor.

The opponent's blade had sliced his shoulder open.

It was an unfair fight.

Spartacus was sure that the younger man was likely a citizen, a trained soldier from a good family, and had entered the arena perhaps to win a bet or some other twisted reason, for no respectable men sought glory in the arena—at least not yet. The sponsors made sure he had every advantage. His opponent's steel was sharp and new. A dull-gray iron helmet with just two holes for eyes protected his face. Heavy dark-orange leather and bronze-plated shoulder patches and cuirass protected the center. Tall, ornate thigh and ankle guards, made of beaten bronze, protected his legs.

Spartacus fought hard, but his *sica* struggled against all the protection, and the opponent was skilled enough to avert strikes into his few exposed areas. Eventually, Spartacus' age made its presence felt, and he had collapsed after the injury to his shoulder.

In three days, the shoulder had swollen like a melon, purple and black, with a copious amount of pus oozing out of it. The physician cleaned the wound and used a combination of herbs, salt water, vinegar, honey, and many healing prayers to keep the infection in check. But the number of men coming to the *ludus* severely injured was increasing, which meant the physician's attention to any gladiator—however prized he may be—was decreasing. Seeing how the skin and muscle were split, he employed a suturing technique that was becoming popular in the schools. A hot needle, thread cleansed with boiled water, a generous application of honey, and a thick rag stuffed into the mouth.

The half-hearted bandaging and insufficient cleansing had then caused a severe infection, and it was only through Canicus' intervention that the *dominus* stood at risk of losing Spartacus that Vatia had hastily allowed Antara to care for her husband.

She sat beside him, praying to the gods as she did several times a day. She compelled them to heal him as he lay bathed in his sweat and damp in his urine. She cleaned his body and excrement. And then she prayed again. She begged and pleaded with Canicus to procure more medicinal salve, and the German finally managed to steal some and bring it to her. Vatia only visited once—he peeked into the cell, wrinkled his nose at the odors, and left.

As was always the case, injuries from blades led men to the brink of death. Some went over to the other side, and some recovered. Spartacus' body had fought for days, and the wound had begun to seal, even if it made his hand immobile. The cut was not too deep, which was the only reason why Vatia had spared him. And it was the reason why he was recovering.

When his mind began to return, the familiar dread came along with it. There was no path for him to keep fighting and live until his freedom—if that news was even true. No one questioned the supposed decree—for men simply believed it and spoke no more of the matter.

And once his wobbly feet made their way to the field, Antara was compelled to return to the kitchen, and Messenius remarked that there would be no next time. *Your days are numbered*, he said.

The desire to leave only became stronger, even if clouded by the crushing sadness of the futility of the idea.

30

LUCANIA

Cleitus finished his daily duties, which usually ended at sunset. There were several pressing matters that he had to discuss with Porcina. But the Senator was away once more in Rome, and no one knew when he would return.

A slave in the kitchen had become pregnant. The problem was not that a slave became pregnant–it was that the father was *her* own father, and that disgusting man was a long-time slave himself and attended to the many daily operations of the estate.

Thirteen cows had died of some mysterious disease, and there was a scramble to separate healthier-looking beasts from those showing symptoms of illness. And now it was up to Cleitus to ensure that cattle purchases, an expensive affair, were done without a hitch.

A few guards were pilfering from the granary and selling it for profit.

Four creditors had come knocking complaining about delays in debt repayment. The estate's finances were no longer precarious, yet Porcina had deliberately withheld payments to parties he considered weak and unable to extract the money. While Cleitus was not in charge of the treasury or running accounting–that was Marcus Vibius' responsibility–Cleitus' work of auditing books and resolving issues gave him a view of all the happenings in the estate's businesses.

Each of these required that he confer with the Senator and execute his orders—except that the man was rarely in the estate and had not delegated his authority to anyone.

And, of course, apart from all this usual business, there was the most interesting, even if trivial matter, of Felix, the herdsman. It was a delicious one that the Senator might enjoy hearing and might lead to him marveling at Cleitus' exceptional ability to track men and their secrets like a hound.

He had dangled Lucia like a fine piece of meat before a hungry herder, and Felix had opened his mouth wide and divulged that he had pushed the guard to death, almost gloating as he said it.

But that was not even the best part.

Even if it brought back terrible memories, the most wonderful confession was that Felix had goaded his beast to gore Mellius. And that Spartacus was expecting to be accosted, and Felix knew Spartacus would kill them. While Felix had little to do with Spartacus' attack on Cleitus, he could not help but feel enraged that Felix was somehow fully aware of what the savage would do.

Cleitus had promised Felix that all would be well once the Senator returned, and the boy had left with foolish hopes.

Cleitus had fantasized many times about how Porcina might react to this news. Would he elevate his position? Increase his pay? Give him much larger responsibilities in the estate? The possibilities were endless. And one day, Cleitus imagined, he would sponsor and demand a personal gladiatorial game involving Spartacus and watch him die bleeding like a butchered pig before him.

He would then slice off every finger slowly, enjoying it. He would make his wife watch. He would make Spartacus *eat* his fingers.

The very thought excited him.

But Spartacus only did what you would do, too, if cornered that way. You know he was innocent.

Shut up. Shut up. He left me a cripple.

But you caused it! He even spared your life. You live well now, and it is because he did not smash your skull.

It does not matter!

Cleitus cursed his mind, for it always *fought with itself.* The thoughts were like a raging storm—they never stopped.

He was a tidy man—a habit acquired as he tried to put on Roman airs. He put away the papers on his desk, rearranged some bound leather parchments on the shelf behind him, and stretched his aching back. It would be time for dinner. Where was Primigenia?

When he was about to leave, he heard a commotion near the door. Who was here at this time? Before he was about to enquire, Marcus Vibius barged through the curtains with two of his burly guards. Cleitus scrambled to his feet in surprise.

"Marcus, what brings you—"

"Sit down," Vibius said sternly as he pulled Cleitus' chair out and sat on it. Cleitus meekly pulled another stool from the corner of the room to face him.

Marcus Vibius was Senator Porcina's estate overseer and the officer of the Treasury. He was the most influential man next to the Senator himself, and some said he was related to Porcina. Vibius oversaw all financial transactions, approved major purchases—construction, slave and animal purchases, food and business supplies, balanced the books, and made hiring and dismissal decisions. The humorless, immensely fat man rarely interacted with Cleitus, though their paths sometimes crossed if there were problems with accounting.

"I am honored—"

Vibius held his hands up, palm facing Cleitus. He adjusted the toga by his shoulder and rubbed a palm on his pepper-gray hair.

"You bring me grief, Cleitus. Grief," he said. Vibius' voice was like cracking pots—no word completed smoothly.

"Sir?"

"It seems you are going about investigating some theft in the granary."

Cleitus was confused. Of course, he was—that was his job, keeping the Senator, and even Vibius, safe from thievery. Why was he looking mad then?

"I have been looking at issues against purchases, and they do not match. Surely—"

"Might be just poor record-keeping. Not everyone we have is a thorough curmudgeon," he said dismissively. "Your yack-yack makes it sound like there is a scheme."

What was this fat bastard's problem?

"They cannot be mismatched for months, sir. The quantities are similar, and the method follows a pattern."

"Explain."

Cleitus hoped to showcase his astute observations. "Well. As you know, we purchase corn, barley, olives, and wheat. All the incoming quantities and prices paid are meticulously recorded, as they must be. But the curious thing is, consistently, the recorded incoming is higher than the outgoing and the reserves. It is as if we are paying for the grain we are not receiving, or something is being taken out without records."

The Treasurer looked frustrated as he took a deep breath. "There are hundreds of entries. Do you think this is nothing more than a clerical error?"

Cleitus smiled. *I am not so foolish!* "Not at all. The discrepancies are consistent month-to-month, and when I look at the classifications, it is often evident in the most expensive grain—mainly the wheat. There are periods where we should have bags in the hold, and yet we have none."

"Have you visited the granary to check?"

"Yes, sir. What use is suspicion if one's own eyes do not confirm it?"

Suddenly Vibius' demeanor changed. Gone was the lazy, nonchalant receipt of the news. He huffed and chewed on his lips. His fleshy fingers gripped the chair.

"You think you know all about complex accounting rules and methods?"

Cleitus was surprised at this angle of questioning. "I might not know all the complexity of running estates and armies like you do, sir," he said deprecatingly.

"Then how are you confident about your assertions?"

"This is simple record-keeping, Vibius. What comes in, what goes out—"

"Do not lecture me. It seems you are making something out of nothing!"

Why was this hippopotamus so frustrated with a simple case of pilfering? Did he not care?

"They are pilfering the estate, sir! Surely you would want that to end!"

Vibius' jowls shook when he opened his mouth. "Are you saying that my nephew is a cheat? Is that what you imply? My family is a bunch of crooks trying to take advantage of Publius?"

Cleitus was taken aback. *This elephant-eater's nephew kept granary books? No one had told him!*

He tried to salvage the situation. "Well, I have been kept in the dark about your esteemed relative managing the books. I am in no way implying he had anything to do with this! Perhaps someone he delegates is cooking the books or is up to no good, smearing your fine family's name!"

Vibius' face only became redder. His jiggling hand shot up, with his fingers mimicking a rapidly opening and closing mouth. "You fucking barbarian. You *know* very well that *only* he manages the granary. Everyone knows. And you go around pitty-patty, and now tongues are wagging. There is nothing wrong with the granary operations!"

Does this meal-muncher have something to do with this?

"I am only trying to protect you and the Senator, sir. You are honorable–"

"Shut up, or I will fucking chop off your remaining fingers. Do not let your dirty Thracian mouth go fuckery-fuck dragging my name or my family's through the sewers! I do not know how Publius put you in audit, because if there is anyone corrupt here, it is you with the lowly pig blood flowing in your veins."

This furious-farter is in on the scheme. Bastard.

Cleitus tried another tactic. "I have sworn an oath to protect the estate and your names, sir. If a jackal is putting you to risk, do you not want to know?"

Perhaps he would trample his corrupt nephew and save his fat arse.

"I do not need a son of a low-class barbarian whore trying to protect my family with his jibber-jabber. You just stay away from this affair and not a word from your mouth."

Fuck you, Roman. Fucking savages who think too highly of themselves.

Anger bubbled up Cleitus' belly and throat. He had had enough of these insults and attacks on his integrity. He had done *nothing* wrong.

"You have no right to stop me from my duties, sir! I am only beholden to–"

Vibius gestured to his thugs. Cleitus had no time to reach for the dagger hidden in his tunic, tucked away behind his thick leather belt. The men were strong and thorough–they pummeled him with blows before dragging him to the floor.

"Stop! Vibius, you cannot–"

The haze of pain from his punched belly made it impossible to think clearly.

One man tied Cleitus' hands behind his back, and the other secured the legs. This location was far from the main house, and no one would hear him if he shouted. And likely, no one would care either. Who would go against the second most powerful man in the estate?

Then one of them got near his face. "Listen, you fucking little Thracian weasel. Stay out of our business."

Vibius squatted near him, straining against his weight and breathing heavily. "You think you are a high-born, big official in the estate. You are just an accountant poking his barbarian nose where it does not belong."

"I am only doing my job! Let me go!"

Vibius nodded to the man again. Cleitus strained to look back, but the second guard put his feet on his neck and down his head. *What are you doing, you whoremongers?*

A panicked Cleitus tried to kick, but his tied legs only met air. These men knew what they were doing.

What–

No! No, No, No, No, No!

The searing pain was terrifying yet so familiar. The sharp knife sliced through the tendons and bones of the ring finger. And Cleitus continued to howl as they then cut off his little finger. The red mushroom of agony engulfed Cleitus as he bundled up and began to retch.

They hoisted him back to his feet and put him against the wall. One of the men wrapped a cloth around the bleeding stumps.

Cleitus felt faint.

Vibius' fat face was close to his. "Now you listen to me, fingerless little mongrel. Do your audits but keep your mouth shut, or it will be your cock the next time. Do you understand?"

Cleitus nodded fervently, terrified.

"You are no Roman, and do not imagine yourself one. You will cooperate and enjoy a fine life with your slave and this little house, do you understand?"

"Yes," he said weakly.

"Be a quiet little dog, bark at things that do not touch my world, and all will be right. I will even have your salary increased. Do you understand?"

"I understand!" Cleitus said and heaved.

"Filthy pig," Vibius said and stood. "Your slave will care for you. Tell Porcina you were attacked outside the estate."

"Yes!"

"Untie him," he ordered.

Cleitus lay in a puddle of his own piss as they walked out. It seemed Primigenia was held elsewhere, for she came running soon after.

Cleitus felt no shame as he cried in his slave's arms. As his chest heaved, Cleitus cursed the Romans.

For having inducted him into their army.

For having pulled him into a scheme to kill Spartacus.

For sending him on a useless quest that resulted in his injury.

And now, for having treated him like nothing but a low criminal.

He cried, and he cursed.

But he knew that the gods were sending him a message.

31

LUDUS OF VATIA

A flimsy bandage keeps a festering wound at bay for only so long, for the noxious poison that rises within the injury will burst out sooner or later. And such was the case with the peace in Vatia's *ludus*, just as Spartacus suspected.

The men trained and fought, and some died, and for a few months, not much transpired except the usual quarrels and fights on petty matters—tribal arguments, personal insults, perceived disrespect, and so on. Vatia made good coin on his loans and sale conversions as gladiators died fighting unjust surprises. But then he began to add more to the school without expanding the barracks. Two men in a room changed to three. And some newcomers were forced to share as four or five. Only a few men who were afforded the privilege of their room kept theirs—Philotas, Canicus, and Oenomaus. Crixus and Spartacus, the target of Vatia's ire for their past transgressions, now had cellmates. When a cell had five, two men struggled to sleep on the mattress, and three pressed against each other on the floor. And such close quarters amongst unfamiliar men was like lighting a matchstick in a room of dry grass.

Fights broke out regularly, ruining the peace. The severity of punishments increased—men were flogged until they were ruined, some were starved for days, two died in the box, left there by their unmerciful master, and two were executed summarily on the training fields. Unlike only a year ago, life went cheaply, and it was clear Vatia could bear the losses without hurting himself too much in the process. Throughout it all, Vatia visited to assure that new constructions would begin soon. "Asina's school has it worse, and they face it like real men. Which of your leaders is inciting this dissatisfaction?" He scolded them. "Many of you have only a few years to walk with pride, yet you are testing the will of the Senate. Do you want them to reverse the new decree?"

No one had confirmation of the terms of this decree. Canicus' woman had brought news from outside–she had heard nothing of the sort, but then a cook knew little of the affairs of the Roman Senate. She had not reconnected with Pollio, who was away for long periods on business. But Spartacus was convinced that this was all a lie and no such decree existed.

And throughout this, Spartacus was spared from fighting as his shoulder healed. He returned to training. But how long that would last was to be seen as new stars emerged. Oenomaus was amongst the most celebrated. He was said to be ruthless and explosive in his style, combining the best of Spartacus and Crixus in the speed and ferocity of his attacks. There were a few others, though some ascendant figures were extinguished in the cruelty of the games.

And as Spartacus bade his time and watched, knowing that many men were beginning to realize they were being misled, the first new horrifying news emerged.

In an event in Rome, a condemned woman, naked and with her hands tied behind her back and hoisted on donkeys, had been pushed onto the *spectacula* and used as target practice by archers. There were variations of this incident. In one, she was first raped before the baying audience before being put on a donkey. It was not the archers, but dogs were set on her in another. In another, the dogs raped her, and a bear ripped her. Whatever the case, there was no dispute in the story. Now condemned women were being sent to the arena purely as entertainment, where they were killed in heinous ways. The shift in the audience's demands was becoming clearer—no longer did they seek only principled fights and skill. The games had become grotesque manners of entertainment, where people were sent to die in twisted ways. This news created much consternation—did that mean that the gladiators would now face much worse manner of challenges that made a mockery of their training? It was always understood that weak, unqualified men faced beasts and died for comical intent, but the *real* fighters had so far been spared such ignominy, even if they often faced unjust circumstances. Was all that changing for the worse?

"What is the point of training?" one man complained. "Why dream of glory if we are sent out with a stick and made to face lions and bears?"

"What glory and adulation are there if I have to sleep with my cock pushing up against another man's unwashed bottom and then fight four armed midgets with my bare hands," another bitterly remarked.

And so real and rumored horrors of the arena began to circulate. During Spartacus' initial days, the conversation was mostly centered on the quality of the opponents, the fighters' skill, how close a fight was, and so on. And now it was about the terrible ways men died unfairly. This, in turn, depressed the ardor of practice, and men began to look to their leaders for assurances that *something* would be done.

"What about the decree? Is it real?"

Many began to harass Philotas, who had first announced this, and he maintained that it was all true. Spartacus' respect for the man had diminished. Why was he so intent on keeping peace with lies? Why take Vatia's side as the situation worsened?

But when cornered by Crixus, Canicus, and Spartacus, Philotas had his reasons and defended himself robustly.

"What would you have me do, you idiots?" he hissed. "I convey what I hear, or Vatia will have my head. Would you rather have riots and get massacred? Instead of condemning me, you should be thanking my attempts to douse these foolish fires. Many of those rumors are entirely untrue, and you *know* that!"

"How do *know* that?" Spartacus countered. "It is no secret that the nature of the games has changed—is changing—quickly. Virulent ugliness is spreading from game to game. These are no longer only honorable funeral demonstrations or glorious fights of skill. Every game is a mockery!"

"Not every game!" Philotas shouted at him. "Don't most men return? The reality is that only a few events are unjust, but most are still what they always were. The rumors make it seem like the games are just a death spectacle."

"They will soon become only death spectacles," Spartacus said. "Say something, Canicus!"

The German was taken aback but reluctantly joined. He and Philotas had a long history together, but that did not stop him anymore. "Even one or two unjust fights are enough to put us at grave risk, Philotas. You surely see that. There should be *no* such unfair contests. None. Does the decree not guarantee fair fights? How valid is a decree if men are sent against a posse of lions or twenty armed men? That is no path to freedom!"

"No real fighter has gone up against a posse, and no—"

"I was made to fight *two* men, and then fought against a heavily armored man while I was left defenseless!" Spartacus said, his jaws clenched painfully.

"How real is the story of the woman sent to death?"

Philotas looked uncomfortable. Would he try to lie or find reasons to justify that?

"That was a travesty. I have learned that she was put on a donkey."

"How did she die?"

"She fell, and a bear was set upon her. But these are extraordinarily rare—"

"Rare now! It will not be soon," Spartacus said. "Do not be naïve, Philotas. None of us will be spared for the circus."

But Philotas was a stubborn mule who would not budge. *This is all temporary. The gods have better plans for us. We must wait for the right time. Vatia is coming to his senses.* And so on he went until Spartacus left him in disgust.

Then came the outbreak of disease. When men are clustered too close, and little care is taken for their cleanliness, the gods punish them. Spartacus had seen this many times during his marches in the army. And when this outbreak struck, men fell ill where they were, their bowels emptied without control, and the dense cells became filthy and unbearable as men were often locked in for long periods.

Finally, as more violence came to the fore due to this intolerable living condition that threatened more loss of life, Vatia allowed all men to the field, with no weapons or even wooden sticks or wicker shields, and let them lie on the ground under open skies. The physician allowed baths. Those who died unable to hold food or water were taken away and burned on a pyre to prevent the spread of sickness.

Vatia also arranged for prayers to the many gods of the tribes and the Roman gods. They tied frogs to the necks of the most diseased and made incantations that did not bear fruit. They took the dying men into incense-filled chambers and left them there with food and water, but to no avail. A few died, and others recovered, indicating that the gods favored those men.

Finally, after days of this, on a night when few lamps lit the field and the sky was dark with clouds, Spartacus gathered a small group led by Crixus, Canicus, and himself. After seeing that there had been few disputes in the last several days, the guards had left the field. After all, sick men enjoying open skies at night were likely to do little mischief and lose that privilege.

Spartacus had convinced Canicus to join him. Philotas was in his quarters–a luxury not allowed to almost anyone else. Besides, Spartacus was tired of Philotas' weakness and felt it best that he addressed these men in Philotas' absence. Crixus would speak too, and so would Canicus. The leaders trusted this group of Thracians, Illyrians, Germans, and Gauls.

Spartacus began gently. "The gods have blessed me with your willingness to listen," he said. "For there must be a reason for strong and fearless men to lend their ear to someone."

He could barely see the faces in the flickering lanterns, but what he saw was enough to spur him on. The silence and gentle affirmations conveyed their desire to hear his opinion. As Pollio had warned, Spartacus no longer cared if there was a snake in their midst. It mattered little.

"We roamed free once, like the lions and the wolves. We lived by our rules. We dispensed justice in a manner that pleased our gods, and we loved our elders, our wives, and our children. And above all, we held our head high and bowed to no one except our gods."

Nodding heads. Murmurs.

"One day, we were chiefs, warriors, guards, herdsmen, carpenters, metal smiths, soldiers, and messengers. We were fathers, sons, husbands, lovers, and brothers. And now? We allow someone to call us slaves and treat us not as those vanquished in battle or those who have come upon hardship, but entirely as someone unworthy of life. As if in one day, all the greatness bequeathed upon us by our gods has vanished."

"Are not all vanquished people subject to the laws of those who have conquered them?" someone asked.

"To work on their farms. To tend to their houses. To braid their hair and tutor their children. To fight for them and to tend their cattle. But to sit in cages for years and fight in their circuses? To die a slow death while living as a person, but with none of the dignity of one? How many of those that your people vanquished lived like us?"

"None!" came the response. In tribal wars, the results were often simple–those who fought died or were allowed to live free under the rule of the victors. Some became servants in households, and some miscreants were executed. No one knew of systematic, cruel enslavement, the way Romans subjected their conquered.

"They call us barbarians. And yet how many of us have nailed men and women to the cross for transgressions and let them rot on the wood? How many of us put unarmed women on animals and set dogs on them for entertainment? How many of us laughed and watched a lion chase a fighter deprived of his weapons?"

Spartacus knew that those amongst the condemned were of the most terrible minds. Rapists, murderers of children, bandits who killed innocent travelers without remorse, thugs whose only joy came from ruining others. Yet those were few. Most came from households that did nothing except raise their arms against an invasion *on their lands*. And in many cases, unfortunate ones who did not even fight and yet were condemned.

By now, he had their attention. Men leaned forward. Even Crixus held his tongue, and he solemnly spoke his language, translating Spartacus' words to his men. Canicus waited his turn and spoke in his. There had never been such cooperation—and it had finally taken disease, overcrowding, and troubling news to get them to listen.

"The Romans think their grief is real, for they hold funeral ceremonies and games in their celebration, and in those very games, we die! Is our grief not real? Is our death to be laughed at and mocked?"

"Hear! Hear!"

"We were told that our redemption was our valor. And that like men with warrior blood, we must fight with honor and let the mercy of our master lead us to freedom. But how many here have been freed? How many fights are now honorable? And why has there been no firm, official confirmation of this decree? It has been a long time since we were told of it, yet has anyone seen a declaration?"

"No!"

"But Philotas says we have to be patient!"

"For how long? Maybe he is being lied to!"

"What if it is true?"

Spartacus waited for the questions and arguments to settle.

"We have heard many promises. We were promised fair fights, and yet we face uncertainty. We were promised a path to freedom, yet no one can confirm the veracity of those announcements. And what about payments? Have we not heard that there would be deposits in our name if we won? Has anyone here ever met a treasurer?"

More men agreed. Spartacus finally felt that he was making progress. The question was how willing everyone was to risk their futures with bold actions.

"And here we sit, like eunuchs of royal courts, speaking of glory while living in the most inglorious ways. Speaking of strength while kneeling before men who treat us like dogs. Speaking of power while we dance like primates before a howling audience. Speaking of greatness by spilling our blood on sand that is unworthy of it, and for someone else's amusement. What glory is in that?"

"And it is an insult to me the kind they send to fight," a Thracian said. And this was another topic of contention and disgust amongst the fighters who valued their skill.

"An insult!"

Agreements. Shaking heads.

"What of those fights where we were set upon untrained men? And to the cheers of a hateful crowd, I had to lay waste to them and watch as their heads rolled. They ran at me like they no longer cared for their lives, knowing that I would end them swiftly. The crowd had no mercy and left me with no choice. Tell me, all you brave men, what glory did I cover myself with when I walked out? Nothing but foulness."

"Only fit for butchers who take joy in that," someone murmured.

Energized by the reception, Spartacus continued.

"What of the stories that somehow *we*, the gladiators, are different and will be treated better, and that only the wretched weaklings will be sent to that travesty? Today we kill them in the arena, and how sure are we that one day, when our body ages or our limbs no longer demonstrate the dexterity due to time or injury, we will not be the ones sent for death amongst laughing crowds? How many here can win against an armed, armored gladiator if he were sent with inadequate power? Everything they have told us so far has been a lie, yet here we sit, believing lying Roman mouths."

There was silence. Every man there knew all this to be true, and the unmistakable evidence was all around them. He waited, letting them hang on to his every word, letting the pause weigh on them as they waited for what he would say next.

"And how many of us speak of the men who took their own lives within their cells? What of the German who choked on the toilet sponge to avoid another fight? What of the Odomantean boy who smashed his head into the nail on the training post, never to wake up again? What of Procamus, who snapped and was nailed to the cross as a warning to us? Why do men end their lives if they believe in glorious destinies?"

Spartacus decided to offer one last thought before leaving it to them to ponder. "Who here has not dreamed of sitting by a warm fire and holding their child on their lap? Or the sweetness of the embrace of a woman? Or even simply walking through green meadows as raindrops wet your faces? I see happiness in that."

The silence told him of their acceptance.

"But I know that many of you have hearts that beat for glory in the battlefield. Every Thracian, German, Gaul, and Syrian wants a taste of his enemies' blood and their gods' approval. You seek glorious death! Who here has not dreamed of a battlefield littered with the corpses of your enemies and the cries of their women?" "Yes, yes!" came the chorus.

"Who here has not dreamed of rushing your true enemies while screaming like madmen and watching them flee in terror? I see greatness in that!"

He took a deep breath as the clouds above thundered gently, and little raindrops fell on them all as if the gods were giving them a sign. The exposed lamps flickered, danced, and then went out as the drops turned into a light, steady rain, wetting them all.

The sign from the heavens.

Finally, the words rang from a dark corner. "What do you suggest, Spartacus?"

He had to measure his words carefully, for this was treading dangerous territory. The conversation was no longer only with the smallest groups of men, many that he had known well, but with a larger group with many unfamiliar characters.

"Who here does not want the taste of freedom, even if it comes with the danger of being pursued by Roman legions and sleeping with empty bellies under open skies?"

32

LUDUS OF VATIA

"What is it again, Philotas?" Vatia asked impatiently. There was enough to deal with, including this disease outbreak that had descended like a curse on his school. But he soon learned that it was not just gods' displeasure on his family but the whole city. Vatia had reduced the number of prayers and offerings, knowing that he had not himself caused great offense to divine powers, but the whole city had. Perhaps he could appease them with even grander shows with bigger offerings of blood. His finances were recovering, but not yet where they had to be. After *years* of toil, his ability to loan more men and charge more for his premium fighters was finally beginning to pay.

"I beg you to consider my words this time, *dominus*," he said. "For the danger that lurks in the training quadrangle is not the disease of the bodies, but what is festering in their minds."

"You speak big words, Philotas," Vatia said. "But I keep you well for what you tell me. Walk with me."

As they took slow steps through the colonnaded corridor, Philotas put on a serious tone. "I know that the *dominus* is aware that the talk of escape and violence is persistent in any gladiatorial school. You have told me so many times."

"So? What do you have now that is more pressing then?"

"The talk of freedom and finding ways to escape captivity is louder. It is no longer like the sound of brushes, *dominus*. It is the beating of drums."

Vatia was annoyed. Had he not warned Spartacus to keep such thoughts away? Had the Thracian opened his mouth again?

"You seem to be perfectly content throwing your fellow men to the jaws of danger," Vatia said, smiling.

"I am content serving your wishes, *dominus*. None of these men are my kind or family."

"True. So what are these drums you speak of?"

"The disease has given rise to much discontent, adding to the overcrowding in the barracks."

"They know how to live like animals, so why is this of any surprise? It is no different in other schools."

"Yet never before in your service have I heard of men conspiring so brazenly."

Vatia grew concerned. He had had this discussion before—such talk was nothing of a surprise. When men were held, they always sought means to escape their captivity. It was always the same, whether it was a *ludus*, a mine, an estate, a farm, or a military prisoner convoy. But rarely did such ventures bear fruit, except perhaps in some lightly guarded estates and farms where slaves ran away. And still, most were brought to justice. Breakouts from gladiator schools were very rare, and his facility was well prepared to handle it.

"You say all this, Philotas. And except for the usual fights and arguments, many of which have been dealt with severely, the men seem content. They train as usual and squabble as usual. The tribes have no unity, and most do not know each other's language. How do you suppose they will be successful in *anything*? I have no time to deal with foolish conspiracies and spread more bitterness. I have paid well for many of these savages, and I will not have them be subject to harsh punishment merely on suspicion and lose their ability to fight! And that too when we are finally making a good profit."

Philotas stood his ground. "But it is not the illiterate fools that conspire, *dominus*. It is the leaders, and surely they know how to engage each other."

Spartacus. That bastard still thinks he is chief.

"Is it Spartacus again? Is he pretending to be the king of his people?"

"He is certainly the most vocal, and his poisonous influence corrupts the others."

"Canicus and Crixus?"

"And more. Even Oenomaus the Gaul seems now taken by this Thracian, putting aside their tribal quarrels."

"Oenomaus is quick to feet but weak by the mind. He follows Crixus like a puppy, and if Crixus listens to Spartacus, there is no surprise that Oenomaus would do the same," Vatia said. Oenomaus had been purchased along with Spartacus, and the Gaul had risen quickly as a prized fighter who did what he was told and took pride in his achievements.

Vatia gestured for Philotas to follow him, and they walked up a staircase. A viewing balcony extended from the central building overlooking the training quadrangle. On this day, men made their ordered entry and exit from the kitchen, and few were in the space, milling about, stretching, or talking to each other.

"Can you warn them to stop this talk unless they want to be flogged to within an inch of their lives? I find myself in a vexing situation. I have investments from influential men like the new Praetor-potential like Glaber and cannot have the school in flames or lose its best men through rash actions."

"These men are not easily deterred by threats on their bodies, *dominus*."

"And you think Spartacus is the main instigator?"

"Certainly the loudest."

"I will not have him killed yet, for he has not yet generated all the profit I need. But there is something that should put the fear of his gods in him."

"A threat of crucifixion, perhaps?"

"He may not be swayed by those threats, knowing crucifixion is not easily sanctioned absent concrete evidence. Besides, such hollow threats can be bad for business, and the magistrate might frown upon wanton use, for it can incite other restlessness due to wagging tongues. You may not know this, Philotas, but the council of schools receives news of insurrection, rebellion, and conspiracies almost *every day*, and almost nothing happens."

"You know the right ways, *dominus*. Is there a different path?"

Vatia tapped on the balustrade and chewed his lips. *I have not risen to be made a fool of by slaves who think they are emperors.*

"There is. It is a matter of time."

33

LUDUS OF VATIA

Antara lay by his side. She was allowed infrequently to his cell, and recently it required more entreaties to Philotas and once to Vatia himself to allow her by his side. And since then, she was allowed more frequently—once every ten to twelve days—as he prepared for a major festival in Pompeii, one of the three cities that the *ludus* usually sent its fighters.

She looked radiant despite her exhausting routine. She woke early each day, spending hours in the kitchen, then serving, then cleaning, and often tending to other duties in the estate on the orders of an overseer—a freedwoman who was not cruel but was certainly harsh. They often inflicted the same pain upon those they lorded that they experienced themselves. But since Antara was fed each day and slept without restraints, her health had not deteriorated. And no matter that pain her body bore, her eyes shone brightly, and her mind was resolute.

"Each time you leave, I worry you will never return," she said, tracing a finger on his beard.

"And yet the gods keep me alive, fight after fight. They throw trained men at me, they throw armored fools at me, they throw hapless prisoners in gangs, and yet I have prevailed," he said, smiling. While he rarely admitted it, sometimes the crowd's adulation was a heady sensation. There was no doubt why some men preferred to fight and die in the arena than seek freedom.

"The gods come to me in my dreams, husband. They always say you are destined for greatness. But they show you roaming like a beautiful beast in a lush forest, not one that paces within a cage."

"I do not consider myself great lying within these walls. And yet we must find the right time to act."

"How close are you to the plans?" she asked with some worry. "You are aware that should you cause the *dominus'* death, then all slaves will die. Is that a burden you are willing to take?"

"The talk is about finding ways to escape. Vatia will find justice but at another time. I am aware of the Roman laws."

"Everyone leaves or none."

"Not a condition if we only seek escape. But running without sufficient force would be a foolhardy venture that will only cause unnecessary loss of life and worsen the condition. If we must venture to such boldness, it must be with a guarantee of success."

She nodded.

"And yet you must show utmost discretion. Never speak a word of it until it is time—not even to your dear friend Methe."

"She knows nothing. All I speak of to her, in hushed tones, is her desire to seek freedom. And she would happily do it if there was any certainty of success."

"How does she fare? Has she escaped the lustful overtures of Messenius?"

She shook her head sadly. "He takes her once a while, and there is no one to support her cause. What can anyone do? The *dominus* does not stop him, and she is not the only one he harasses."

"And you? Do they maintain respectful distance knowing the arrangement?"

"I face derision and groping, but none has so far attempted to force themselves upon me. But I fear that can change anytime, and certainly if I were to lose you."

He hugged her close. "You say the gods speak to you, and have they told you that I will never return?"

"No," she said, smiling. "You will one day be great, Spartacus. That is what the gods have planned for you."

"Their plans have only included squeezing my balls every day," he said, laughing.

She slapped his shoulder and pinched his ear. "Speak no such thing!"

They both lay quietly. He wondered what the upcoming major celebrations in Pompeii would entail. Would it be a true celebration of gladiatorial sport or another mockery?

He had heard that the games in Pompeii would be the biggest and most impressive, sponsored by two newly elected Praetors, including Glaber. Glaber was an investor in Vatia's *ludus*. The other man Spartacus did not know. Praetors were important officials of the Republic, next in power to the Consuls. This meant that the games were attracting attention at the highest levels of Roman power, and to Spartacus, that meant only one thing: more cruelty and twisted notions of glory.

They embraced each other as she whispered encouragement for his next battle and prayed that he would return whole.

34

POMPEII

They stood before the tall dignitary podium on which sat many men in togas and their wives and other women, all in resplendent fabric and shining jewelry. A few plumed officers sat behind, and on either end of the platform stood armored, heavily armed centurions, clearly distinguishable by their attire. This was the first time Spartacus had witnessed such extensive arrangements–whether the size of the *spectacula*, now with even more levels of wooden benches or the dignitary section that was filled with the scum of the Roman society—all here to take joy in the savagery that they wrought upon others. Vatia sat in the second row of benches beside some men he could not recognize.

Even the perimeter of the arena was different. The poles with thick ropes had been replaced by a solid wood-plank wall over six feet tall, and the spectators were protected behind it. Armed guards stood at intervals between the bench sections. Tall poles with red and blue flags brought a sense of festivity and purpose to the event. There was even a fake eagle standard near the dignitary podium to signal the power of Rome.

Spartacus remembered well the large wall painting announcing the celebration.

THE MOST THRILLING DISPLAY OF GAMES ALL WELCOME TO THE SPECTACULA OF POMPEII COMEDY, SPORT, BARBARIAN BATTLES, JUSTICE SURPRISES SPONSORED BY PRAETOR GAIUS CLAUDIUS GLABER SPONSORED BY PRAETOR PUBLIUS VARINIUS AWNINGS PROVIDED

RENOWNED FIGHTERS FROM LUDUS OF VATIA ASINA LUCULLUS PONTUS

Justice. Spartacus knew that it meant executions. Some games had begun to include public slayings of criminals and other ejects from the society, a rarity once but rapidly picking popularity. It was as if a display of warrior sport had devolved into something far uglier in just the last two years.

Six gladiators stood beside Spartacus–Oenomaus being one from his school and the others from different schools. All the men looked capable by their posture, physical characteristics, and the small flairs of ornamentation on their bodies. He did not know what was planned for the event or what surprise he may face this time, for there was no question from the pomp and splendor of the event that the crowd expected much. They had all been called out by name from the holding quarter and asked to stand unarmed before the dignitary section. The restless crowd was making noises for the games to begin.

Finally, with the trumpets silencing the crowd, a man raised his hands to announce a speech. There was no announcer in the center of the field–those nearby could hear this important man, and the rest might draw their cues from the behavior of those that could listen.

"What a glorious day to be before the fine citizens of this great city," began the man. "And what better than spectacular games to celebrate the ascendance of important men who will take this Republic to even greater heights?"

He then spread his arms to point to two men on either side. "The generous Gaius Claudius Glaber, now a Praetor, benefactor of Capua, with much affection for Pompeii!"

Tepid claps rang from several quarters, and a tall, thin man nodded and raised his hands in acknowledgment. Pompeii did not have much love for Capua, or for that matter, any city. And even now *Praetor of Rome* did not evoke great sweetness in these people. The other sponsor, Varinius, received a better reception, for he was known in Pompeii and had financed several public works.

With that out of the way, the man in the center continued. "The gladiators who stand before you are renowned in their craft, and today they will display their ferocious power. Those that face these men are what every barbarian nation feels when faced with the mighty legions of Rome!"

A big cheer went up in the nearer sections, and the rest followed. Spartacus had an inkling of what this meant, and he would find out soon.

The announcer completed his speech and bade the games begin, and the gladiators were all guided back to their holding quarters. This time, the fighters from different games had been separated–but Spartacus was surprised to find two men from his school, newcomers, waiting in the holding area. Messenius stood near the door with four men, scowling. "No one will speak!" he said, even as his men secured Spartacus' hands and feet. *A mighty warrior outside, just a shackled slave inside.*

The first fight was against a heavy Gaul from Lucullus' school in Pompeii. Spartacus had become used to the deafening noise and distractions and knew enough to entertain the crowd while keeping his life alive. Even the attire and protection had changed–they had given him a respectable thick leather guard for his right hand and a thick iron sheet for his left thigh. He also wore an ill-fitting, badly beaten iron helmet. The opponent was protected similarly, though the color of his loincloth, the gladius in his hand, and his oblong shield separated him in style. He was a shorter man, for few in the arena ever matched Spartacus' impressive size, but the opponent was powerfully built and younger by the freshness of his skin.

But the heavily contested fight, which certainly deserved the mantle of a respectable game, came to an abrupt end when Spartacus' *sica* cleanly severed the Gaul's neck after he relentlessly attacked Spartacus with murderous intent. Mercy could not be reserved for those bent on inflicting fatal injuries—and the Gaul had no intention of a fight for skill and pushing his opponent to a display of mercy. He wanted to kill, and now he lay dead to a deafening roar of the crowd.

Many threw rose petals on the ground. Spartacus looked around, reveling in their adulation but increasingly angry at *everything*. His mind had been consumed in recent days by the thought of escape, and nothing doused the flames.

The gods require me to do greater things.

And now, everything felt ugly except the prospect of a life without constraint.

He was ushered through another exit and taken to a separate holding cell where only one other fighter from a different school waited. *What now? Where was Oenomaus? What of the others?*

Messenius walked in soon. "Spartacus, you are not done."

He was incredulous. Fighters needed sufficient rest! Was Vatia preparing to end him today?

"Am I going on another fight?" he asked, his voice rising. *Could he attack Messenius, take his weapon, and escape?*

Where would he go?

And what would happen to Antara?

He suppressed the urge and waited for the overseer to explain.

Messenius seemed distracted. "I do not know. But you are going to the arena again two hours after lunch. You will sit here, eat soon, and wait. I know nothing more."

He hurried out and shut the door, leaving a lone guard inside. Spartacus was frustrated–this had never happened before. His anxiety began to rise as a thousand questions swirled in his mind.

Was he being sent for execution?

Was he–

"I am waiting too. Same," said the other man. Big with a hairy chest and an expanding belly, the smooth-skulled, clean-shaven man stared at him.

"Did you finish a match?"

"Yes," he said. "And then they brought me here."

He was a Samnite by his appearance and accented Latin.

"Spartacus."

"Crasulus."

"You were told not to speak," the guard said from the corner.

Spartacus ignored him.

"I have heard about you," Crasulus said. "It seems you have made a name for yourself."

"Means little," he said. "Do you have a purse from your *dominus*?"

"Will not even buy me a whore for a week," he said, grinning and shaking his head.

"Hey, I told you to shut up," the guard said and advanced at them menacingly.

Spartacus turned to him. "We are only making small talk after a tiring fight. Surely you have no–"

The young guard held a small whip in his hand, and he struck Spartacus on the back.

I have had enough.

Spartacus' hand shot up and grabbed the guard's neck with such power that the boy-man dropped the whip, and not even a gasp escaped from his terrified mouth.

"Think of what will happen if you cause injury to famous gladiators for whom the Praetors have paid good money, and the crowd wants to see. Do you want to go to the mines?" he snarled.

The Samnite gladiator made no move.

The guard's eyes began to roll, and he tried to nod his head. Spartacus relaxed the grip. "If you so much as speak a word of this, I will tell the *dominus* of my famous school that a guard sought to harm me on the cause of a bribe. Do you want me to?"

He shook his head in terror. Spartacus towered over him as he pushed the man to the wall and stared into his eyes. "I shall let you go, and you will sit here. I am going to speak to that man. Do you accept?"

"Yes," the broken, fearful word came from the reddened face. Perhaps the boy was no older than seventeen, and it was as if life flashed in front of him.

Spartacus knew he had the upper hand. The Samnite nodded, which meant their story would be one. The guard collapsed to the bench and sat breathing hard while rubbing his throat. He dared not look into their eyes. In normal circumstances with older guards or with more around, this would be grounds for severe flogging to incapacitation, or perhaps even an ejection into the arena for execution.

But not today.

Spartacus moved closer to the Samnite and whispered, away from earshot and in the dull but incessant noise from above, so the guard would not be able to hear. "Do you have the promise of freedom?"

The man looked at Spartacus quizzically. "Six years. No end in sight."

Spartacus knew he had little time before more guards came inside as routine. He would take this chance.

"What of the decree? Are you not eligible for your separation?"

He looked confused. "What decree?"

"The decree of the Roman Senate that those who have served five years with a certain number of wins are allowed to go free?"

The Samnite looked at Spartacus as if he were an idiot. Then all his teeth showed as he began to chuckle. "You believe that?"

"I speak of what I was told."

"I have heard that more than once. It is something the school owners spread to keep the new men subdued with the promise of a bright future. Do you think the Romans care about a gladiator's freedom when you see these games? It will get worse, not better. Only one man decides the freedom—and it is your master. It is his will. That is all that matters. Keep rubbing his cock until he is pleased, and until then, this is all we will do."

That was the confirmation Spartacus needed. There was nothing more to be said on this subject.

"How is it in your school? How are men treated?"

"You mean when we are not starved or beaten? Like anyone else. We train, and we sleep in crowded cells chained to walls. Is your *dominus* better?"

Spartacus rubbed his chin. "Ours lets us sleep under the open skies when the barracks are filthy with shit because most have caught a disease."

Crasulus laughed. "Not lying on a bed of excrement, how magnanimous!"

The guard gave them a quizzical look, wondering why they were laughing, but he kept to himself. Perhaps plotting revenge when the chance presented itself. He would probably take out his frustration on another hapless soul—that is what these power-drunks did.

"Do you know what comes next? Why are we here? Are we fighting each other?" he asked Crasulus.

"Then why keep us here separately?"

Suddenly it felt like the ground would shake as the crowd thundered outside. The cheers and howls were evident. It was as if there was pandemonium—but given no one had rushed into their cell, it seems whatever it was, was just entertainment.

"What is going on?"

The guard said nothing, and he sat in oppressive silence, imagining what fate had in store for him. Was this it? An ignominious end before any masterful attempt at escape? At least he would die bravely in the arena, and his wife would stay unpunished. As long as she worked the kitchen and estate, she would remain relatively safe, and he hoped that Vatia would not subject her to greater misery.

He prayed to Zibelthiurdos. *My wife says you have greater designs for me, god. Show that it is true!*

Two guards entered the room, and the one inside left quietly, giving the gladiators a deathly stare. Whether he would open his mouth outside and send retribution was yet to be seen.

Spartacus could not control his curiosity. "What wonderful event is transpiring now, sir?" he asked politely to the senior man.

This guard seemed open to simple conversation. "It is madness. Too bad I could not wait until I was sent here to guard you thugs," he said. "I have seen nothing like it."

"What is it?"

"They unleashed two bears, a lion, and two wild dogs, all at once, into the arena. What mad mayhem! And then they sent in ten prisoners holding small wooden sticks to 'hunt' the beasts," he said, chuckling. "It was comical. This was no beast hunt. But the audience seems to be enjoying all the running, crying, and watching limbs being ripped." He began to pick on his teeth and chuckled as he shook his head.

Even as his mouth was frozen in a grin, his companion closed his eyes to rest. "Too bad I could not enjoy the whole thing. Imagine your balls in a dog's mouth, or your back getting branded with hot irons. It seems the audience had quite the joy!"

"It is not over yet. They have more of this coming. Who knows what they will make you do?" the leader said, and they both shared a good laugh.

Spartacus had to control himself from flying across the room and smashing the men's heads. He was much larger than them and far better trained. Instead, he turned to Crasulus. "It seems we will face the jaws of death. What a way to die—not as free men hunting them in our lush forests, but here," he said and spat on the ground.

Crasulus shook his head. "You think wrong. Have you not learned the ways of Romans, Spartacus?"

"What do you imagine, then?"

"I do not imagine. I *know* how they think. This event is all about a few true gladiatorial fights, but the real excitement for the audience is the butchery of the condemned. It is a blood comedy that makes their heart sing. You just watch. They will bring us back to the arena, announcing our grand victories today, and then put us to the grim task of killing a few more—only this time, quivering men."

"Set us to execute criminals?"

"Criminals? Some of these have committed no crime worth mentioning. Their only crime is not having been born here and finding themselves in the clutches of these vicious bastards. Do you think a child stealing bread to assuage his hunger is fit for murder in the arena? Because that is what they have begun to do, and these people love it," Crasulus said bitterly. "I hang my head in shame to the ugliness of what was once a sport of honor and skill."

"And they call *us* barbarians!"

"What are you two muttering about? Be quiet," the leader said. Spartacus decided not to contest this time.

So they waited in the damp and cool room for the weather was still cold, waiting for the onset of warmer days. Spartacus pissed in a bucket, kept to the side, and kept his head down, praying.

The thoughts of a life not lived never left him now. Could he have been a chief back home? Or perhaps even the king of Thracians *if only they listened to him!*

Fucking Romans.

Marching where they should not.

Poking their nose in others' business, and then stealing it entirely.

Pretending to be above others while conducting themselves in manners well beneath anyone they conquered. As if their buildings and roads could excuse what they did.

He leaned back and dozed until awakened for lunch—the bland and thick gruel of barley.

And then he waited.

Someone slapped his shoulder to awaken him. "Get up! You. Get up. It is time!"

He slapped his cheeks to energize himself. The Samnite Crasulus was already up, shaking his body, stretching, jumping up and down to prepare himself.

"If we fight, may you find peace in the afterlife, brother," he said.

Spartacus nodded. "And you in yours."

They both washed their faces in a pail of water, and Spartacus regulated his breath to ease the stress. The difficulty was not the fight but the wait.

The uncertainty.

The unpredictability of it all.

Finally, an organizer opened the door and peeped in. "Both, prepare."

Several guards walked in along with two slaves holding armor and weapons that were the same as the ones in the morning. Once they were attired, they led the two gladiators out to a blinding afternoon.

A big shout went up when they walked to the arena, separated from the other. But unlike previously, a posse of armed soldiers walked behind them.

What was this about? Would they be fighting legionaries?

In the center of the arena were all the signs of a massacre—disturbed sand and numerous dried blood spots. There were even many little chunks of red and pink material all around—the cleaning crews did not even have the time to do their job.

But closer to the center were two tall, embedded posts, separated by a considerable distance. Attached to each post was an iron chain with a waist clasp.

"You, here," a guard ordered Spartacus to one of the posts. Once there, they attached the clasp around his waist, which meant he could only go so far and in an arc in one direction. Crasulus likewise was anchored to the other post.

Both were far enough away that it was clear they would not be fighting each other.

"Who are we fighting?" Spartacus asked the man, still securing the restraint and checking it.

"I do not know," the man said. Once satisfied that all was in good order, the guards retreated from the field, but two remained—one behind Spartacus and the other behind Crasulus.

Spartacus turned to Crasulus.

He smiled. "Whatever comes through the gates, may the gods be with you," he said.

What a strange sense of kinship, Spartacus thought. The announcements had been made before they arrived in the arena, so he had no idea what to expect. The crowd was noisy and shouting with impatience.

What were they looking for?

He did not have to wait long.

The gates on his side opened.

Lions? Wild dogs? Bears?

And after a few anxious moments, out came four bewildered prisoners, chained to each other at the neck with a common rope. They were entirely naked, and each man held a crudely fashioned gladius.

What was this travesty?

Two slaves ran behind the chained men, holding hot branding irons whose tips glowed even in the sunlight. And when one of the condemned men hesitated, slowing the others, a slave poked the man with the iron, causing him to yelp and run toward Spartacus again.

The crowd hooted with laughter and amusement.

Once they were close enough that he could see the terrified yellows of their eyes and the perspiration on their scared faces, the man behind Spartacus addressed them loudly.

"Use your weapons and take on the gladiator. If you do not accomplish the task of subduing this Thracian before the count of one hundred, then he will be unleashed on you!"

That was why he was chained. Like a dog to be set upon these hapless men.

The men nodded fervently.

Spartacus paid attention to one of them.

Not a man.

Just a child.

His hair was reddish-brown and frizzled. His cheeks were still pink and freckled, like some of the Celts of the north. The boy had little flesh on his bones, for his ribs jutted out, and his hands shook unsteadily as he held the crude, unsharpened gladius. He must have been no more than ten or eleven–still a child. The Thracians inducted fighters from when they were thirteen, and the Romans sometimes had fourteen-year-old legionaries. But ten? The bones were weak, and the mind was still unscripted for violence. What had he done to find himself here?

The other three were like wild animals–their hair unkempt, bodies unwashed and dirty with hair, dirt, and streaks of blood from the abuse prior to this game. Men who perhaps once had lives of laughter, people that loved them, and now only a sad amusement for bloodthirsty Romans. The more Spartacus looked at them, the more he was filled with rage—not because they sought to kill him to save themselves, but because of what they were forced to do for the laughter of others.

But the gods left him no choices. The men began to hesitate and hop forward, waving their gladii. *This would be a massacre!*

He heard some noise behind him but could not turn. Crasulus must have been bewildered at this, too, seeing what he was expected to do.

The guard now screamed at them. "Move! Faster! Be burned or fight. The choice is yours!"

Spartacus knew he had to be careful and not underestimate this stupidity. The danger was not the pathetic skill of these frightened men—it was that a single misstep allowed even the dullest blade to cut deep. Four wildly slashing men, desperate and with nothing to lose, could still prove deadly if one let down his guard even for the briefest moments. The blood loss from even an accidental hit could prove fatal.

The slaves behind prodded the chained men, and Spartacus heard the *sizzle* on one of the older men's skin. He screamed and wobbled—and then he lunged at Spartacus, dragging the others along.

It only took one powerful strike on the gladius to dislodge it from his hand and then a singular thrust through his chest to end the man's life, even as Spartacus swiftly raised his shield to protect himself from a surprisingly quick swing from the side.

A fighter amongst them, like a fox among chickens.

The boy was being dragged along, but Spartacus turned his attention to the one who had swung a near-fatal blow. His crazed eyes showed deadly determination, and his swift arc of the weapon showed a certain skill.

Gaul!

That was how they swung their blades in a twisted fashion, curling the handle and using the weapon as a club. Spartacus kicked another man to his right, ignoring the howling boy, and then shielded himself from another blow.

Not this way, Zibelthiurdos, and not in this ugliness.

When the Gaul swung again, Spartacus knelt with lightning speed and then cut the Gaul's belly open with his curved blade. The ruptured abdomen erupted in a stench, and the man collapsed. But with two dead men weighing down, the remaining two became almost immobilized.

And they stood paralyzed in fear, their eyes seeking safety where none existed.

The crowd was screaming for blood, not being satisfied by the butchery they had just witnessed. The trumpet sounded, implying that time had run out. The guard ran behind Spartacus and removed the lock, letting him free.

Unshackled, he advanced on the older man, who frantically swayed and swung his sword.

Why are they not seeking mercy? Do they not know the rules?

Perhaps there were no rules.

This was just execution.

An ugly, sad end to pathetic lives.

He struck the man's sword with a powerful uppercut, and it flew off the handle.

Fool! At least die with dignity!

There was no way for him to walk away from the carnage. The only path was to give him a merciful end. But to do that, he needed the man to acquiesce.

Spartacus would not perform casual butchery on an unarmed man who was neither soldier nor gladiator.

But how, without drawing the ire of the sponsor or the baying crowd?

"Do not run," he screamed at the man.

The crowd cheered.

He walked closer and hissed in a low tone. "Do you seek a valiant death by the edge of a sword, a shameful one on a cross, or a thousand burns on your skin?"

The man's shoulder sagged once he realized the inevitable.

"Pick up your sword and fight me. Now!"

He did as he was told, walking toward his fallen gladius and picking it up.

A brave man, even in the face of this travesty.

Meanwhile, Spartacus ignored the boy, who just stood immobile.

With a guttural cry, the man charged at Spartacus, who expertly parried the attack, let the man take a few swings, thus bringing himself a dignity before death.

And then, with a powerful thrust clean into his heart, Spartacus ended his life.

The crowd seemed somewhat satiated, and some of their attention turned to Crasulus. Spartacus turned to see that Crasulus was bleeding from a deep gash on his cheek, and he was engaging two men.

He turned toward the boy, who transfixed where he was and staring into Spartacus' face with utter terror.

At that moment, Spartacus saw someone he had known long ago.

Felix.

That boy in Lucania.

Abandoned by his mother and condemned to a life of abject misery.

Spartacus knew what he would do. He raised both his hands and shouted. "A boy? They send Spartacus a little boy?" he said, drawing the crowd's attention. "They send a little rabbit to a bear! What entertainment is in this?"

There were several hoots from the stands.

"They want this feared Thracian," he bellowed, thumping his chest and rubbing his generous beard, "the destroyer of Hercolanius, the German twins, the Samnite lord, and more, to *chop* off a *child's* head? Is there no one worthy of my name and the great Glaber's name?"

Someone began to chant, *Thracian! Thracian!*

And more joined. But no one was screaming for the boy's blood–Spartacus' drama just amused them.

Fucking Roman scum. Entertained by all this.

But he was not done. The boy did not attempt to flee when Spartacus leaned toward him. "Kneel before me. Do it now, and you may yet live!" he said, and the boy understood the Latin words.

He fell to his knees.

"You fall to your knees like I am your king!" Spartacus said loudly to the willing ears in the stand. From the corner of his eyes, he noticed that Crasulus had stopped fighting, and those sent to fight him were dead.

The only remaining show was Spartacus and the boy.

Spartacus walked close and raised his *sica*, turned it to its flat side, and lowered it near the boy's shoulders. "Be quiet, boy, and stay that way," he hissed.

The child flinched and began to sob.

"It is not for me to forgive you, boy, for I am no king of Rome!" he announced, knowing that from this position and the silence of the crowd that his words would reach the dignitary podium, including Glaber's seat. The Praetor watched intently.

Spartacus pointed his *sica* toward the seated praetors. "They must decide to spare the life of one nothing but a child, for a warrior must only face men and send them to the afterlife!"

He turned theatrically toward the crowd that seemed to be reveling in this audacious display.

It was a final gamble.

"On your words, honored praetors! By your will alone shall this minnow find his mother in the worlds beyond our reach!"

Would a praetor order the death of a little boy deemed unworthy as an adversary by a slave gladiator?

"Let the little one go!" someone shouted from the stand, perhaps now broken from the blood lust and madness of the game, for all that remained was a small, thin, crying child sitting amidst bodies and before a fearsome, weapon-wielding barbarian.

"Yes, yes," joined a chorus, made shriller by women's voices in the audience. Did they see their own children? Were these Romans even capable of such a thing?

There were very few voices for execution, and Spartacus simply stood staring at Glaber. *Praetor, he calls himself, enjoying the slaughter of unskilled, unarmed men and boys. Face me, you bastard.*

Someone ran to the podium and listened to words from above. It was unusual for a sponsor to make decisions of life or death–they often suggested their desires to the organizers and let the referees deal with such matters. But with the games becoming showcases for political aspirants, this was changing too–the sponsors were sometimes forced to make a call before an audience.

Finally, Glaber stood reluctantly, as evident by his hesitating style. He spread his arms and made a grand gesture. "I have decided," he said, his weak voice barely projecting. "May the boy live!"

Some of the audience cheered while the others watched quietly. The mood was somber.

Spartacus dramatically thrust the *sica* into the ground. He bowed exaggeratedly toward the dignitaries.

"Rome spares you, child. Return to your life!"

A slave ran toward the boy and grabbed him by the underarm. Another one loosened the noose and set him free. To the crowd's cheers and jeers, they ran out of the arena.

What might happen to him? Spartacus did not know. The reality was he might be put up in another game for a less kind crowd or a more ruthless fighter. Or he may go to a farm and die. Like that boy *Felix*.

When Spartacus walked out of the arena, his *sica* pointing to the crowd and his fist thumping his chest in a show, he was sure of one thing.

The gods had brought him to the edge of patience.

35

LUCANIA

It took cauterizing the stumps with hot metal and days of agony for Cleitus to recover. While the pain dulled, the hatred for the Roman had burned bright, yet the helplessness to do anything about it was humiliating. The news of his misfortune had spread—and no sympathy was forthcoming. The plebs in the estate found great joy in mocking him—often showing their palms and spreading fingers and laughing or calling him the Thracian stump.

Cleitus had forgotten all about Felix and every other matter as Primigenia attended to him and brought him back to life.

Cleitus kept his mouth shut about the treasurer's pilfering, and in return, Marcus Vibius slightly increased Cleitus' pay and added another slave to his household. The days returned to normalcy, and the familiar restlessness returned. The monsters from the past reared their ugly head.

Felix.

Cleitus had come *so close*. The idiot herdsman believed Cleitus' promises and revealed the truth about many things. All that was left was a fine afternoon with Porcina and receiving accolades. And between his conversation with Felix and the Senator's return after a long absence from the estate, another guard had gone missing. Once again, Cleitus *knew* it was Felix's handiwork, yet he had managed to stay out of suspicion.

Summoned before the Senator for regular briefings, Cleitus' mind churned with many thoughts. Thoughts of revenge against many who had wronged him, thoughts of finding clever ways to enrich himself, thoughts of ingratiating himself with the Senator to elevate his position.

And now he sat before Porcina, who looked ill from exertion. He had grown paler. *Had the trip to Rome to kiss more buttocks gone badly?*

"Well, Cleitus, it has been many days," he said, his raspy voice like scratching a board with nails.

"Yes, Senator. I am very pleased to see you again and honored to be in your presence!"

Porcina muttered something to himself and then stared at Cleitus' bandaged hand. "I heard," he said, pointing.

What had he heard?

Cleitus only bowed, not wishing to inadvertently utter something in conflict with what Porcina might have heard.

"You should be careful when you go out on errands," he said. "Lest you return without an entire limb next time."

"Yes, sir."

"I have spent money on healing you once before. Do not make this a habit."

Bastard. I have done much for this estate, and lost my fingers in service!

"Yes, sir. It was in service of the estate—"

Porcina waved. "I have no desire to hear your story. Tell me about the latest."

Cleitus was deflated. He mattered so little to the Roman despite doing so much. There was no hint of concern—no questions about what had happened, no words of care, nothing. If Cleitus were left in a ditch next time, Porcina would only piss on him. He regained his composure and reported the many matters. Porcina sat disinterested through it all. The reality was quite stark: crops were failing to disease, revenues were under stress due to competition, and Porcina was barely making enough to service his debts and run his estate.

"It seems no matter how hard I try, I am always in some debt or the other!" he said, irritated.

"I have heard that some other owners are not faring too well either, sir," he said.

Porcina nodded. "Does not change that the gods have decided to fuck me anyway. First it was Sulla, and now it is something else. Anyway, do you have anything else?"

"There was another–" Cleitus began, hoping to discuss an elevation in his position.

And then Marcus Vibius walked in, huffing and puffing. He seemed startled to see Cleitus.

"Publius! I only heard now that you had returned!"

"I sent word for you," Porcina said. "It seems you were unavailable at your house."

"Other pressing matters. But here I am! I see that Cleitus, our fine Thracian auditor and accountant, is already in your ear," he said, assessing Cleitus' reaction.

Cleitus' hand thrummed with pain, as if remembering what Marcus had wrought upon it. *Fucking pig.*

"We were just discussing matters of the estate," Porcina said. "Sit down. I am concluding my conversation with Cleitus here."

"Excellent," Vibius said and groaned as he sat on a chair nearby. He then looked at Cleitus. "What happened to your hand?"

You pig fucking whore mongrel.

"Miscreants during one of my errands, Marcus."

"Make sure they do not take your cock next time," he said, grinning.

Cleitus' cheeks burned with humiliation, but he kept his control.

Porcina turned to Cleitus. "How is the slave woman I gave you?"

"Primigenia?"

"Whatever her name is."

"She is a diligent worker, sir."

Vibius grinned. "I am sure she is diligent in other ways too. Though I wonder what good comes of a cripple Thracian's cock dipping into any cunt."

Porcina chuckled.

Cleitus wanted to jump from his chair and throttle the fat bastard.

"Fine," he said again and absent-mindedly drummed his fingers. "Is there anything else?"

Vibius stared at Cleitus.

Cleitus considered his words. It had taken him days of painful thought to arrive at this conclusion.

"The herder's boy. Felix, sir."

"Which—oh, that one. What about him now?"

Cleitus ignored him. "I have a request for you regarding him, sir."

Porcina looked annoyed. "Take slave matters where they belong, Cleitus. Do not bother me with all that. Have him lashed—"

"No, sir. I am asking that he be transferred to my house. I may have better use for his service."

Porcina looked confounded. "You? What can a herdsman do for you? Is he not fit for his task?"

"Do you want a boy for yourself now?" Vibius said from the side as he stuffed some dates into his fat mouth. "Doing *tasks* your slave girl cannot do? Like fuck you in the—"

"Now, Marcus," Porcina admonished the treasurer.

"He has weakened, yet he possesses a keen mind for the land. Instead of keeping where is no longer fit like other boys for the long and arduous work, I can use him to scout for better pastures for the Senator's estate, put him to swift errands within, and use him for my trade travels."

Porcina stared at him, trying to discern the reasons for the strange request. "You once thought he had a hand in that Thracian's escape and that he led a guard to his death."

"A notion since dispersed since speaking to him at length and examining his whereabouts."

Vibius, slighted by Porcina before, tried to assert his position. The stupid jokes were gone and instead replaced by his meanness. "You fancy yourself quite the interrogator, do you not, Cleitus?"

Cleitus shot back. "Skills I have gained by Senator's grace."

Porcina ignored the tone between the other men. "And through this conversation, you have realized that he is no threat but could be of help?"

"Yes, sir."

Porcina rubbed a palm on the wooden table before him, contemplating the ask.

"It is an unusual request to seek a slave you once doubted. But then you are an unusual man. I cannot discern the minds of your kind," he said.

My kind. Barbarians in your eyes.

"Unusual, indeed. Everyone else has all their fingers," Vibius said as if he were a petulant child.

One day you will pay, pork.

"Fine. You may have him. Should he create difficulties this time, then have him sold," Porcina said. "Now leave us alone."

"Thank you, Senator. I am filled with gratitude," Cleitus said and rose from the chair.

He could feel Marcus Vibius' gaze burning his back, and he left the Senator's chamber.

Cleitus decided what he would do next.

36

LUDUS OF VATIA

Even as Spartacus seethed from the disgraceful event at Pompeii, he was further incensed by the news that reached his ears. Crixus had been dispatched to an event near Rome and made to fight two others from their own school—leading to the fighter's death. Crixus raged, for he had trained the dead man himself. Canicus, like Spartacus, was forced to partake in a public execution, taking on six men who fought holding clubs spiked with nails. And one of them had grazed the waist causing a painful gash. Vatia was unquestionably making good money from these spectacles while simultaneously trying to get them killed in dishonorable ways. It was a clever and vicious ploy.

As he waited for Crixus so he could hold an urgent conference, Spartacus remembered the speech he gave to men under the skies. It felt like it was ages ago, forgotten, and the fire and fury in his words dissipated into the grim air of the *ludus*.

He saw now despondence and hopelessness, with the veteran men increasingly recognizing that the misery would only increase and freedom was nothing but a cruel mirage. The crowding had not eased—and both Spartacus and Crixus had been surprised by additional new men into their cells, depriving them of the modicum of privacy they once enjoyed.

But why? What was Vatia hearing, and from whom?

Crixus finally made his way just before lunch as if he were coming for a casual conversation. They both knew they had to be careful in this new, unpredictable environment where the situation was changing rapidly for the worse. The *ludus* training field was crowded with more men in each rotation, making it easier to slip into unmonitored discussions.

"You have returned whole by the will of gods. Talk but not linger too long," Crixus said. He looked tense, his bushy eyebrows knotted and his jaws tight with anger.

"How much longer, Crixus? Do we die for amusement, or shall we die fighting while fleeing?"

"When? Are you getting help from that Roman of yours?"

"He is no Roman of mine, and I care little for what benefit he gains so long as he helps us—we have to think of what we need from him."

Crixus looked around, gently tugging on his beard. "Most of my men will come."

"How many of yours?"

Crixus counted his men methodically. The ones he could trust. "Twenty-six."

"I can bring thirty-four Thracians."

"Canicus? Germans?" Crixus wondered.

"We have to speak to him," Spartacus said. He found Canicus' demeanor confounding. The Germans, those from the east of a great river called the Rhine, were contemptuous of other tribes and always ready to fight. And yet their leader exuded supreme calmness and refused to indulge in any reckless adventure. The Germans were fierce warriors, and having them join, or at worst, not stand in the way of a breakout, was critical. Spartacus had not yet had the chance to make urgent plans with Canicus.

"What of rest? Syrians?"

The Syrians—a term they used for all men from the east of Thrace—were a mixed lot. They rarely mingled or brawled with the rest, preferring to keep to themselves. Spartacus had tried to make a connection with their leader, one named Nisarpal, and barely succeeded. Nisarpal spoke passable Latin but had no interest in indulging with Thracians or anyone else. He considered Romans, and everyone west of him, *barbarians*.

But would he act and join, should Spartacus make a bid for escape? No one knew.

Just then, Philotas snuck in from behind, surprising both men. "Plotting?" he said, smiling broadly. "If you want success, then you need my knowledge!"

Crixus was about to lash out, but Spartacus signaled him to be quiet. Had Philotas come around?

"The situation is dire," Spartacus told the Macedonian. "What do you hear from Vatia? He rarely comes to the training arena these days."

"He is busy—is it not obvious from what you see? Demand is rising for men—"

"Just men," Crixus said, furious. "Not gladiators! Just men to die."

"You speak the words on my tongue," Spartacus said encouragingly. "Hear of my recent fight. They say we bring greatness to this school. And yet when I walked into the *spectacula* the last time, I was greeted not by a man of equal strength or station. Not one whose skills were forged in an army or the arena. They sent four shivering men, shaking and wetting themselves as the audience laughed. And one of them was just a boy, not even ten, his thin limbs unable to even hold his weapon. Who knows what crime they had committed? Perhaps nothing deserved such an end, for I no longer believe the words out of Roman mouths. Them they sent with dulled gladiuses, ones these fools knew not even how to hold. One of them, from *our* school—I had seen him. He died by my hand."

Philotas acknowledged the words, surprising them both. "Old days are truly gone," he said. "Some gladiators, rest nothing."

"When new stars rise, we will be nothing," Spartacus said. "Do you not see it, Philotas? You as well."

He did not respond.

Spartacus continued. "I spoke to a gladiator from another school in Pompeii, and he said the decree is just a ruse."

Philotas' eyes did not flicker–almost as if he expected it. "Why would anyone believe it?"

Crixus lost control. He swung at Philotas and rammed his fist into the man's face. Philotas sprawled on the field before Spartacus restrained the Gaul. "Stop it! Stop, you intemperate idiot!"

"You lied to all, knowing the truth!" Crixus bellowed, and by now, many others had gathered around the commotion. Philotas nursed his jaw and smiled, even as he lay on the grass.

"Everyone, go back before the guards get here, now!" Spartacus ordered those who had crowded them. His commanding presence and Crixus' stare were enough for the men to disperse and return. Canicus was nowhere around.

Spartacus lent a hand to pull Philotas back to his feet. "Crixus speaks what is on my mind."

Philotas took a minute to gather his wit. "What is my job, you fools?" he said. "I am tasked with keeping the peace against impossible odds. And sometimes, that means even if I suspect Vatia's words are false, I am forced to convey them. You did this many times yourself, Crixus. Do not pretend you are without blame!"

"Not so much. You lied not to a man or two, but everyone!"

"Crixus, keep your voice down before Messenius comes here," Spartacus said. No good came of Messenius' involvement.

Once they calmed down, Philotas turned to Spartacus. "So, what are you proposing?"

37

LUDUS OF VATIA

"Fucking backward stains who think they are kings," Vatia raged as Philotas stood beside him. The situation had taken a new urgency—the embers of discontent had not been extinguished by any means, and now it was as if dry wood was being thrown onto it to light a fire.

Not now! Not when he was finally making a name in many cities! Not when his political aspirations were finally bearing fruit, and he had the chance to leave his ambitious brother behind in the race for an office. He felt besieged—his father-in-law, wife, brother—everyone bothered him. He had worked hard to silence wagging tongues through a steady growth in his school—the loans and death conversions had grown, and he had found a steady supply of slaves, fighters, and miscreants through a rich supply pipeline from the praetors and other commanders who gave him early access and good prices.

And now this.

But he was again trapped in the situation—Spartacus had grown very popular, and he, along with other gladiator leaders, brought in more profit than most others *combined*. Going after him now or making an example of him just by the words of Philotas but without any real evidence of wrongdoing could go wrong. If news of his actions spread, opportunists like Asina would argue that Vatia was useless in grooming true gladiators and compel magistrates to restrict access to the best in the markets. Besides, other gladiators may act hastily in fear and create much trouble at this delicate time. Vatia's image was growing, and so was competition's, and all it would take was unrest to turn his name to that of an incompetent pimp of men. Not only that, Vatia had been unnerved by Pollio's attempt at mingling with Spartacus and his men, a matter he had casually dismissed before but worried now that something worse might be afoot. The news was that Pollio himself was investing in a *ludus* and also sponsoring minor games. Who knew what that son of a street whore was up to?

"How bad is it? How urgent?" he asked Philotas.

"If Spartacus' ardor is not dampened, I fear there will be an attack sooner or later."

"But how will they fight the guards? Many are locked up during the day, and there is no access to the armory!"

"All it takes is a few enterprising men to snatch weapons from the guards, subdue them, and open the barracks and armory. We have designed everything to prevent a few miscreants from getting adventurous, *dominus*, not a large breakout."

Vatia paced around. He was agitated. *How do I teach these mongrels a lesson?*

"Who are the leaders now?"

"Spartacus and Crixus, *dominus*. I do not know where Canicus stands, but Oenomaus listens to Crixus and respects Spartacus."

"Oenomaus as well?" Vatia clenched his fist. *Give me a sign, Apollo.*

"Yes, *dominus*. I have a suggestion."

"Why should I listen to you anymore, Philotas? You have failed utterly in keeping these men in obedience so far."

"Messenius—"

"I will deal with him. He is expected to wield his whip effectively, and you, your tongue. And by the gods, both of you have proved useless!"

"And I beg your forgiveness. It has been difficult with the recent disease outbreak and overcrowding–"

Vatia had no desire to listen to more excuses. "Do not use overcrowding as an excuse. These men have lived like animals, and this is no different! What is your suggestion?"

Many of these dogs had lived on the fields, foraged like animals, slept in unsanitary and crowded barracks and tents, and now suddenly, it was all *inconvenient?* Fucking slaves should accept their fate!

Philotas perked up. "Why not find an occasion to have Spartacus fight Crixus to death so you may end one threat while making a handsome sum?"

Vatia considered it. "Interesting proposition. Except that few men are willing to pay for such an event. Besides, would that not create resentment amongst the gladiators and bring to question if more might be put against each other?"

Philotas nodded. "What about quietly whisking him away and putting him to death? Or maybe send him to an execution?"

Vatia was annoyed. "And all those cases cause losses to me. I will not have him die while costing me–that is a defeat and an insult to my standing! And why quietly anymore, Philotas? No more of *quiet!* The gods have given me sufficient grief with these so-called *leaders,* and it is time to make an example of them and end it all!"

"Without damaging the *dominus'* business," Philotas said, baring his yellow teeth.

Vatia paced around some more. "No one should have a hint. None!"

He rubbed his eyebrows and rapped his fingers on a pillar nearby. He turned to a guard nearby. "Tell Messenius to come here."

They waited for Messenius to arrive while Vatia continued to walk around impatiently.

But with every step, his rage grew.

What was once an irritation had turned into a blazing fire in his mind.

His throat was tight with anger.

He could barely breathe, and his stomach hurt.

The *insolence*.

The *insubordination*.

The lack of gratefulness amongst these base barbarians who were only alive and eating and living because of *him*. Fuck Spartacus and Crixus, and whoever else dared to even *think* of breaking out!

Messenius arrived huffing and puffing. The brutish overseer took great pleasure in inflicting pain on the slaves, and he would undoubtedly be very willing to take matters into his own hands—but like any dangerous dog, he had to be controlled lest he did something that ends up putting his own master at risk.

"You called, sir?"

"How long will it take for us to round up a group of legionaries from the local garrison and bring a cart of weapons with them?"

Messenius looked confused. "We have enough in the armory, sir?"

"Just answer my question!" Vatia screamed at him. *Everyone questioning his fucking orders, by gods!*

Messenius bowed. He stammered. "At least three days, sir. They are stationed far outside Capua, and arrangements will need time."

"Send someone you trust in advance. Not a runner—use one of our horses."

"Yes, sir."

"Tell them we need this support for five to seven weeks, and that I will manage their living quarters and food."

"Yes, sir."

"If the commander objects, ask him if he wishes to hear directly from Glaber himself."

"Yes, sir."

"Double the guards by the armory. No one in the field should have weapons—just clubs."

"Gladiators or—"

"Guards, you stupid bastard. Listen carefully! No weapons for the guards on the field until I say! Reduce the number in the field by half, and put the rest, fully armed, near the kitchens and the exit."

Messenius nodded vigorously. He was beginning to get it. "I will do this as soon as you dismiss me, sir!"

"Yes, yes, but wait here. I have more. And do this very discreetly. No one should feel any different from normal changes."

"Yes, sir."

Vatia yelled at a slave woman nearby to bring him some wine. He stretched his neck to relieve the stress.

"Did we not hear that Publius from the Astorum estates is sponsoring an execution in a few days?"

"Yes, sir."

"Beasts involved?"

"Wild dogs, sir. The usual. The audience is not yet bored with them. And then a few usual fights and execution rounds."

"He sent a request for men from my *ludus*, but the cheapskate will not even pay half of what I usually command. Send word to him that I have a delightful proposition, if he would be so interested. A true drama and spectacle at the right price."

Messenius grinned, no doubt imagining something hideous.

"Inform Crixus that he is to prepare for a great show in a few days, and that I have ordered that he be confined to his barracks to rest and eat. Lock him in alone."

"Yes, sir."

"What of Spartacus?" Philotas, who had stood quietly so far, asked.

Vatia's blood vessels pumped in his temple. But the gods had finally given him a most delectable idea. "We do not know how deep this conspiracy is. Let him train as usual–do not give him cause to suspect anything. Once Crixus is gone, I will make a glorious example of Spartacus. We will all watch him as the demons devour his soul before I put him on a cross."

They both grinned, knowing he had something truly creative in his mind. What might it be?

They would all know soon.

38

LUCANIA

Felix was bewildered. He stood in his loincloth, swaying, rubbing his shoulder, unsure what to say to Cleitus.

"Did I not say I would bring you here?" Cleitus asked the gangly boy.

Cleitus' guards had made the boy wash in the bath before sending him to Cleitus. Felix no longer smelled like a mixture of mud and cow dung. His bushy hair was still dirty, and his teeth were an even greater abomination than Cleitus'. *But he has all his fingers, and his face has a sweet youthfulness to it,* he thought, briefly jealous.

Not only that, Cleitus had had the boy's slave collar removed, assuring the estate overseer that he posed no danger.

"*Dominus.*"

It felt strange, but in an oddly pleasing way, for him to hear his slaves call him master. And yet Cleitus could not *imagine* being one who would call someone that way in a capacity as a slave. Porcina was his *dominus,* but more like a man who paid for his services rather than as a master to his slave.

"Your truthfulness has earned you a better life," Cleitus said proudly. This kindness made him feel surprisingly good. He could not even remember when he had done such a thing before–perhaps long, long ago.

Felix nodded.

Felix's uncommunicative style was irritating. But what was Cleitus expecting–that the herdsman would get on his knees and thank him? That he would kiss his feet in gratitude?

"You will no longer chase the beasts on fields or spend hours guarding your back."

Felix finally smiled—it was the slightest of a curl of his lips—but knowing that the boy *never* smiled, this was a powerful indication of his gratefulness.

Having had enough of the silence, Cleitus finally asked. "So, do you believe that gods have favored you?"

Felix looked at him for what seemed like an eternity.

What is this idiot thinking?

Finally, the boy spoke softly. "They have shown me kindness beyond my imagination, *dominus*."

Cleitus was very pleased.

But he was not done yet. He was thrilled at what his mind had conjured. And for his plan to bear fruit, he had to make sure Felix was overwhelmed and entirely compliant.

"Their kindness is not yet over, boy," he said. He turned to the closed curtain and yelled, "Primigenia!"

His slave girl stepped through the flowing curtains, grinning. *She was so beautiful. It was terrible that the law prevented them from getting married. She cared nothing for his missing fingers.*

"Well, it seems Felix here believes the gods have been kind to him."

"Yes, master."

"But have they been kind enough?"

She giggled loudly. Cleitus was enjoying himself immensely—it was quite a sensation indeed.

He had even briefly practiced this little performance.

Bringing joy to someone else—what a strange thing!

Felix looked utterly confused, and he attempted to laugh–not knowing whether this was a mockery at his expense or if it was something genuine.

"You think a new cruelty will be inflicted upon you."

Felix nodded, his eyes darting frantically. Cleitus desired to know what was going on *inside* his mind.

"Well, there will be cruelty–"

The boy's face fell, and his smile died. He turned behind quickly to see if anyone was about to seize him.

Cleitus continued. "Look here! Yes, there is cruelty, but not the type you think, he said," grinning.

Primigenia was being an idiot, giggling even louder. Cleitus turned to her and slapped her ample bottom, causing her to squeal.

Felix was bewildered–his face alternatively changed between a suppressed smile and utter confusion.

Cleitus nodded, and Primigenia darted behind the curtains.

There was a ruffle and some voices.

More giggling.

And then the curtains parted.

Felix's eyes grew as wide as the afternoon sun. He let out an audible gasp.

39

LUDUS OF VATIA

Methe stood paralyzed behind the door, unsure whether to come into view or let another maid take wine to the *dominus*. But she had heard much and was sure some others had too—for there was unease at the loud voices and what was being said.

She knew so far that Crixus was going to be sent away to some dangerous spectacle involving beasts, but there was more–though the men had not explicitly discussed it. But Spartacus' name had come up repeatedly, insinuating that something terrible awaited him.

Methe had grown greatly fond of Antara, Spartacus' woman, and her friend in the stifling life of the *ludus*. The Thracian woman was of great spirit and never abandoned her gods–she had told Methe her story, and Methe, hers to Antara. The women had grown a kinship bonded by the hardship.

Only recently, Antara had tearfully confessed how Messenius had become increasingly inappropriate with her despite her protestations and how they were not allowing her to meet her husband. But they had not attempted to get the word out to Spartacus, fearing his reaction and worse things to happen to them all.

And now there was this ominous conversation about misfortunes about to come.

Methe hurried to the kitchen but did not find Antara. She returned to the barracks. Antara was there by her flimsy bed, praying between her breaks.

It would soon be time to serve food to the gladiators and then clean the areas.

"Antara," Methe said urgently, disturbing her friend's prayer. When she ignored the call, Methe decided to interrupt by shaking her by the shoulders.

"What is it?" Antara said irritably. "I am praying, Methe!"

"You can pray later," Methe said. She looked around to make sure no one was around.

Antara recognized the urgency in Methe's tone. "What is it?" she asked.

"Do your gods tell you of ill tidings?" Methe asked, holding her friend's hands in hers. "I fear something terrible is brewing!"

She told Antara what she had heard. That there was something about to happen in a game sponsored by Publius of Astorum and Crixus would be there, and that something terrible was awaiting Spartacus, though she had only heard fragments and did not know what all they meant.

Antara was frozen with fear. Methe knew she could not take the news to Spartacus. She knew no guards she could trust, and now learning that Philotas stood in the same room with Vatia and Messenius, she would not know whether to send a message through any of the gladiators.

"What do you want to do, Antara? Speak to the *dominus* to forgive your husband for whatever he did?"

Antara's eyes showed steely resolve. "No. That would only invite his wrath. The gods have planned greater things for my husband, but they ask that I play my role as the dutiful wife. Begging Vatia is not one of those roles."

Methe admired Antara's strength. "But what else can you do?"

"There is something I have never told you, Methe, and may the gods forgive me for that. I only hid it for your safety. Will you guard what I tell you?"

"You know I will, Antara! What?"

"Anicia, the pleb who also works in the household—the pretty one with long hair—"

"Yes, I know Anicia well. What about her?"

"She desires Canicus with all her being. And it is she who sometimes goes to Pollio to convey or bring messages."

Methe was shocked. "Anicia? That clever one! She looks so coy and innocent!"

Antara smiled. "She has a good heart and one that is kind to the slaves—"

Suddenly Messenius walked into the room with a guard. His lecherous grin was revolting. "It seems the ladies are gossiping. It might be better if you got on your knees and sucked me instead."

Methe turned away, and Antara held her head low. The brute would only get worse if anyone talked back.

Messenius stepped forward and gripped Antara's forearm. "Well, as much as I would love to fuck you and watch you call your useless gods, I am still a faithful servant of the *dominus*, and I doubt he would want me in a Thracian cunt."

He looked at the guard and winked, and they shared a laugh. Methe said nothing, but her heart thudded with intense fear. What did Messenius want from them? Antara kept her head low, but her lips trembled.

Methe herself was panic-stricken—had anyone seen her? Did Vatia know she was nearby and heard him?

"You, Spartacus' woman. You are coming with me."

"Where are you taking me?" Antara managed to squeak out a few words as Messenius yanked her hand.

"You will find out soon enough," he said. "Move."

Antara turned to Methe. "Tell her to take the message to the gods about the next festival!"

Messenius grunted as he pushed her forward. With one hand, he circled her waist and squeezed her breast. "Your man is lucky," he grunted as he marched her out. "Just a few days. But such a waste. The hold will not be too long!"

And then they were gone, leaving behind a frightened Methe. It took her a few moments to recollect her memory of what Antara had told her.

The gods had condemned Methe to this life, but they had not taken away the sharpness of her mind. At that moment, Methe knew what Antara had asked of her and where Messenius was taking her.

She hurried, for she knew any delay might be too late for her friend and her husband.

40

LUCANIA

Felix almost choked.

Lucia!

The girl he dreamed of every day smiled shyly as she stood beside Cleitus.

Felix could barely breathe. An intense heat enveloped his being, rising from his loins to his cheeks. He could not believe what was happening–first, the removal of his collar, then his advancement into a household, and now, the woman he was infatuated with beyond measure standing before him.

Cleitus was grinning. "Well, Felix. Perhaps you wish to greet her?"

Felix did not know what to say. Greet her with what? He barely managed to eke out a grunt, and then the corners of his lips felt like boulders were hanging off them when he tried to smile.

And Lucia knew the effect she was having on him, for her eyes twinkled, and her mouth remained in a coy yet mischievous smile. Primigenia stood beside Lucia, goading her on, pinching her arm, and giggling.

Were the gods playing another terrible trick on him? Was all this about to vanish in a fleeting moment, only to be replaced by something vicious? Cleitus was a dangerous man. Felix knew that much. He had relentlessly tried to find out the truth behind Felix's involvement with Spartacus and the guard's disappearance, and he had succeeded. But after that, instead of any severe punishment, Felix was now confronted with this confounding sequence of events—none of it made sense.

His excitement was suddenly replaced by fear. Should he attempt to run? Should he beg forgiveness for something he had no idea about? Do something else?

But Felix would not debase himself before Lucia. He would not so easily break down before *anyone*, for he had endured much and would continue to do so if it was the will of his gods.

"Have I done something wrong, master?" he asked Cleitus, keeping his voice steady.

Cleitus shook his head. "You have done no wrong to me, Felix. I am a man of my word, and this I had promised," he said. "And I expect much from you below my roof."

"Yes, master."

Cleitus turned to Lucia. "The boy knows nothing of the world or women, so teach him."

Lucia bowed. "Yes, master," she said, but with a grin. All of Primigenia's teeth were on display—she was enjoying herself.

Felix felt like his feet were bolted to the floor, and he stood transfixed as Lucia walked toward him. Cleitus nodded, and he and Primigenia made a loud remark as they left. "Do not scream too loudly!" she said, giggling away, and Felix heard the familiar sound of Cleitus' palm slapping her bottom.

Lucia!

She smelled like scented balsam. The heady fragrance combined with the beauty of her cool glassy eyes, her red lips, and her body's contours beneath her fabric was too much for Felix to take. There was no one else in the room, and the doors were shut. *They were all by themselves!* No Mellius or his whip, no one threatening to flog him or hoist him on the cross, no one mocking him from the side. What if someone burst through the doors to crash his joy and watch his misery? Is this not a joke?

It was as if Lucia had read his mind. "No one seeks to do you harm," she said. Even her voice was so soft and gentle and wonderful. And then she held his hand.

Felix, still unable to speak and unsure of what to do, was suddenly aware of his intense erection—something Lucia noticed immediately, for his loincloth was barely sufficient to hide the embarrassment.

She just giggled.

And when he stammered and stuttered with embarrassment, Lucia only drew him into an embrace and placed her lips on his. "Do not be worried and do not speak," she said. "Just listen to my words."

He grunted and clumsily placed a palm on her breast—but she did not resist. Felix's mind was a storm of sensations when she slowly parted her fabric and removed it. He had seen naked women clandestinely, when they washed in the stream or when growing girls ran around naked, but never this way where the display was *for him.*

He prayed to his gods that this shall never end and that this not be a cruel dream.

With his head still spinning from the unfolding events and his entire body feeling like it was on delicious fire, all it took was for Lucia to remove his loincloth and brush her fingers against his painful manhood before he exploded in an orgasm unlike anything he had ever experienced.

She assuaged his embarrassment, only saying that she was pleased by his excitement.

And then Lucia took Felix to worlds he never knew existed.

Cleitus and Primigenia stood grinning outside the door, listening to the giggles and groans from the room, knowing that Felix would perhaps not walk straight for a day by the time Lucia was done with him. As a slave, she was fulfilling Cleitus' instructions to give Felix the greatest pleasure, but her affection for the boy ensured that the act was done by volition than compulsion, and the most wonderful sensations came from that willingness.

He looked at Primigenia, who was still very immersed with her ear to the door, and felt affection for the simple girl. She had taken exceptional care of him after his encounter with Vibius, and she never complained. And slowly, he had come to accept that perhaps even if she had affection for another man, it mattered little, for she was unquestionably devoted to him and his needs. He grabbed her by the waist, surprising her.

"Come," he said, and she nodded with a big smile.

As they went to their quarter, Cleitus' mind returned to Felix. The boy was no fool, regardless of his wretched station. He was a cunning character.

And one Cleitus would fashion as his weapon for what he was about to do next.

41

LUCANIA

They all sat before him, Primigenia and Lucia cross-legged, and Felix squatting as usual. Cleitus beamed with satisfaction–it was an odd thing; none of them were Roman, and yet they were *his slaves*, but he saw himself as their leader than a master. For Cleitus, all these feelings of magnanimity, grace, and ownership were new, and he liked it. They were his followers, disciples, *his*.

This was a meeting he wanted to call, but something had created urgency. The estate was hinting that they wanted Primigenia back in the services of the Senator's household–and the suggestion had originated from the bastard Marcus Vibius.

Cleitus could no longer wait.

The time since inducting Felix and Lucia had gone exceptionally well. Felix was brilliant at his tasks–carrying messages, running small trade jobs, caring for the few cattle Cleitus had procured for himself, keeping the areas surrounding Cleitus' home clean; nothing deterred him, and he never complained. He ate his food daily, as if it were a feast, and he was still a blubbering idiot around Lucia.

Primigenia was loyal to him, and never once had she mentioned affection to another man, and increasingly Cleitus was convinced that she did indeed *like* him. And Lucia? The ever-obedient Lucia never attempted to see her mother, and she did her work diligently–and she seemed happy being here.

But Cleitus was not the one to forget sleights, and the monster storm that had raged in his mind for days had calmed down, allowing him to think clearly for the first time in years. It was as if his decision had quelled the waves of uncertainty. They may be surprised, shocked even, but he would leave them with no choice.

"I have something important to discuss," he said, scanning his captive audience of three. Primigenia furrowed her brows, Lucia let out a loud breath, and Felix gently swayed as he squatted.

"Who believes they will be safe and free below Porcina's roof?"

No one answered.

"Who here knows what happens to slaves should someone cause harm to the Senator or his family?"

All of them nodded.

"Who here has seen the land they came from?"

No one answered. But their demeanor indicated they understood what Cleitus was hinting at.

Cleitus decided to reveal his thought. "Who here thinks Porcina's estate is the heaven bestowed upon you by gods and that living here is sweeter than walking away?"

They all took deep breaths, and yet none displayed shock or dismay. Were they expecting that he would one day speak thus? Or did they worry about trickery?

"I am not a slave, but I am seen no better than one," Cleitus said. "But it seems none of you care much about staying here."

And still kept quiet, anxiety writ large on their faces but none willing to speak a word.

He smiled. "Have no concern that this is a plot to entrap you. I have no such intentions. Any favor I had for this estate vanished along with—" he said, as he held out his fingerless hand and pointed at the stubs with his other hand.

They were all still silent until Primigenia stirred. She smiled, though the strain showed on her face. "Some of us have known little else, master," she said. "And I have longed to know what life is without the shackles."

Cleitus nodded. "And may you know that the estate is demanding her return, away from me."

Primigenia was downcast, and Lucia looked horrified. She reached out and held her friend's hand.

But encouraged by Primigenia's words, Lucia was more explicit. "I wish I was there to gut that bastard myself. Many have suffered by his hands. While I will miss the comfort of a fine roof and the estate kitchen, I will enjoy breathing the air not corrupted by these pigs."

Lucia had taken a leap that Cleitus had not even expressed yet. She had spoken plainly about leaving.

Felix simply grinned like a fool, watching Lucia's face. He had the most to gain of them all by getting away, for he had suffered most grievously, and Cleitus knew that Felix would die sooner or later if left here.

"You speak my mind, Lucia. How hot and oppressive this air feels. Who here will walk boldly with me, knowing the dangers of running away?"

Finally, Felix spoke. He had found his voice and, in recent weeks, did not hesitate to state his opinions, even if in his reserved, quiet manner. "What better has it been, being here, master?" he said and turned slightly, showing them the scars on his back.

Lucia gently placed a hand on his back and caressed him.

"But where will we go?" Primigenia asked.

"I can take you to places no one will find," Felix said proudly. "And keep you alive!"

Cleitus smiled. "There are many places where we could melt in the crowds or hide in the forests. Imagine lying down on the grass looking at the stars, knowing that you will not wake to the screech of an overseer in the morning."

They grinned. Together, Cleitus thought, they would find a way out of Italy, back to Thracia. He would marry Primigenia, wed Lucia to Felix, and grant them freedom—after all, in *his* land, would he not have the freedom to do that?

But you think so small! Do you wish to be a farmer?

What happened to your grand ambitions? These people are expendable! Use them!

Quiet! Quiet!

And Spartacus? Just let him go?

Think, Cleitus! What brings you glory?

Being a good person! Leading them! Freedom!

So weak. What happened to you?

Quiet! Quiet!

Cleitus calmed the screaming voices in his head. *Enough!*

He came back to his bearings as they watched his face intently. Cleitus immediately plunged into an energetic discussion of how to leave, what they would need, and what the household must do in preparation.

But there was one more thing.

"There is one unfinished business," he said gravely as his eyes turned to Felix.

"And Felix, I need you to join me to do what I must."

42

LUDUS OF VATIA

It was late in the morning, with lunch only an hour away. Spartacus flexed his arms and practiced with the wooden post with his Thracian contingent. The Gauls were absent from the field. A few Germans had just entered, and a group of Syrians practiced in another corner.

But something felt amiss. He felt it in his bones. He had not seen his wife in the kitchen for a few days, nor her friend Methe. Philotas was only sporadically around, always giving excuses that Vatia wanted him on errands. But the most unusual thing was the subtle change in the security patterns.

The number of guards had reduced, and he had seen more near the kitchen and the doors out of the kitchen to the exits of the estate. They were no longer armed, instead only holding wooden clubs and watching the training men with unease. Not only that, the number of guards near the armory had increased. *Someone was leaking their conversation and plans to Vatia or Messenius. Who? And why hadn't Vatia acted upon it?*

He wanted to talk of these changes with Crixus, but the man had been confined to a separate holding area for the last few days. This was sometimes done to keep fighters well-fed and rested before a major spectacle, yet no one had announced a new game. Canicus knew nothing of what was going on and Oenomaus, usually not of the mind to indulge in much talk except the bawdy variety, seemed not to have noticed a thing.

The only one who felt the changes was Nisarpal, who had developed a mild affinity and respect for Spartacus. He simply stated, *something is not right, something big,* in passing as he walked nearby.

The air was cool but noisy with the grunts of men swinging their wooden sticks and striking the wicker shields or the worn wooden posts.

He looked around.

Where was Castus? Canicus?

He put his disturbing thoughts away and focused on the wooden post ahead. The main leaders had spoken in increasing urgency to *do something,* yet had not found an opportune moment. And much to his frustration, the plans remained just that–plans. They had to act–but when? Was he being too slow?

And now something was going on, and he had no idea what.

He could guess, except he had no evidence.

His shoulders felt the jolt when he struck his heavy wooden club to the practice post. His skin was slick with sweat, and his hair itched. The scabs on his healing wounds irritated him, but he paid no heed.

And then, from the corner of his eye, he saw Canicus emerge into the field from the barracks entrance–his face grim and jaws tight.

Canicus' eyes flicked around the field until they found Spartacus'.

The German quickened his pace and hurried. *What concerns him?*

Canicus made no greeting when he reached Spartacus.

"Have you seen Crixus?" he asked.

"No, but that is a question I wished to ask you. Where have you been?"

"Listen to me, Spartacus, and make no movement or act rashly. But listen to me carefully."

Spartacus was alarmed. If the thoughtful Canicus, who already knew how Spartacus was a methodical man, thought he would act rashly, then something serious was afoot.

"What is it," he asked, his anxiety already rising. They moved away from the training men nearby.

"Make a promise to your gods that your next actions shall be made with thought, if you wish to have a favorable outcome."

"What—"

"Do it, now!"

It was rare for Canicus to act this way, and at that moment, Spartacus knew that something terrible was about to happen—and the gods would put him to the test and see if he were the man destined for the right actions in the face of extreme misfortune.

"I swear by all my gods, Zibelthiurdos, Sabazios, and Dionysus, that I shall heed your words Canicus, but I expect you to be truthful to me no matter how harsh or ugly the matter might be."

Canicus bowed. "Pay close attention. Your wife is now in a hold at the estate, waiting to be transported to an event."

Spartacus' heart almost exploded. *What?* Blood rushed to his face. He let out a gasp.

Canicus placed a hand on his shoulder. "Her friend Methe overheard Vatia, Messenius, and Philotas—"

"Philotas?"

Had to be him!

"Just listen, Spartacus! Be quiet and let me finish."

Spartacus nodded, controlling his rushing emotions.

"Vatia has requested for a detachment from the local garrison. Soldiers and a cart full of weapons, to be placed in the estate for a few days."

"I noticed the change in guard and suspected something."

"It is just the beginning," said Canicus. "Methe overheard the men speak of you and Crixus. Vatia will extract everything out of you and Crixus and finish you off. Castus, Oenomaus, and I will probably follow. Your clever wife asked Methe to speak to my lover, Anicia, to find out about the next event by Publius of Astorum."

"And?"

"Anicia sought Pollio's help, for your friend was back in Capua. And he has found two things. Now be calm, Spartacus, for now is the time to–"

"Stop telling me to be calm, Canicus. I know what is at stake," he said, irritated. He could barely speak and did not need the man nagging him.

Canicus ignored the rebuke. "The event at Astorum is to feature the usual gladiatorial fights, but it also includes a fresh surprise involving beasts."

"So?"

"Four wild dogs, a Gaelic hunter, three Samnite bandits," Canicus said, crowding Spartacus, "and a Thracian god woman tied to a stake, to be rescued by the valiant Gaul or die by the jaws of the dogs or the spears of the bandits."

Spartacus' legs almost gave out. *No! No, no, no, Zibelthiurdos, why?*

Canicus held his shoulders, not speaking.

No.

No.

How long will you punish us for my one indiscretion, Sabazios? Have I not suffered enough? What has she done?

He could not believe the sheer viciousness of Vatia's conduct. Had Spartacus not earned much for the owner?

Philotas, that treasonous bastard who wormed his way into their discussions, pretending to be one among them as the "peacekeeper!"

"How certain are you?" he asked, struggling to breathe amidst the thundering in his chest and roaring in his ears.

"I convey what Anicia said. And I could have withheld this from you, Spartacus."

"You are a true brother," Spartacus said. "When is this event?"

"In three days," Canicus said. "And that is why Crixus is confined–they will ship him out along with your wife."

Spartacus realized what the event could be.

The Roman degenerates would tie his wife up to a stake for the amusement of the ugly audience. They would send in Crixus to "defend" her from the beasts–wild dogs and Samnites, and he would die against the overwhelming odds. And then her bloody end would come too, quickly if the gods were still in his favor—or it would take time, ripped limb to limb by the jaws of vicious beasts, or jabbed and stabbed, depending on what the sponsors and audience demanded.

Spartacus breathed in and out, trying to regain his composure. But Canicus was not done. "That is not all. They have something in mind for you, Spartacus, and while Methe did not know what it was, it is depraved."

Spartacus could not imagine what would be worse.

Would they also drag him to the event and make him watch?

Would they tie him to a stake in the perimeter so he would be next?

Would they chase him with branded irons to force him to kill her?

Would they hoist him on a cross as side entertainment?

What else could Vatia think of?

It was not unusual for soldiers to rape wives and daughters of the enemy and force their men to watch.

But Spartacus, and now Canicus, knew that the wait was over. The gods had presented him with the ultimate test—he could succumb like a coward and let the river of fate run its course, or he could turn its direction, just as his wife always said.

A terrible calm descended on Spartacus. Canicus was right—flailing about and lashing out at the first Roman before him would do no good. It would only get him killed, and then the rest would die anyway.

That was not what Zibelthiurdos expected him to do.

What did General Sulla do when presented with insurmountable odds? He pretended the odds did not exist. As much as he hated taking encouragement from a cruel *Roman*, the General exemplified what it meant to go against everything and everyone and still win.

He turned to Canicus. "Are you ready to fight with me, brother?"

"As surely as my gods have told me, Spartacus. There is nothing worth fighting for in this *ludus*," he said and spat on the ground. "To think I once thought that our condemned lives were deserved and that my glory was in the arena."

"Let us not dwell on the past! Speak to Castus. I shall talk to Oenomaus and Nisarpal."

"Will the Syrians—"

"If we do not ask, we will not know."

Spartacus cursed himself again. *What a coward I was! Waiting and waiting for the perfect time. Always averse to risk and lazy, waiting for the most opportune moment. Perhaps that was why Zibelthiurdos confronted me with this most terrible situation.*

What kind of leader am I if I cannot assess the future and take decisive action!

Help me this time, Zibelthiurdos! Support me, Sabazios! I shall be as decisive as a general from now!

The sun rose to its zenith and the air hummed with demonic menace.

It was time.

43

LUCANIA

Estate treasurer Marcus Vibius had the same routine most days. He left the estate around sunset for the day and walked alone or with a guard to his house. The long walk took him through a wooded path with either side flanked by tall, leafy oak that provided a lovely canopy of relief on hot days. But in the evenings, it rendered the road dark.

He loved peace and solitude. It relieved him from the day's stresses and respite from the relentless drudgery and conflict at his work. He sometimes had a slave-carried carriage take him home when he had no desire to walk, especially after a large meal or a drinking excess. His mind was busy with many thoughts–a Tribune was scheduled to visit in a few days, and Porcina had put Vibius in charge of putting on a good show. Wine, women, and food, all of which cost good money. Some of which he was pilfering away arousing no suspicion, now that Cleitus kept his mouth shut. And then there was raising new loans to buy land abutting the estate. Securing money was a distasteful affair that involved much cajoling, begging, and making promises Porcina could not keep.

The cool breeze chilled his back. He shuddered.

"Miserable. And it is about to worsen," he said, and the guard behind him agreed.

The sun had not yet set so there was still a gentle drapery of dull orange in the sky. A lantern would be needed soon.

His thoughts turned to more personal matters. His sons were doing well for themselves. One in Rome and another in a town far north, both tradesmen with fine wives and children. It was a shame that neither wanted to join him and help open a new business. Sooner or later, Vibius would announce his gratitude to Porcina and leave—at least before the greedy bastard found out who was stealing his money, anyway, Vibius thought with a grin.

The canopy felt like a tunnel ahead of him, like an open jaw of an unseen beast, but blowing cold air. He loved it, and he hated it.

It was not too long before he noticed a figure walking toward him—the sliver of light penetrated through the trees and reflected on the white toga.

Cleitus.

What was that Thracian mongrel doing here, at this time?

"Greetings, Master Vibius," Cleitus said in his raspy voice. His face was barely visible, not that Vibius cared to see the broken-nosed, missing-toothed ugly dog who thought too highly of himself.

"What brings you to this cold path, Cleitus? Isn't your house on the other side?"

"Sometimes a man has to take a walk on these quiet stretches to refresh his mind," Cleitus said, standing directly ahead.

"Of course. Anyway, I trust all is well at your work," Vibius said, hoping to end this small talk and proceed.

But Cleitus would not get out of his path. *What is the idiot—*

"The work would be excellent, Vibius, if fat bastards were not pilfering from whom they serve."

This fucking son of a bitch! The gumption!

"Watch your hippity-hoppity mouth, bastard! How dare you—"

Vibius heard a rustle and a choking sound behind him. It took him a moment to register what he saw—his guard on his knees with a ghastly gash across his throat and blood spurting from it, shiny and dark under this play of night and sun.

Behind the guard stood a tall, gangly boy. Vibius could not place the assailant—where had he seen him? He held a thin metal wire looped around both his wrists.

Vibius turned back to Cleitus in panic. What was this pig doing? He tried to scream, but barely a squeak escaped his throat.

Cleitus advanced menacingly. "Open your mouth and let your voice take flight, Vibius. After all, no one thinks much of screaming slaves when they are flogged or raped, so your protests will be just another sound."

"What do you want?" he asked, frightened. "I have increased your pay, and even—"

Cleitus backhanded the treasurer with his ringed fingers. The sharp strike cut his lip and drew blood. Vibius yelped and swayed where he stood.

"My pay? You mouth-stuffing little pig. You took my fingers, and you speak of your pay? I was only doing my job!"

"But all is well now! Let me go, and your fortunes will rise even higher!"

Cleitus backhanded him again, and Vibius' ears rang. "Well? Your men and all you Romans have done nothing but look down upon me from the first day. Nothing is well, Vibius!"

He was feeling weak with fear, and there was nowhere to run. "I am old, and my bones are brittle. I seek to do you no harm, Cleitus," he said, sounding pathetic.

A dagger glinted in the Thracian's hand.

Run!

Vibius turned to flee, hoping that the bushes on the side would provide cover in the darkness. But he barely managed to get to the edge before he felt Cleitus' leg trip him. He sprawled face-first into the gravel and mud ground and scraped his face against a thorny bush. "Cleitus, stop!"

Cleitus stomped on Vibius' stomach, and he doubled with pain. It was as if his innards had ruptured. *Fucking ingrate!*

He caught his breath. "I can make you rich!"

Cleitus knelt on one leg beside him. "I have no desire to make money off of you or Porcina or any fucking Roman."

"I thought we had settled this!" he gasped. Whatever dispute was between them was settled long ago!

"No, Vibius. *You* settled it. And you did it by taking something from me that I can never earn. You deliberately inflicted upon me what you thought brought not just pain but a reminder of my past. You reveled in my humiliation. You went way beyond a threat."

"What past? It was just—" he tried to lie.

Cleitus smacked him on the face. "Oh, Marcus Vibius. And still you try to mislead."

Vibius had had enough. He tried to scream. "Help! Thracian slaves are attacking—"

Cleitus nodded to the boy who hovered near his head. The boy swooped down and stuffed a filthy rag into his mouth. He struggled and tried to get up, but Cleitus kicked him in the chest, causing him to fall and slam his head on the ground. Pain shot through the back of the skull to the front. Vibius screamed through the rag.

His mind cycled through a rapid string of incoherent thoughts.

Had they pissed on the rag?

Let me go, you low scum! Wait until someone finds you!

He felt the boy part his toga below his waist.

What are you doing! I am an old man!

He began to kick, but they avoided his legs and flailing hands.

And then Cleitus plunged his dagger deep into Vibius' fleshy thigh and sliced it like a butcher's meat. He screamed into his rag, his eyes bulging out of his sockets. The springing warm blood wet his skin, and incredible pain shot up his body.

He could barely hear what Cleitus was saying when the Thracian dog flicked the blade's edge near his scrotum.

No, no, no! Jupiter! Someone, help!

Vibius was barely coherent when Cleitus sliced away his genitals. Even as he rolled around in that extreme agony, the Thracian gripped him and whispered into his ears. "Remember you said I should be glad that no one had taken my cock? You laughed, didn't you? I will keep this as my trophy."

And then they left him there, bleeding profusely. His entire body lit up by suffering, Vibius tried crawling back to the road, but the severity of his injuries and the copious blood loss made it impossible.

He heaped curses on Cleitus and all his people as he lay there. He regretted the day he went to Cleitus and cut off his remaining fingers on the damaged hand. He regretted many things in his life, and as his body began to weaken and the agony dulled, Vibius knew he was soon to be not of this world.

The deed completed, Cleitus dispatched Felix to his house to get the women to prepare to leave. They had taken Vibius' keys. He went to the treasurer's room in the estate, where he knew the fat bastard kept bags of coins and some gold and hastily gathered as much as possible. At this time, no one questioned him, for he often went to his work area and Vibius' and was no stranger to the few men posted outside the main buildings.

When he returned home, Primigenia and Lucia waited anxiously, and Felix had done a commendable job preparing several carry sacks for their journey.

There was a hum of nervous energy in the air. Lucia helped Felix wash the blood and discard his clothes for a fresh tunic. He no longer wore the tattered, flimsy attire and loin clothes of his past, having been given a respectable tunic that would not make him look like an obvious slave, hiding his many scars on the back and chest.

All of them knew the consequence of their actions–that if any suspicion were directed their way, slaves were automatically tortured and put to death depending on the mood of the *dominus*, and Cleitus himself would be at severe risk. He did not know if anyone had witnessed the act or if Marcus Vibius had ever spoken ill of Cleitus, thus leading investigators to his doorstep. The death of the treasurer, an influential man, and Porcina's relationship would not be easily overlooked.

Felix's slave collar was gone. The branding on Primigenia's thigh was easily concealed. Lucia was unblemished. Cleitus was a free man and thus could announce that he was traveling with his slaves. There was palpable excitement under the flickering night lamp—they would all leave well before sunrise and vanish into the mountains that Felix knew quite well. While he knew little beyond the estate, the areas he was familiar with were still too large and treacherous for search parties. They would make their way to a bigger town and find ways to hide amongst the crowds, and then Cleitus would take them to Thracia.

Those were lofty ambitions, but none cared much for the practicality or the lack of it—all that mattered was this day and the next. Felix said plainly that he would murder every Roman who came his way and would die happily, having finally had Lucia in his embrace.

That neither woman was pregnant or with child was a relief.

They looked to Cleitus as their leader, which Cleitus had longed for and never received. But strangely, it made him happy, even if carrying the burden of that responsibility. He had come far from being someone else's dog.

Fuck Porcina and this estate.

They sprayed pig's blood on the ground and littered the floor with women's garments to suggest a violent action against the house's denizens. Whether anyone would believe it or not was beside the point—it would sow doubt and hopefully spare the slaves still on the estate from being subjects of cruel interrogations. Lucia's mother, who was estranged from her daughter, was still in the house—and there was no question Porcina would seek to know if the mother knew anything if such suspicion was aroused.

And as they quietly melted into the night, Cleitus mused at all he had thrown away so quickly, but he regretted none. Vibius had finally pushed him over the abyss. It felt like Cleitus was doing his own bid—not Durnadisso's, not

Spartacus', not Florus', not Curio's, not Porcina's—and it felt wonderful. He had done a spectacular job of convincing his household to go along with his plan, and Felix, grateful for what Cleitus had done for him, had done his bidding without question.

You are your own man! The leader!

Didn't Spartacus lead you all?

Quiet! Forget about him!

But he rebelled, just like you, and you took so long.

Quiet! Quiet! Quiet!

In that fleeting moment, as gravel crunched beneath his feet and the air had nothing but the loud breathing of his companions, Cleitus wondered if Spartacus was right in his conduct all along.

44

LUDUS OF VATIA

It was a gloomy morning with the sun winking through the ominous clouds that draped the sky. Spartacus had barely slept the night before, his mind a storm of emotions and thoughts. He ate his morning gruel quietly, and when they finally opened the latch on his door, he stepped into the dark corridor still cool from the night winds.

About forty men trained on the field when he stepped on the grass. The earth smelled of rainy mud, for it had showered briefly the previous night.

Canicus stood huddled with his men. Other men trained on the poles.

Nisarpal sat alone away from the other Syrians.

Crixus was still confined, and Philotas was not on the field. Oenomaus paced as the unarmed guards watched. Castus was in barracks as this was not his training shift.

Spartacus let the cool wind and open air invigorate him and clear his eyes. He casually walked up to Canicus. "Oenomaus joins us. Have you spoken to Castus?"

"It is not easy for a German like me to get the ear of a temperamental Celt who will only listen to Crixus or you," Canicus said, half smiling. "But he stands with us."

"Excellent. Has there been any change in the guard duty since you have been here this morning?"

"No. Not much getting out of the estate either. If the game at the Publius' estate is in two days, we should expect Crixus to be shipped this afternoon or tomorrow morning. Same with your wife."

Spartacus swung the stick in his hand to pretend to be training as a guard began to walk their way.

"Should we expect the kitchen to be guarded the same as yesterday?"

"Yes," Canicus said. "They are spread thin. But if the detachment arrives, and they are expected this evening, then everything changes."

"Do the gods look over your shoulder, Canicus? Will they now?" Spartacus asked.

"The dreams indicated favorable omens."

"Go back to your station. I shall speak to Nisarpal."

Spartacus went to the Syrian, who looked up as he neared. "Thracian."

"What say you, Nisarpal?"

"It seems you are about to rain disaster on us all," he said, smiling.

"The gods and Romans are better at it," Spartacus said, grinning at him. "What says the leader of the Syrians?"

Nisarpal pretended to look away as he stretched his back with a training pole behind his neck. "Better fuck than being fucked, no?" he said, showing his teeth.

Spartacus nodded and returned to his corner with Thracians. No words were spoken—it was time for lunch, and the whistles would sound soon to herd them toward the kitchen.

As Spartacus tried his best to focus on training, his stress increased with each passing moment. And before the usual time for lunch, he noticed Philotas standing below the awning near the entrance and watching them all.

Motherfucker.

Philotas caught his eye, and Spartacus smiled, catching the Macedonian by surprise. He nodded his acknowledgment.

And then he vanished into the corridor.

The clouds were getting darker, and thunder rolled from a distance.

Phreeeeeee!

The whistle for lunch.

Spartacus and Canicus walked quietly into the kitchen seating area. Not much had changed since the previous day. Ten guards surrounded the eating hall—double the usual and more heavily armed. Messenius sat on a stool in a corner, staring at Spartacus as he entered. Fourteen Thracians, ten Germans, and nine Gauls—Spartacus counted them all, for he was among the last to enter the mess.

Nisarpal and some of his men remained on the field. *On this day, we eschew lunch in honor of the gods,* he said to the puzzled guards.

The routine was always the same. The men sat on the benches, many of them prayed, and then the women came around with clay bowls of porridge and cups of sour wine or vinegar and ash water. Men were forbidden from chit-chat and were only allowed to make one request for more food. Once in a while, the gladiators who had better relations with the guards made small talk.

"Are we planning a new event in the *ludus*?" Spartacus asked Messenius.

Messenius was taken by surprise by the question. He scowled at Spartacus. "Why do you ask?"

"There was talk of extra security arriving, but no one told me if an event was planned here."

The overseer looked surprised but quickly tried to hide his reaction. He grumbled and answered, "Yes, a lovely event is about to happen, Spartacus. You will be the first to know all about it," he smirked. "Glaber's contingent will be here by sunset to ensure all is well."

Spartacus pretended not to understand. "The *dominus* has always honored other schools, yet we have never been given a chance to show our skills here, on our grounds!"

"Surely we merit recognition?" Canicus added. "Where is Philotas? He usually knows about this."

Messenius grinned, and another guard joined him. "Well, the Macedonian is enjoying a fine afternoon in his room wetting his cock in Procamus' wife—that is, she *was* his wife before she became Philotas' whore after her husband went up on the cross."

Spartacus feigned indifference even as his rage bubbled inside. If Crixus were here, he would undoubtedly fly off the bench and attack Messenius. These men took pride in wanton cruelty and exercising power over those they believed to be helpless. Condemned. And mongrels like Philotas were happy to take refuge beneath their master's boots and seek advantage.

The women began to serve.

"The *dominus* has not graced us with his presence either," Spartacus said, still looking at Messenius.

The overseer was getting irritated by the talk. "Shut your mouth and eat, Spartacus. He is a busy man."

"May I speak with him today?"

"He is busy with matters of the *Ludus* and will remain in his quarters. Now shut up."

"I have not been allowed to see my wife for many days. And she is not here in the kitchen."

Messenius' malicious grin returned. "You will meet her soon. Very soon," he said and smirked. "She is preparing for a special event. And you will participate in one as well!"

"The wings of gods are upon us," Spartacus said.

Messenius was confused. "What—"

Most men dropped their spoons. Those words meant something special.

May I have your mercy now, Sabazios, and may my men show fidelity to their words.

Spartacus turned to Canicus and met his eyes.

They nodded to each other.

Spartacus sprang from his seat and lunged at the nearest guard who stood lazily with his shield touching the floor and his gladius barely in his grip. A great roar rose from the rest, and men exploded from their positions and turned on the guards. The women's screams drowned in the cacophony.

Spartacus grabbed the guard's face and smashed it to the wall, causing him instantly to lose consciousness. And before the next one could draw a sword, he snatched the fallen guard's gladius and swung it in an upward arc, decapitating the other. The shorter and smaller men, ill-trained and caught by surprise, stood no chance before his hulking presence and lethally honed skills forged in the battlefield and the arena.

Around him was mayhem. Many gladiators rushed the kitchen, pushing the workers out of the way and getting their hands on anything they could get their hands on. Brass utensils, heavy pins, cutting knives, skewers, two swords, wooden boards, needles, cleaning cloth that could be used to twist and strangle, and even grain mills. Every man that managed to wrest a gladius or dagger from the guards immediately went to attack others—and within minutes, the floor of the kitchen was wet with rivers of blood and severed heads and hands. Only one gladiator was on the floor, severely injured.

Where was Messenius?

Spartacus had previously given clear instructions that Messenius must be held and not killed at the first opportunity–and Canicus had subdued the terrified overseer who lay on the ground, his forearm almost hacked away. Spartacus quickly retrieved the barrack keys from the overseer's belt–the same keys opened all the rooms–and looked for Oenomaus.

"Oenomaus!" screamed Spartacus. "Go free Crixus and the other men!"

Oenomaus, busy smashing the skull and splattering the brains of an already dead guard, took a deep breath and nodded. He picked up a shield and gladius, gathered a gang, and headed down to the barracks after collecting the keys from Spartacus.

Nisarpal was awaiting his signal. If men came rushing through the barracks, the Syrians would rise too–helping the rest and causing as much damage as possible. While they cared little for the Gauls, the Thracians, or the Germans, the Syrians had reached the same conclusion: no more glory and no path to freedom. And when he saw Oenomaus emerge from the corridor and wave to them, the Syrians first murdered the scrambling unarmed guards, breaking their necks or bashing their heads into the walls. Then they joined Oenomaus as he opened every door.

"Come with us or die here!"

"If you stay, do you think they will spare you?"

"Those who stay behind will go up on a cross!"

"Get out, out, out!"

It was a blur of madness as those who knew of this day's plan darted out with glee, and those who were kept unaware were bewildered and yet forced to action. No matter how dull a man's mind or how despondent, they all understood one thing—whether they had a role in the uprising or not, any man that remained behind would die a terrible death.

The newly gathered mass rushed up the corridor to the kitchen—the path to the exit.

"Where is she? Where are my wife and Methe?" Spartacus screamed at Messenius, grabbing his neck. Some of Spartacus' men surrounded him to protect him.

Messenius' choking voice was still full of disdain. "Fucking slaves, you will all die!"

Spartacus knew that the man would not be easily reasoned with, and the more time spent here clashing with guards now streaming in, the greater the risk to them all.

"Manage the men here!" Spartacus told Canicus. By now, scores of men battled guards at the exit out of the kitchen—pushing each other with shields and trying to stab over them.

Messenius was a hefty man, but Spartacus was far larger. He and another Thracian gladiator hauled Messenius to his feet and dragged him to the kitchen where a fire burned in a hearth. A few women cowered in a corner. A gladiator lay dead face down. A ghastly stab wound through his chest.

"Hold him," Spartacus said to this companion. And even as Messenius struggled and shouted, Spartacus yanked his right arm and thrust half of it into the fire. Messenius screamed—the first time Spartacus had heard the brute howl in agony, for it was always him who inflicted it upon others. The stink of charred skin and burned muscle was instantaneous.

"Where is she?" he asked, his face close to the man's wide eyes. "Or I will burn you limb by limb!"

Messenius shook his head rapidly. Whether he was in agony or trying to say something was unclear. Spartacus prepared to push the other palm, and Messenius panicked. "No! No. Yes, she is here!"

"Where?"

"Holding! Women know where it is! Stop!"

"When is the detachment arriving?"

"I told you. Later today!" he said, gritting his teeth, saliva dripping from the corners. Messenius was no longer the confident enforcer. His legs were shaking, and the man could barely stand.

This was the man who had laughed while nailing Procamus.

And *knew* what was about to happen to Spartacus' wife and had taken much pleasure.

And without question he knew what was planned for Spartacus.

The gods deem this as just.

Spartacus grabbed him by the neck and smashed it into the burning coals and flame before Messenius realized what was happening. He held Messenius' face there as the overseer's hair lit up like a dry torch, and all the flesh burned away, along with his eyes–Messenius' scream was barely audible, and it took not too long before he stopped moving.

Spartacus grabbed his gladius from the floor and turned to the women–many who knew who his wife was. "Do you know where the holding is?"

One of them shook her head fearfully. "You, come with me! Others, you can either leave with us or stay here under the mercy of your master. But you know what will happen!"

Two men protected Spartacus' flanks as he took the woman with him. Crixus, along with another large group of gladiators, including the Syrians, broke into the kitchen—it was now a crowded spectacle. The guards were all dead, but a battle raged in the exit with a large group of guards with shields pushing against the fighters on this end.

"Make way!" Spartacus ordered—and they listened to him as if he were a commander. Quickly Spartacus nominated five men, all taller than the rest, to join him in the front. With his commanding height, it was easier for Spartacus to see above the heads of the guards and also to stab them in the face from above his shield—a craft well-honed during his campaigns and battles against skilled legionaries and perfected as a gladiator. Once a few guards fell with their faces stabbed or eyes punctured, the rest collapsed and fled. Now the gladiators rushed through the corridor—the critical thing was for people not to slaughter other slaves or turn to looting, for that was a sure way to lose control. Those designated as leaders kept their men in check, acting as their commanders, knowing well that a few would not follow orders but so long as the rest stuck to the instructions, they would emerge mostly unscathed.

"Crixus and Canicus, keep some to guard the rear, and the rest head down to protect the exits!" Spartacus ordered them. A broad staircase ahead descended and eventually led to a quadrangle, from where another short path led them out of the building.

Spartacus and ten men followed the woman through to the women's holding area, which was nothing but a small windowless room separate from the women's barracks and at the ground level. A lone guard stood there fidgeting nervously, having surely heard of all the commotion above but not knowing what was happening. He tried to run before being cut down.

Spartacus kicked the flimsy door open and peered into the stifling darkness now lit by the dull sunlight from outside the door.

Where is she?

In the far corner sat Antara, staring, afraid, and surprised. He rushed to her.

Antara had been washed and wore a beautifully embroidered shimmering blue stola, and her face was thick with cosmetics. *Dressing her up for a procession to slaughter.*

She was speechless as Spartacus scooped to grab her in his arms.

"What is going on?" she stammered.

"No time to explain! Come with me."

He held her waist as he ran out with her. The gladiators occupied the lower area, killed a few more guards, and held seven Romans hostage—four women and three men.

"Where is Methe?" Antara asked anxiously, but her friend was nearby with Canicus. They embraced joyously.

"What do we do with these people?" Crixus asked about the Romans wailing as the gladiators kept them pinned beneath their feet.

"Who knows them?" Spartacus asked the slave women who knew the innards of the house of Vatia better than the fighters. It took little time to learn about their activities and relationships with the slaves—two women and one man were allowed to leave but were locked into a room. The remaining men were quickly executed, and Spartacus forbade any man to drag the women for their pleasures. "There will be no molestation," he said sternly to a few disappointed faces. "Our freedom will earn us what we seek."

The other two women met their end after being condemned by a slave woman who had suffered. Someone had set fire to a few columns by then, and the blaze spread.

"There is one more thing," Spartacus said.

They found Philotas cowering near a staircase along with Procamus' wife. Spartacus and his men seized the Macedonian even as he loudly protested that he was for the rebels' cause and was only *protecting* Procamus' wife.

With smoke filling the spaces, there was not much time to indulge him.

"What a treasonous bastard you turned out to be," Spartacus growled at him. "To think I trusted you so long, even after your vacillation and pacification. You were just doing Vatia's bidding."

"I had no choice!" Philotas complained. "He offered that as my path to freedom. Now I can join you, and we can—"

Spartacus punched him so hard that Philotas crumbled on the floor, doubled up, and could not breathe.

"Filthy vermin. How low could you get? That you would coerce the wife of a man Vatia so gleefully crucified, and then you knew about Crixus and my wife. How much of it was your instigation?"

Philotas shook his head but did not answer.

Spartacus turned to the fearful woman. "Were you taken of your own will?"

She did not answer. Instead, she walked to Philotas and kicked his face so hard that his nose splintered and began to bleed. "Fucking bitch!" he cursed her.

That was all Spartacus needed.

They tied Philotas' hands and feet, even as he shouted his innocence.

Spartacus then dragged him like a corpse toward the fire that raged below.

"No, no! Stop, Spartacus! I can be of help! No!"

And as Philotas struggled, Spartacus lifted the flailing man and threw him into the fire.

Philotas lit up like dry grass.

"They wished to burn us, and now they are consigned to the flames," Spartacus told Procamus' wife over Philotas' screams as he rolled in the fire. "Messenius and Philotas have received their justice."

"Everyone, this way!" Methe shouted, joined by Anicia, Canicus' woman. It was unclear whether the Roman girl would remain with the escaping group.

Some men and women grabbed what they could, but none were so foolish to be left behind searching for loot, only to die later. Those instructed to grab bread and barley from the kitchen had done their duty–which meant there would be some food for the night, even if the rations would be meager.

"Where is Vatia?" Canicus asked.

They learned that the owner had escaped along with his wife and a few others when the struggles raged in the corridor.

His time will come.

They set fire to more wood–if nothing else, they would turn the bastard's facility to ruins and push him into deeper financial debt.

And then, with Spartacus leading from the front supported by Crixus, Canicus, and Nisarpal, a total of seventy-four gladiators and eighteen women, including two Romans, dashed into the open courtyard with an unlocked gate that opened wide into an empty field. Only two children—one nine years old and another a baby, accompanied them.

The remaining guards had fled—there was no one to stop the group from exiting the estate.

Spartacus looked up to the heavens—the cloudy sky offered immeasurable comfort.

It felt strange. Unbelievable even, after all this time in captivity.

Their first steps into the open of their own will.

45

CAPUA

Vatia's estate and *ludus* were outside the city. The one muddy road took them away from Capua, making it easy for the escaping slaves to evade capture or face resistance.

There was but one problem.

They had not the time to raid the armory, for the keys were nowhere to be found and the breaking into it would take too much time. It was likely that Vatia had escaped with the keys. This left them vulnerable as they were not sufficiently armed and would be at a considerable disadvantage should they be confronted by a contingent.

Spartacus ordered everyone to spread into the grassy and bushy fields next to the road and lie low. No one knew yet where they would go, though Spartacus had an idea. But first, they needed weapons.

"What do you suggest?" Crixus asked.

Canicus grinned. "We missed you for the plans, Gaul," he said. "Now we ambush the detachment!"

Crixus grinned. The Gaul had since learned of what fate awaited him, and now he was set to seek revenge on everyone Roman—and both Canicus and Spartacus knew they had to control the man, for his temper often ran ahead of his senses.

But an attack on Romans, and getting his hands on fine weaponry? Crixus was thrilled.

It took not too long for two horse-driven baggage carts to turn the bend and enter into view. But they paused, for the drivers had surely seen the rising smoke and fire in the estate. Spartacus and his men were prepared—a few were hiding behind a small knoll near the bend, and they set upon the unsuspecting soldiers.

Surprised by all sides and without time to set to formation, the detachment was like a lamb led to slaughter. Every man was savagely cut to pieces. Spartacus's rage overcame him as he repeatedly stabbed an officer in his chest until there was nothing left in the open cavity, and he was himself drenched in blood.

Vatia was a fool. He had underestimated how many soldiers were needed in times of a *real* uprising. Even his order of weapons was woefully inadequate. Or the garrison commander had refused to send as much as was asked—but Spartacus surmised that the greedy *ludus* owner may have miscalculated.

The cart had forty pairs of good enough oblong shields and worn but perfectly adequate gladii. The thirty dead soldiers were sources of some armor, footwear, knives, water cans, clothes, fire-making equipment, ropes, and some food. All were stripped entirely, and the materials were distributed—the ablest fighters getting the weapons and footwear, and then the rest split by tribe and left for the leaders to decide. The Syrians were already arguing about where to go next—and they favored a straight escape to Brundisium to take a ship to sail by the coasts of Greece. It was too early to make lofty plans, but Nisarpal had a problem containing them.

The sun would set soon, and they needed shelter for the night. But before the shelter, they had to get away from the open fields, for a larger armed force would surely appear at the first light of dawn.

The men had accepted Spartacus as their leader, with Crixus as the next in command. They all knew that this hasty arrangement was fragile, but it was the best move for now, with all their lives at risk and uncertainty about what to do next. Of all the men in that group, Spartacus was the most experienced in matters of organized conflict and leading men.

Zibelthiurdos, perhaps this is how you wish me to seek my destiny!

The first step was to escape to the thickets near the base of mount Tifata, away from any civilization. The clouds from the morning had dispersed after a light rain during the day, so at least they would be dry for the night. The biggest challenge after finding shelter would be water and food, but they would plan for that once morning arrived.

"Women in the middle. Castus and Canicus, spread the Germans along the right flank and the rear. Gauls to the left. Syrians in the center. All Thracians in the front—"

Canicus stepped closer to Spartacus and lowered his voice. "It is only right that you have us in the front."

Spartacus bristled at the ask but understood the reason behind it. Leading *from the front* was prestige, and men easily took offense. He could already see the Syrians arguing with Nisarpal—perhaps about being asked to be around the *women*. The Germans looked unhappy, and Crixus nodded to Spartacus.

"It is glorious that every tribe wishes to be at the front and lead others to safety!" he said, drawing some smiles. They quickly made adjustments—a mix of all tribes in the front, and the rest spread along the little column with their leaders sprinkled.

The politics will only grow as we grow. That is if we do not splinter like weak branches before then.

And thus, the slave rebels under Spartacus the Thracian began to trudge away from Capua and Vatia's villa toward the safety of the forests, by the footsteps of Tifata.

Antara walked beside Spartacus, and she quietly wiped the blood off his forearms and back from time to time. "I never doubted you would arrive, husband."

"Your gods gave me strength," he said. "They lit a flame in my belly and woke me from the coward I was."

"You are no coward!" she protested. "The gods tested you, and now you have shown what you are capable of–bringing all these men together to a common cause."

"It will be a challenge keeping us together," he said. "That will be my greatest test."

"No test is so great that my husband will fail," she said, smiling and gripping his arm.

Spartacus laughed, and even on this fateful bloody day, he felt great joy knowing that they walked free, even if just for now, and that she was beside him. She had lost weight, yet the same determination blazed in her eyes.

At dawn, they would decide what to do next.

46

LUDUS OF VATIA

Vatia ranted and raged at his ruined *ludus*. Nearly half of his estate had been burned to the ground, many of his staff executed, his guards dead and rotting in the debris, and the degenerates had ravaged what was remaining. They had even made their way to his room and office. They had torn the curtains, smashed the urns and mirrors, pissed on the floors, defecated on the bed and couches, stolen jewelry, damaged the walls, and even scraped the paintings. Four gladiators had died, and only two men of the entire population of the *ludus*, had remained behind. Useless dullards who knew nothing of the event and had died protesting their innocence. Messenius was charred almost beyond recognition, and Philotas, or what was left of him, was just a burned black mass and a wide-jawed skull.

Gone!

Everything he had worked for so far. All gone! Fucking ungrateful animals, unworthy of any human compassion. He had given them life and a future, and yet they had found their true beings under the violence of that pretentious slow-speaking Thracian. How he longed to put each on a cross and watch them die slowly, begging for release!

His wife had promptly left him and fled to her father. No doubt, sooner or later, the old bastard would be on his case again. Followed by his attendants, Vatia went to every corner—and the only two places left unmolested were the armory, for which the low monkeys had not found the keys, and the inner temple, for they still somehow feared the gods. Nothing else was sacred.

What a fool he was to ignore Philotas' warning. Who knew that these men would rise to such belligerence?

Or did Spartacus learn of his wife's fate?

How?

Who leaked that information?

Publius? But why would he, and how did that news travel to the gladiators?

Tired, he sat on the floor and put his hands on his head. "Get me some water from somewhere!" he yelled at a slave, who scampered away.

The creditors would be after him. He was a laughingstock in the town–the fool who could not control his slaves.

But then, Vatia had not grown to where he was by just giving up. He had too much to lose. His prestige. His ambition to political office. His debt to his investors, and the consequence of not repaying them. His relationship with his wife and father-in-law. Making his father proud and his brother envious. *So much! He would lose so much! His life and everything he had worked so far, because of these low, mongrel slave motherfuckers!*

He would have them butchered like pigs! Flay them and wear the skins as garments!

He would find the means to have them hunted down.

And he knew just the person to do it.

47

CAPUA

In the first few weeks on the run, no one was on their heels. The sparsely populated regions outside Capua provided the best hiding spot for the group that had slowly grown to a hundred-twenty due to a few roadside banditry attacks and ravaging a few small, barely guarded estates. The strict protocol Spartacus implemented helped their cause—no rape, no murder of children, orderly execution of the *dominus* and his wife as decided by the house slaves. Guards and other able-bodied men and boys were not allowed to leave alive. They also took horses from the stables, for among the Thracians and Syrians were expert horsemen who would now be able to patrol the column and convey messages. They had enough water and food supplies—grain, bread, unspoiled meat, milk, and wine. Spartacus and the other leaders had to quell the rampant indiscipline with a few beatings, and he did what he had learned during his time in the Roman army.

Set people to purpose.

During their stops, everyone had a task—digging protective ditches, preparing or scouting for food, guard duty, conducting training, running raid parties, scouts, and watchers—all that kept the quarreling and arguments to a minimum. But Spartacus knew that without clear organization, none of this would last too long.

Uncertainty of the future and the reality of their fate tempered men's passions and brought to the fore the biggest question—what to do next and where to go. And now, with the group ensconced in a safe section in the folds of the mountain and with a clear view of Capua and surroundings, the leaders called a conference late into the evening.

"Straight to Brundisium," Nisarpal declared, even before the men opened a discussion. They all sat on rocks— Spartacus, Crixus, Oenomaus, Castus, Canicus, Nisarpal, and Thrumbosus, another Thracian who had gained Spartacus' favor due to his superior organizational skills.

"Straight to Roman gallows and crosses," Castus retorted. "What a foolish idea."

"Only cowards—" started Nisarpal before Spartacus raised his hand and admonished them to silence.

With all eyes on him, Spartacus began. "If we must come to the right conclusions, then let every man speak his mind and be received respectfully," he said, staring at Castus. "Whatever the idea, evaluate its merit rather than whose mouth it came from."

Castus grumbled, and Nisarpal grinned. But now they focused on him, for they knew that only he had traveled the road from Brundisium to Capua as part of a military march.

"Brundisium or Tarentum is our way out of Italy, but for whom? For the Thracians and the Syrians. It will be a long way away, and fraught with danger for our German and Gaelic contingents."

Nisarpal nodded reluctantly.

"Besides, while your idea is right for those tribes, Brundisium is the pathway for every returning general from Greece and elsewhere, and the roads have a heavy military presence. All it takes is news to travel, and our column will be easily apprehended."

"We disperse," Crixus finally spoke. "Each tribe goes its own way. Vanish."

Spartacus knew that many hoped for this to become true—that somehow they could *vanish* and reach safety.

"How will each tribe go its way, Crixus?" he asked the Gaul. "You are all easily identified. Most have been branded. And none of you have release billets. Where will you hide until someone learns of who you are? Sooner or later, you will be discovered, even if it means a year or two. All major roads are guarded. All ports are guarded. Perhaps a few will stay alive, unseen, in some benevolent master's house where the *dominus* does not inquire about their presence."

Crixus scoffed. "No benevolent master."

"Precisely. No estate owner will hire a slave that shows up from the wilderness. And big cities are dangerous to venture into if you do not know if there is a bounty on your head. Perhaps no one will know, or perhaps they are waiting for us. Will you take that risk?"

"Can we make our way north?" Canicus spoke. The thoughtful German looked as energized as he was from when he sprang to action at the kitchen. Spartacus had grown great respect for the man. "If we reach the great snow mountains, the Gauls and my tribes can turn to the west and the Thracians and Syrians to the east."

"That would require traveling undetected through the length of this land," Castus said. "But it may be the best option until we are outside the reach of the Roman armies."

"How will you manage food and shelter while traveling undetected for weeks knowing that the news of our escape would have reached every garrison by then?" Spartacus countered.

"South? Go to Sicily," Nisarpal said. "We came that way."

"Explain," Spartacus said.

Nisarpal had a profound knowledge of the seas and some sense of the lands. "Heard but not seen Brundisium," he said.

"But we ship from the coast near my home, come along Greece, then the boat goes down to Sicily. From Sicily, narrow water channel to the tip of Italy. Then we come north."

"But that benefits you," Crixus said, irritated.

"No," Nisarpal shook his head. "Benefit *both*. Thracians and Syrians take boat to go east. You," he said, pointing at Crixus and Canicus, "go west, and then go north.

Spartacus smiled. This was a brilliant idea. From his own outdated but limited knowledge of the geographies, he knew that Roman presence in Sicily was not as dense as in the paths to the north, and if they were to get on open water, they could all disperse easily. The challenge, of course, was not only about getting to the southern tip, but finding enough coin to buy boats and crew.

But that was a problem to be resolved later.

The idea had merit.

"We cannot go north," he said. "We are too few and easily fought. Many open plains where we are easily observed. We must build our *army* first."

They looked at him in surprise.

"Army?" Crixus said. "King Spartacus?"

The men laughed, but once they realized Spartacus was serious, Canicus was the first to speak.

"An army of *slaves*? And then do what, Spartacus?"

"An army of men and women freed from their masters. No longer slaves, Canicus," Spartacus said forcefully. "An army needed for safety as we move through this country. Did we free ourselves, only to try to vanish like cowards and then be hunted down like dogs, one by one?"

"We all seek freedom," Oenomaus said, finally opening his mouth.

"We are free *now*, but we are not truly free as long as we are running from apprehension, are we? Are we in our homes? Are we with our wives and children? Are we serving *our* tribes? Are we in conquest against our enemies? We are now just bandits on the run. And so long as we are just bandits, we are easy to destroy. Armies are harder to destroy."

"Armies will attract attention," Nisarpal said.

"To Romans who have suffered ignominy by runaway slaves, it makes no difference whether it is an army of slaves or a gang. They will come after us. If we are by ourselves in little splinters, they will quickly extinguish us. If we mobilize and move with purpose, it will take them much longer to organize and come after us—and that will give us the time to make the right decisions."

They argued some more, but the men were convinced eventually that surviving as small bands would be exceedingly difficult, and not just that, it was dishonorable for those who considered themselves warriors. Besides, Spartacus had repeatedly appealed to their *outrage*. "Did we escape so we could become like little drops on a hot stone, or do we want to be the torrent that breaks dams?"

Crixus seconded Spartacus. "I agree that we must build strength. And staying here, so close to Capua, is dangerous."

Spartacus nodded at Crixus. It was critical to have one leader supporting his opinions, for if one stood behind him, others followed. "I have spent time speaking to men who had served in the farms further south. We need land rich in farms, cattle, and small and unprotected estates. These places have many slaves treated terribly, shepherds and other herdsmen left to fend for them themselves, and hardy farm workers shackled to their barracks for years—just like us. Food, livestock, milk, and people to join our ranks—that is what we must aim for. Do not forget that I once spent time in an estate further south."

Canicus grinned. "And women. Many who yearn for us."

"Anicia will chop your cock and ship it to Rome," Crixus said to laughter.

Spartacus knew that indiscriminate pillage and rape were the easiest way to alienate any local population—and he had to be wary of such madness, even as they grew stronger.

But for now, finding a place to swell their numbers and keeping them fed was the most important one. Important for what he had in mind but had not fully revealed to the men who rarely thought of issues greater than themselves.

Small minds.

Antara had given him hope, and she had given him ambition, and seeing her safe and now managing the women gave him much joy.

Spartacus turned to the men. "You ask where we go next, and I know exactly where."

Crixus, in his characteristic belligerence, shouted. "We march on Rome! Kick them like a donkey's bum!"

Oenomaus slapped his shoulder, and the two Gauls laughed heartily. Spartacus waited for the silliness to settle.

"Do I have your ears?"

Chastened, they all turned to him.

"In only a day's rapid march south from here is a great region with a lofty mountain and rich vineyards, orchards, much well-spaced farmland, and estates. Perfect for vantage, and for our aspirations."

None of the men had come from the south, and Nisarpal had no idea.

Spartacus turned to look far into the distance. The mountain was not visible from here. Mist and clouds hung low in the intervening space.

He would lead them on this fateful journey as ordained by the gods.

"We go to Mount Vesuvius," he said.

END OF BOOK II

THANK YOU FOR READING

———◇———

Thank you for reading the second book of the series! You should grab "Savior," the next book in this trilogy. We will journey with Spartacus and his rebel army.

Your reviews and ratings make a huge difference! I would be immensely grateful if you took a few seconds or minutes to either rate the book or leave a review if you enjoyed it.

You can also go to https://jaypenner.com/reviews for easy links.

A detailed notes section will be available at the end of the trilogy and cover various aspects of the book—fact, dramatization, and the rationale for certain decisions.

Did you know? You can go to https://jaypenner.com/maps to do a Google flyby of all locations mentioned in the book.

Join my newsletter https://jaypenner.com/join to know when the next book releases, or follow me as an author on Amazon and you will be notified.

Until next time!

-Jay https://jaypenner.com

REFERENCES

The following works provided helpful historical references and commentary on the Third Servile War (the Spartacus War).

1. Spartacus and the Slave Wars - A brief history with documents (Plutarch, Appian, Sallust, Livy, and others), by Brent D. Shaw

2. The Complete Roman Army by Adrian Goldsworthy

3. The Spartacus War by Barry Strauss

4. Spartacus by Aldo Schiavone

And numerous papers and articles on the time, the man, and his circumstances.

Printed in Great Britain
by Amazon

17100426R00199